The Courageous Exploits of Doctor Syn

Black Curtain Press
P.O. Box 632
Floyd, VA 24091

ISBN 13: 978-1627555494

First Edition
10 9 8 7 6 5 4 3 2 1

The Courageous Exploits of Doctor Syn

Russell Thorndyke

1

THE YOKE AND THE FLOATS

In the days when Doctor Syn was Vicar of Dymchurch-under-the Wall in the County of Kent, a period which covered the latter years of the eighteenth century, the Coffin Shop, presided over by his Sexton and general factotum, Mister Mipps,
was one of the chief centres for village gossip.

Situated at the cross-roads, and overlooking the vast expanse of Romney, it was the first building encountered when entering the long
straggling village street.

It consisted of a low and extenuated shed, housing a forge and carpenter's bench, and joined to an old cottage, the ground floor of which was utilized as a general store.

Though the cottage was known officially as Old Tree Cottage, from an ancient trunk which reared itself proudly before its casements, the whole building was always referred to as the Coffin Shop.

And it was in the Coffin Shop that Mipps could always be found when at home. Anyone wanting to buy anything, from a jar of pickled onions to a marline spike, would ask for it across a tresselled coffin, and wait while Mipps retired into the store, and finally delivered it upon a coffin lid, for there was always one coffin there, which Mipps explained as being in readiness for the next stocksize corpse that might come along.

Mipps was a thin, wiry little man, with a pointed nose like that of an inquisitive ferret. As though to balance it, his scraggy back hair was screwed into a queue, stiffened with tar, a fashion he had adopted in the days when he had served as a ship's carpenter.

With the exception of Doctor Syn, who always seemed to have the best advice for everybody's problems, there was no one who carried more parochial respect than Mipps. Old and young would drop into his workshop with their wants, or their gossip. Like his master, the Vicar, he was ever ready to listen to anyone's troubles, and his whispered solution would be followed by a nod and a look of satisfaction as his visitor departed.

These whisperings in the Coffin Shop had sometimes been looked upon with suspicion by Revenue men, which was a great source of amusement to Mipps, who defied them to find anything against him.

"Prove that I'm the Scarecrow," he would say, with a chuckle, "and I'll be ever so proud. Besides I'll be able to retire from the undertaking business when I finds myself the head of the Romney Marsh Smugglers. I've heard you say that their profits are ver good indeed. Mine ain't very good, so a change will do me wonders."

Very often Doctor Syn would hitch the reins of his fat white pony over the gate-post of the Coffin Shop, while he went in to discuss parochial matters with his Sexton, and on such occasions the villagers would tactfully wait for his departure before presenting themselves to Mipps.

It was on such an occasion that several villagers, more than anxious to receive a whispered message from Mipps, waited dutifully till their spiritual leader should mount his white pony and ride away.

They quite understood that the Vicar's business must come first, since Mipps was the Vicar's man, but to most of them there was something more important than parochial matters, namely, their next orders from the mysterious Scarecrow who had led them for so many years against the Revenue men, without betraying his identity. Even Mipps professed ignorance on this subject. Certainly he was often used as the Scarecrow's mouthpiece, and passed messages that had not been able to be given at the last meeting of the Night riders. Sometimes, too, the Scarecrow found it necessary to change his plans, which he was able to do through the medium of the Coffin Shop.

On the March morning in the year 1781, the Vicar's consultation upon parochial matters with Mipps seemed to those anxiously waiting unnecessarily long.

In the ordinary way the little knot of fishermen and farm hands would not have minded how long they were kept gossiping outside the Coffin Shop. It was pleasant to sit on the old wall of the bridge that spanned a broad dyke opposite the closed shed from which they could hear the swish of the plane as the old carpenter worked. Dymchurch was a sleepy enough village in the daytime, whatever its activities might have been at night.

But these were anxious times. As they talked in low voices, they watched the evolutions of a squadron of Dragoons, who were exercising their horses across the green meadows of the Marsh.

They had been in the village for some days, encamped with horse-lines behind the Ship Inn, in a large field that ran to the sea-wall. They had been applied for by the Preventive Officer, who had not enough men at his disposal to deal with the strong force for smugglers that worked under the Scarecrow.

With their plumed brass helmets and scarlet tunics, the Dragoons lent an exciting touch of colour to the village, and since the Scarecrow's Night-riders had thoroughly worsted them, with two runs on a big scale since their arrival, their harmless manoeuvres did not worry them.

But a new source of danger was looming over the village, which made the gossipers all the more anxious to see the Vicar mount his white pony and ride away, so that they could discover from Mipps exactly what the new rumour meant.

They had just gleaned the news of the arrival that very day of men from the Royal Navy, who were to augment the already established Dragoons.

The majority had more respect for the Navy than for the Army, and so they took the rumour which Percy had imparted to them on the bridge very seriously.

Percy was one of the most important members of the village community. Although most of them regarded him as the village idiot, by reason of his being overgrown, lanky, loose-lipped, roundshouldered, and slow of speech, discerning folk realized that amongst the may sluggish cells in the brain of this seventeen-year-old lad were some that could act with the most acute perception. In other words Percy was not always the fool that he looked.

His physical strength enabled him to eke out a reasonably comfortable living for himself and his widowed mother, by carrying buckets of fresh water from the village well to the various cottages. With their men-fold working on the land or sea, for most of them were either at the fis hing or farming trades, housewives were only too happy to save themselves the walk to the well and the labour of drawing and carrying by paying Percy his moderate charges for two buckets full of well water delivered three times a day. The humblest cottage employed him, for it was an accepted fact that he had the monopoly of the well.

From one of his clients Percy refused payment for his services, and that was Mipps, who had long promised him a yoke to enable him to carry the pails of water the easier.

Mipps had measured it to fit the lad's hunched shoulders, and it was on this particular morning that he was putting the finishing touches to the work, planing it smooth while the Vicar talked to him in whispers.

The little knot of gossipers sitting outside upon the bridge wall would have been astonished could they have heard the drift of this consultation, which

had to do with the Scarecrow's business.

"I tell you, my good Mipps," the Vicar was saying, "that we shall have to adopt even more carefully laid plans in the immediate future. We are used to the methods of the Dragoons which we have dealt with before when the Government has seen fit to billet them upon us. But the Navy is a different proposition. This Captain Blain, who has been detailed from the Guard Ship at Dover to break up our Night-riders, is a man whose record I am well acquainted with, and believe me he has a strategic brain. He is an opponent worthy of our steel."

"And he comes today, does he?" asked Mipps.

"And has been invited to the Court House as Sir Antony's guest," nodded the Vicar.

"I don't envy the Squire," said Mipps. "He's already cluttered up with the Dragoons officers. Let's hope they pay well for the hospitality they receive.

"The Squire feels that the Cobtrees can hardly receive compensation for hospitality," returned the Vicar, with a smile, "so I gather that the Government allowance of rum for the troopers."

"Well, so long as the Squire keeps the officers away from the Vicarage," said Mipps, "all the easier for us, eh, Vicar?"

Doctor Syn shook his head. "That's not my view at all," he said.

Mipps looked at his master, and checked the query that was on the tip of his tongue. His master was thinking.

Mipps knew Doctor Sy n better than any. Had he not served under him as ship's carpenter when his master had walked the deck of the Imogene as Captain Clegg, flying the black flag? Watching the long thin face now he realized that the Vicar was working out a problem, and would speak in his own good time.

Doctor Syn was an arresting figure as he leant against the coffin. He was tall, slim, elegant and alert. A smile suddenly broke over the pale intellectual face, and Mipps was fascinated, wondering what was coming.

"I have made up my mind that Captain Blain shall not be billeted with Sir Antony Cobtree at the Court House," he said. "He shall be looked after at the Vicarage. We will keep a close eye on him ourselves. It might even be necessary to see that his door is fastened on the outside. Yes, we'll put him in the little panelled room because the door opens outwards. A wedge, eh, Mipps?"

Mipps nodded. "Maybe as well to have him clapped under our own hatches," he said, and then added miserably, "but I'll wa ger that when the time comes you'll be letting him out so that you'll have an opponent worthy of you steel, as you calls him, working against us when the Night-riders are out."

Doctor Syn chuckled. "The Night-riders may scare some folk from the Marsh when a 'run' is on, but I fancy it will take more to frighten Captain Blain. Their illuminated faces, the phosphorus on the horses, their wild trappings, as they circle in and out of the mists, will not impress Blain. No, Mipps, we must think out new methods to deal with this Captain."

From the village street came the monotonous wail of the lad, Percy, crying out, "Water, water." The gossipers saw in him a means for interrupting the conversation going on between the Vicar and the Sexton.

"Hurry up, my lad," one of them sang out. "Old Mipps is cursing in there for want of a pail of water for his work."

"Percy's on time," rejoined the half-wit. "In a fine hurry he is, so don't be hindering him with you talk now. The Sexton has promised the yoke this morning, and Percy's lost a good pint of slopping walking fast. All over my breeches. The yoke will keep the buckets from bumping my legs."

"You get inside," said one of the fishermen, "or old Mipps will be out of temper, and you'll get no yoke at all."

"If you stop, talking, and don't go hindering," drawled Percy, "I'll go."

Percy, continuing his trade wail of "Water," pushed his way through the Coffin Shop door, and was reprimanded by Mipps for daring to enter when he had seen the Vicar's white pony tethered to the gate-post.

Doctor Syn came to the rescue by saying kindly that he was glad to be there when Percy received his present of the yoke, which Mipps had so kindly made for him.

"Let's see you put it on," he said.

Percy stood the buckets down and took the yoke in both hands. It was finer than he had imagined. He stroked the smoothly shaped wood with his finger-tips, and felt the neat splicing of the ship's rope that gripped the strong iron hooks. He gave a gurgling moan of appreciation as he finally lifted the yoke over his head and gently lowered it till it fitted his hunched shoulders.

"Fits shipshape and Bristol fashion," said Mipps, eyeing his work with admiration. "Pick up the buckets, and let's see if all's easy.

The Vicar bent down and raised the bucket ropes, while Mipps adjusted the hooks. The stooping Percy watched them with anxiety.

"Now then, take the strain," ordered Mipps.

Very gingerly the lad began to raise himself. The bucket ropes were taut and then the buckets left the floor.

When Percy saw them swinging he gave vent to another gurgle of joy.

Then he took a slow step forward.

"Steady 'em with your hands," ordered Mipps, "or you'll have 'em swinging all over the place and slopping water worse than ever."

"That's it," said the Vicar. "Now let's see you walk down the shed."

With wonder and ecstasy written all over his face, and his mouth wide open, Percy started on his walk down the shop. When he reached the end he

turned slowly, and grinned at his own cleverness. On the way back to his benefactor he walked quicker, and began to call out his long-drawn wail, "Water."

"Still slops a bit," said Mipps critically. "But it don't splash his breeches like it used to."

"Just a minute, Mipps," replied the vicar. "Something has come back to me from the old days. Do you remember a native water-carrier, who used to fill up our ship's barrels from the quay of San Diego? I have just recollected a clever dodge he employed."

"A thin-looking, half-nigger in stripe-cotton breeches?" queried Mipps. "I've got him. And I remember a dodge he had, which was nothing less than highway robbery, saying he'd filled the barrels when he'd only drained 'em out, and tilted the same water back again. I remember catching him at it and drawing my clasp-knife across his throat, saying that if pork was in season I'd have him for it. Was it that dodge you was thinking of, Vicar? You was preaching at the Red Injun Christian church at the time.

"No, my good Mipps, though I remember the fellow as a rascal," laughed Doctor Syn. "I'll show you what his dodge was. Saw me this bit of wood in half."

He handed Mipps a scrap of wood which he picked up from the carp enters' bench. Mipps sawed it through.

Doctor Syn took the two pieces and placed one in each of the buckets of water.

"Floating islands," he explained. "Now with these on the surface of the water, Percy will find that the ripples of water will break upon their edges instead of against the rims of the buckets. It will avoid the splashings. I wonder, when I have seen poor Percy's breeches so splashed, that I have not thought of this dodge to save him from catching cold before. Doctor Pepper will be spared a good deal of physic in the future."

When Percy repeated his walk down the shop, he received no splashes from the contents of the buckets, which caused him to utter a succession of admiration gurgles at the new miracle.

Mipps picked the two pieces of wood from the water and threw them aside, and taking another section, sawed it in half, chislled them round, planed and polished them, and dropped them, into buckets.

"Never spoil a good ship for a bit o' tar," he said. "Now then, Percy, get a quick step into you, and see if Doctor Syn don't deserve to have free delivery of well-water same as me."

The miracle worked, and Mipps added tactfully, "This is the reward of our missionary efforts amongst the bloody heathen, Vicar."

"Water, water," cried Percy, as he walked the shop once more in rehearsal for his daily rounds in the future.

"Oh, and that reminds me too," added Mipps. "Your voice, my good lad, gets on my nerves same as it do the Squire and the Vicar. No more of that horrible gloomy cry of yours, because I've whittled you a whistle what you'll blow instead of howling. It shrills sweeter than a Bos'n's pipe, and I've fixed a lanyard for your neck, so as if you blows it out of them noisy lips of yours it won't drop overboard as the saying is. Here it be, so put it on and tell you clients that the cry of water will be no more heard in the land of Israel as 'Oly Bible says."

Over Percy's neck he hung a whitened cord attached to a large wooden whistle, which he thrust into Percy's loose mouth.

"Now then, blow, and blow hard to make it heard by the housewives," he ordered. "And no more horrible howlings when you're rounding the Horn with your craft.

Once more Percy walked proudly down the shop, blowing hard upon his instrument, which sounded shrill and clear.

"Learnt to make whistles, I did," he explained, "from an Injun, when I and the Vicar was preaching 'em the Blessed gospels."

Suddenly Doctor Syn held up his hand for silence.

"I can hear another pipe," he said.

Mipps went to the back casement and opened it, cocking his head sideways. "You're right, Vicar. And a drum tapping, too. It will be them Navy men marching towards us along the Hythe road."

"They are to be billeted in my Tythe Barn," said Doctor Syn. "You, Percy, had better get along there to be in readiness, if you want to get their order for water. You can tell them that you have already got the job with the Dragoons. I think, Mipps, we will ride along to welcome them."

The waiting crowd of gossipers were disappointed when they saw Doctor Syn mount his pony and wait for Mipps who was whistling to an aged donkey that was browsing lazily in a meadow behind the shop.

This animal, who rejoiced in the name of Lightining, because he never hurried, was officially the churchyard donkey, where he would pull the roller over the grass between the grave stones.

Mipps ran to meet him as he slowly walked across the meadow in answer to his master's call.

Slipping an old bridle over his head, Mipps clambered up on to the animal's hind quarters, and grasping a rein in each hand he manipulated his course as though he were steering with rudder strings.

Indeed there was never any doubt as to Mipp's old vocation, even without his continual boasting on the subject, for whatever he did smacked somehow of the sea.

Meantime the sound of the drum and fife grew nearer, and although Percy was anxious to take his first proud walk with his yoke along the village street, he thought it wisest to go the short cut across the fields in order to reach the Tythe Barn before the arrival of the Navy men.

He had made a good contract with the Dragoons. He could not carry all the squadron buckets for horses and men, but he had insisted on his right to work the windlass on the well, and for each ten pailfuls he was paid one penny by the Quartermaster. He hoped to secure an even better bargain from the naval men, and as he swung along over the fields behind the village, he rehearsed what he would say.

While Doctor Syn waited for Mipps to steer his mount on to the road, he exchanged morning greetings with his parishioners, apologizing for having immediate need of his Sexton, and urging them, as they appeared to be at a loose end, to hurry along the street to the other end of the village and to give the strangers a hearty welcome within their gates.

"What with those gallant Dragoons cantering over there," he said, "and these jolly sea-dogs arriving from Dover, we hope that soon our village will be free of this wretched smuggling business, and that the mysterious Scarecrow will trouble the March no more."

"If they catch him, sir," replied one of them, "it will be a great occasion when he comes to be hanged. Would they try him at the Court Houses, sir?"

"Of course," nodded Doctor Syn. "As Leveller of Marsh Scotts, our good Squire would preside, and he would be judged by the Lords of the Level. As you say it will be a great occasion. He has given our good Marsh an evil reputation for too long. They talk about the Scarecrow even in busy London, where you would think they had enough criminals of their own, without concerning themselves with ours."

"But he does concern 'em, sir," went on the fisherman. "They say he not only lands the goods hereabouts and takes it to the 'hides,' but looks after their disposal with the receivers in London. All I can say is that if that's true he must be busier than I'd care to be. It's one thing to ride the Marsh, and scare honest folk from off of it, but another to run the business side as well."

Doctor Syn nodded. "He must be a very busy man indeed. I like hard work myself, but after riding the Marsh all day looking after my scattered flock, I find parochial accounts very irksome in the evenings. What you have said makes me feel almost sorry for the Scarecrow. I only wish he would rest from his ill-chosen labours."

As soon as Mipps had persuaded Lightning on to the road, Doctor Syn led the way along the street, followed at a respectful distance by the villagers, who were joined by others as they passed the scattered cottages and shops, so that by the time they had entered the Avenue on the way to the church, they mustered a considerable crowd, and completely blocked the roadway.

The Dragoons, who had finished with their morning exercise, and had trotted in sections of fours behind their squadron leader, Major Faunce, were obliged to break down into a walk and finally to halt.

The Major by riding on to the footpath was able to bring his charger to the front, where he reined up alongside Doctor Syn.

"Good morning, Major," said the Vicar. "It seems that it is a case of 'All the King's horses and all the King's men,' come to rid us of our parochial danger. I begin to think that it is money thrown away. I cannot think that the Scarecrow is of flesh and blood. Do you really think he will ever be caught?"

"If the Navy catches him," replied the handsome young office, "I will agree that we of the Army are the second service."

"They make a brave show," went on the Vicar, watching the party of sailors swinging towards them along the winding road.

A tall, thin, hard-bitten naval captain, riding a gaunt charger loaned from the garrison at Dover Castle, headed the procession of marching, whistling seamen. Behind him wee two little powder-monkeys, one beating lustily upon a deep side-drum and the other causing a long wry-necked fife to squeal forth a jolly hornpipe to which the company responded with a swin ging step and a carefree manner.

"I'll say this for that naval officer," remarked the Dragoon, "that he sits a horse as though he can ride."

"Which is more than one can say for most that follow the sea," put in the Vicar. "Take Mipps, there, my Sexton. True, he is only mounted upon an ass, but he makes its hindquarters look like thwarts. His is mentally in a boat and not upon an animal. Why? Because he once followed the sea as a carpenter. I agree that officer rides, even though his charger walks. One can see that he could follow the hounds."

"Got a bit of a name, I understand," went on the Dragoon, "as a prize martinet."

"A necessary qualification, too," replied Doctor Syn, "in order to control those jolly dogs."

"The Scarecrow might well be conceited," laughed the Major, "if he could only have seen this arrival."

Perhaps he is here, who knows?" returned the Vicar, looking round upon the staring villagers.

Just then the general interest taken in the approaching detachment was interrupted by a shrill whistling that jarred against the notes of the nautical air, so proudly blown by the sturdy little powder-monkey on his fife.

It was Percy marching beneath his yoke, and blowing lustily upon his new whistle. The crowd roared with laughter as he strutted from the churchyard to the open space before the Court House, where he took up his position immediately beneath the gallows.

The Major leant down from his tall charger and whispered to Doctor Syn, "You don't think he is the Scarecrow, do you?"

The Vicar looked towards the water-carrier, smiled and shrugged his shoulders.

"That's an idea certainly," he whispered back. "I often think that perhaps poor Percy is not quite so simple as he looks. He would certainly have good opportunity for passing his orders amongst the villagers, if any of them should be in this dastardly business, which I can never bring myself to think. Against your theory though, we must remember that both of us have seen the Scarecrow riding, showing a sash that is sadly lacking in that poor lad. No, I don't somehow think that Percy can claim that notoriety. Far more likely that he is somebody used to following the hounds with the Squire, and yet I can think of no one in that

category of daring riders who can show the promised of the Scarecrow's brain. I think the nearest we ever got to a solution of his mysterious identity was when we tried to fit that equally elusive rogue Jimmie Bone into the role. But the Scarecrow quickly put him to rights by robbing him before witnesses of what he had robbed from them. Perhaps the Scarecrow is really the Devil all the time."

The conversation was terminated because the Captain of the Navy men called a halt.

Doctor Syn rode forward saying: "Welcome to you and to you gallant men, Captain Blain. I am Doctor Syn, the Vicar here, and I voice the whole parish in saying that Dymchurch is at your service, sir."

"Thankee, parson," returned the Captain. "Stand easy, men," he rapped out, turning in the saddle. "You're here on shore duty, but that don't mean that man-o-war discipline is relaxed. So behave yourselves, and no chalking drinks at the inns, mind. Bos'n, take charge while I see to the billeting."

Doctor Syn pointed out the big Tythe Barn in the Vicarage grounds, near by, and said that both he and the Squire were in agreement that this was the most suitable place for housing the men.

The Captain merely said he would like to see it, and was setting off with the Vicar when the Major introduced himself, saying that he was very ready to co-operate in the work against the smugglers. To this the Captain made no sort of acceptance, beyond a gruff grunt, and adding: "Till I have had time to look around and get the strength of the situation, I cannot say, sir, whether I shall favour co-operation or no. If I find that I want the help of your troopers, I will let you know all in good time."

Doctor Syn noted that this somewhat churlish attitude from the Captain was resented by the Major of Dragoons, who turned his charger and ordered the crowd to stand back, if they didn't wish to be ridden down. He then sang out the orders for the squadron to proceed to the horselines behind the Ship Inn.

The crowd fell back to let them pass, and then began the volleying of jests between the two branches of the service.

The sailors, seeing that their Captain was riding away towards the church and vicarage, in company with the parson, indulged in such taunts as, "Put your little horses away, and don't let the nasty Scarecrow steal 'em."

"You get back to your little hammocks on the guard Ship," retorted a trooper, riding by. "The Scarecrow ain't afraid of little cutlasses and handspikes.

But he don't like sabres."

"He's never seen 'em," scoffed another of the sailors. "You know little boys ain't allowed out on the Marsh at nights."

"You wait till you see us jumping them infernal dykes, while you slips into 'em, water spaniels."

The Major, secretly amused, nevertheless thought it his duty to stop further bandying, so rapped out, "Silence."

The Bos'n, also amused, nevertheless, thought it fit to show his authority too, so sang out, "Fall in."

The sailors who had rested their kit-bags on the low churchyard wall, hoisted them on to their shoulders once more, and falling into line began to whistle a sea-song, which encouraged the powder-monkeys to fall to again at their instruments.

Some distance away, Percy blew louder on his whistle.

The Vicar, riding by him with the Captain, interrupted his remarks about the Tythe Barn which they were approaching by turning to the water carrier and saying, "That's enough, my lad, for now." They were walking their horses, or rather the Captain was walking his, and Doctor Syn ambled along to keep pace, Mipps following at respectful distance on his donkey.

Though the Vicar was chatting about the barn and pointing out the end of it jutting out behind the Vicarage, he was mentally weighing up the naval officer.

As tall as himself, and sitting straight in the saddle as though he carried a ramrod in his back, his borrowed charger gave him the advantage in height, so that from his little fat pony the Vicar had to look up at him.

The Captain's face, he saw, was hard and deeply lined, but his one eye had a roguish twinkle. He had lost the other against the French. His voice was deep and husky, and his neat-fitting uniform suggested that here was a man who would keep his vessel trim and brisk. The look of the Captain reminded the Vicar of his own past, for just such a man had Doctor Syn once been, when he had sailed under the black flag as Captain Clegg. By the time they drew rein at the barn he had come to the conclusion he had expected to arrive at by what he had heard of Captain Blain, namely, that here was a personality to whom even the dashing Scarecrow had better show respect.

Aye, Captain Blain was certainly an enemy who would give the best a good fight both with strength and wit.

"It's a g ood barn, Captain," remarked Doctor Syn. "Plenty of room inside it. My Sexton here, Mister Mipps, keeps it all shipshape."

The Captain surveyed Mipps critically, then a smile twisted his lips and creased his one eye, as though he found the figure astride the old donkey comical.

Now Mipps only liked to be thought comical when he had uttered a remark which he intended to be funny, so to show his resentment at the Captain's quizzing, he dismounted from his donkey as though he were tumbling ashore from a boat, and touching his hat to the officer in nautical style, remarked dryly: "P'raps if them men of yours was told by someone with sense how close they is to the 'oly churchyard, they would batten down their noise a bit.

There's many a good Dymchurch corpse lying yonder, enjoying a well-earned rest, as the Vicar will agree."

"We shall not disturb your corpses, Mister Sexton," replied the Captain sternly, "unless I suspect that their coffins contain contraband. 'Twould be a good 'hide,' and has been put into practice before now. It is likely then that I shall order my Bos'n to pipe all coffins on deck for inspection."

"I fear, Captain," returned Doctor Syn, " that as Vicar of this parish, I could never countenance sacrilege."

"Contraband in coffins is sacrilege enough, so that I shall be on the side of the Church, Reverend Sir, by stopping it."

As he spoke the Captain became aware of Percy, who had followed in order to obtain an agreement for the sailors' necessary supplies of water.

"And what's that fool staring at?" he demanded.

Doctor Syn explained Percy's office in the village and advised the Captain to follow the example of the Dragoons and employ him.

"I'll refer him to the Bos'n," replied the Captain, "and what the soldiers pay, why, so will we."

Percy shook his head at this and said in his monotonous drawl: "Soldiers earn little. Sailors a lot. And that's proper, as sailors comes first with King George. I never yet met a sailor what a miser, but all soldiers is poor fish."

The Captain let out an explosive chuckle. "The village idiot is not only a flatterer, but a man of business it seems." He then shouted in his sea voice, "Bos'n!"

Up came that rotund sea-dog at the double, followed by his men, and at the Captain's orders he took Percy under his care, and after some haggling it was arranged that water should be brought to the barn whenever the casks needed filling. Since this did not entail the sailors sending fatigue parties to fetch it, like the Dragoons, Percy insisted on a slightly higher rate of pay, which the Bos'n, who was a jovial and good-hearted old dog, respectfully advised his officer to accept.

This the Captain did with a further chuckle at Percy's business capacity, and then ordered the Bos'n to book him a room at the Ship Inn.

This was Doctor Syn's cue to interrupt. "Forgive me, Captain, but I have heard that you are to be invited to the Court House yonder as the guest of Sir Anthony Cobtree, our Squire, who is already entertaining Major Faunce, whom you have just seen, and Mr. Brackenbury, his lieutenant of Dragoons. I venture to suggest, however, that you will find yourself less restricted in my house. You may go and come, just as you please, even in the night hours.

My old house-keeper is used to me setting off at all hours upon this pony to visit my sick parishioners, who are scattered far over the Marsh there."

He pointed out across the flat expanse of dyke-divided pasturages that stretched away until it met either the sea or sky. He then went on, while the Captain appeared to be obsessed in the Marshlands which the Parson had pointed out. It was somewhere there, in that mysterious distance, that the equally mysterious Scarecrow rode at night at the head of his phantom horsemen.

"Indeed," went on the Vicar, "I am setting out now to see a poor old woman who is sick, with my panniers here filled, as you see, with new-laid eggs and other nourishment. But I must not weary you with my parochial cares and chatter, or you will think twice before accepting my invitation, which I sincerely hope you will at least consider."

"I do, Parson," replied the Captain, "and upon my soul, I thank you. Very seamanly of you, I'm sure. As to the Court House, from what you tell me, I shall be glad not to reside there, for I can see that I should quickly come to loggerheads with those officers of the Junior Service. No doubt with the Squire, too, for I hear that he resents outsiders coming to enforce the law upon his territory, since he is the chief magistrate of the district."

"He is of my opinion," said Doctor Syn, "that if the land is used as a smuggler's base, there are none of his tenants who are in any way implicated.

"Which remains to be seen, Parson," said the Captain sharply. "I intend to stamp out a smuggling that is known to exist. And I shall do it in my own way, and only collaborate with those who are willing to take my orders. By the way, Reverend

Sir, without presuming to dictate to you as mine host, I should be glad of a room in your Vicarage which has a casement looking out over the Marsh."

"I think that can be managed," returned Doctor Syn. "And if you can allay the pangs of hunger for another two hours, I can do myself the pleasure of dining with you. I must needs be some little time with old Mother Handaway, who is as greedy for a long reading of the Scriptures as she is for good things to eat. I will send a message to the Squire informing him that you are to be my guest, unless you would rather tell him yourself when you call to present your credentials."

"I have no credentials to present to him, nor any," retorted the Captain. 'I think rather it will be the other way, and that I shall be demanding credentials from one and all. My position is like this, reverend Sir. The Preventive men on this portion of coast, not able to cope with this notorious Scarecrow, who is terrorizing the neighbourhood, frightening folk from the Marsh yonder, while he runs his contraband, first applied to General Troubridge at Dover for some Dragoons, and then, since the Scarecrow still worsted these, they further approached the General's brother, Admiral Troubridge, who handed me the commission, for it seems that the Admiral is anxious to beat his brother at the game of Scarecrowscaring. I presume that most people here realize the vast sums that are involved. Yes sir, vast sums, of money that never find their way to the Revenue coffers. It's money that never find their way to the Revenue coffers. It's my duty to see that this state of things comes to an end, and you can lay to it I'll do that duty to the best of my powers, by thunder, and take no interferences neither. As for you, reverend Sir, I can promise you this. Aboard your quarters I'm your guest, and will not worry you about my business outside. You will find me courteous, and ready to join you in any general conversation, or in a game of chess or backgammon if you've the fancy. Whatever I think of folk in your parish, I'll keep to myself and not put you in an awkward position. That's fair, I take it?"

"Perfectly fair,' assented the Doctor. He then turned to Mipps who had naturally heard the whole conversation.

"Mister Mipps, you will about-ships with your donkey, and give Mrs. Fowey the necessary orders from me for the Captain's accommodation in the panelled room overlooking the Marsh. You will then trot after me, across the Marsh. You will easily catch me up, as I must do little more than a walk, or I shall be breaking the eggs."

"Aye, aye, Vicar," exclaimed Mipps, once more perching himself upon Lightnings's hindquarters, and manipulating the reins as though pulling round the rudder of a boat.

"Queer fellow that Sexton of yours," remarked the Captain. "More like a seaman than a sexton, what with his tarred pigtail sticking out like a jigger-gaff, and the way he steers that animal."

The Vicar laughed. "Mipps has been a ship's carpenter in his day, and aboard a man-of-war, too. As good an old rascal as you'll find upon acquaintance. Aye, Captain, you'll come to like Mipps well enough."

"I dare say. He seems a bit of an oddity to me though," returned the Captain.

"A character certainly allowed the Vicar. "But take it from me, who have known him these many years under trials and blessings, a good one. In spite of whimsicalities he is at heart a good and kind little fellow."

"I know the type well," nodded the Captain. "He is a one-man's servant, and as such would be faithful to the last, no doubt."

Doctor Syn perhaps perceived that the Captain was attempting somehow to drive him into some toil, so he answered quickly: "No, he is faithful and kind to the whole parish, young and old. That water-carrier, for instance, is blessing him at the moment, since Mipps fashioned that yoke for him, to make his work the easier. And he did it too, out of his own leisure time. Even new-born babies take to Mipps."

"Well, if the Scarecrow gets me on the Marsh one of these dark nights," laughed the Captain, "I'll be glad if you will not only read the prayers over my coffin, but write my epitaph, too. If you give me such a character as you give to this sexton behind his back, I think I shall have a better chance in the next world."

"And as Mipps will tell you shortly, Captain," laughed the Doctor, "no one can knock up a coffin better than he, so you see your corpse would be in

the best of hands. But joking aside, I trust that your presence means an end to Death stalking the Marsh at night."

"I'll take the first step in that direction then," said the Captain, dismounting and handing the reins to one of his men.

"And that is?" asked Doctor Syn.

"Billeting my men," replied the Captain.

The Vicar responded to his salute with a benedictory gesture, and then walked his pony out upon the Marsh road.

A quarter of an hour later he was overhauled by Mipps who had put Lightning to the nearest point of a hand gallop which that animal could be persuaded to accomplish.

"Very neat, Vicar, the way you manoeurvred the Captain's lodging," he remarked. "It'll be a close eye on him, eh, sir?"

"That's so, my good Mipps. From tonight it will be watch and watch about between us two. If we know his moves beforehand we can the better check 'em, and I fancy even then that he will give us a good run for our barrels."

In and out the winding dyke-bordered lanes they walked their mounts till old Mother Handaway's hovel appeared in sight, and then Doctor Syn broke a silence that had lasted some quarter of an hour.

"By his suspicion of your coffins, Mister Sexton, I gather that this Captain is too well informed. We may have to employ new methods, and here is one for passing the word to all concerned that has only just occurred to me. You remember those two bits of wood I floated in Percy's buckets? He likes them. They are useful since they prevent the splashing. Make him a present of some well-shaped floats that will appeal to him as a toy appeals to a child. I'll suggest that you make them like the four suits in a pack of cards. Two aces of each. Chisel and polish them well.

"On his rounds, see that he makes your Coffin Shop the first port of call, in order that you may tell him which pieces to float. We will arrange a code together before I return to dine with the Captain. After dark we will meet those concerned at Doubledyke. Before they leave the Oast House, where our meeting is to be, they will all have been instructed in the code, and in future the innocent lad, Percy, can carry the Scarecrow's orders to every cottage in the parish."

"That's a pretty notion," chuckled Mipps, "and I marvel that we never thought on it before."

Doctor Syn certainly did not read the Scriptures to old Mother Handaway, for there was much to don on the Scarecrow's business. Not that the old hag would have profited had he read to her, for she was a mad old thing whom the distant villages upon the Marsh held to be a witch. Perhaps she had every reason to think she was, for did not the Devil himself visit her, sometimes in the shape of the good Vicar of Dymchurch, and sometimes riding past her cottage as the dread Scarecrow? And had he not given her many golden guineas for service rendered? She had had little to do for such high payment, since it was Jimmie Bone, the Highwayman, who groomed the Scarecrow's horse which she guarded in her underground stable, the entrance of which was so cunningly hidden by the stack of dried bulrushes in the side of the deep dry dyke that ran before her cottage. This was deep enough to conceal a mounted man form the Marsh around.

Unless anyone happened to be in the dyke itself, the opening of the secret door could never be seen, but the three men who used it always took the greatest precautions to ensure that no one was about The dry dyke, some said, had been made by the Romans at their first landing, but the stable had been built probably by some independent smuggler years back. Mother Handaway's grandfather had told her the secret of its entrance, and she had kept it to herself till she first hid the Highwayman there, at a time when hard pressed and wounded he had otherwise been caught and hanged.

A good hiding-place and none better, hidden also by the cow-shed, and with grass growing from good soil on its roof. Inside, the roof was groinspanned,

made by masons who knew their business and who were aware that it had to stay for generations. Once, it was lain down, in some local history, that somewhere in the vicinity of the dry dyke was an ancient building of sorts, but naturally the Handaways never allowed the interested parties to search for it.

Certain it was to the Vicar, the Sexton and the Highwayman a most excellent dry stable.

The other dykes in the vicinity of the farmyard were all live dykes filled with water, and there were many at this point of the Marsh that intersected, while the mist ribbons that rose up around their banks gave ample hiding-place to the farm itself. From a distance it was exceedingly difficult to say what was going on around Mother Handaway's. On the other hand, anyone at her cottage could discern anyone moving on the Marsh for a considerable distance.

Although there was on this occasion no need for caution, it was taken.

Inside the stable the tall Highwayman received them, endeavouring to conceal his yawns, for he had been out on the Dover road till the early hours of the morning on his illegal business.

On a rough table at the far end beneath a lighted stable lantern, there was set out a heap of watches, rings, and other trinkets, with a strong leather bag from which a heap of guineas and crown pieces had been spilled.

"A good night's taking," laughed the Vicar. "It seems I am come at an opportune moment to collect my tythes."

"Which I always pay you, you will own," replied Gentleman James.

"Aye, Jimmie Bone is the only honest Gentleman upon the road." Said Mipps.

Both the pony and donkey had been led into the stable, and were quickly stalled. The vicar first entered Gehenna's stall, and made a fuss of the magnificent creature known too well by the Revenue men as the Scarecrow's phantom horse. He then went into the next stall and patted Mister Bone's charger, a black animal like Gehenna, though of quieter disposition, and trained by his master like any circus horse. As for Gehenna, woe betide any who tried to touch him other than the three jolly rascals in the stable. Gehenna had never lost a fierceness which even the gypsy horse dealers had failed to tame.

"Help yourself, my good Jimmie Bone, to the good things in the pony's panniers," said the Vicar. "You'll find some good liquor in one of them, and we can all do with a tot of brandy. Then while you make a meal we will get to work on our new code, Mister Sexton."

The Highwayman, who depended upon Doctor Syn and old Mother Handaway for his safety And food, fell to one end of the table upon a cold capon

which the Vicar's housekeeper had prepared, thinking it was for some poor sick soul upon the Marsh.

Meantime the Vicar, between sips of brandy, dipped a goose-quill into an ink-horn, and wrote out a list of places along that part of the coast. He then began to sketch in pairs of aces against them.

"You must find time to chisel out these eight pieces of wood for Percy's buckets this very day," he said. "We shall start using them immediately, and I should like to have them when I meet the Night-riders at the Oast House this evening, in order to give them their instructions."

An hour later Doctor Syn, with empty panniers, and followed by Mipps, jogged his way back to Dymchurch, in order to entertain the Captain at dinner.

During the meal, their conversation was general, since Doctor Syn sensed that the Captain was anxious not to discuss the object of his arrival on the Marsh. So the talk gradually veered into distant parts, for both men had sailed the seven seas. The Captain in his line of business, and Syn, as he explained, in the cause of spreading the Gospel amongst the heathenish parts of sea and land. By the time they had lighted their churchwarden pipes, both men had acquired a respect and liking for each other, while their various adventures were exchanged.

After their long march from Dover, the Captain had instructed his Bos'n to let the men rest in the barn, as he wished to take them out that very night upon the Marsh in order to accustom them to the dyke-land which he hoped would be their battlefield in the near future. For the same reason Captain Blain retired to his room, in order to snatch a little sleep before the night march, and Doctor Syn prepared to set out once more across the Marsh with his panniers filled with good things for his poor and needy.

Captain Blain set his casement open wide, and for some time studied the lie of the land through his telescope. He watched particularly the route taken by the Vicar and Sexton, jotting down directions in his note-book.

"I'll lay that same course," he said to himself, watching the white pony and donkey as they zigzagged this way and that, "for they seem to have reached the centre of the Marsh and have not once descended into a dyke."

At last they disappeared into a belt of mist which prevented him from seeing their arrival at Mother Handaway's.

Supper having been fixed for ten o'clock, and Doctor Syn, having given Mrs. Fowey, the housekeeper, orders to call his guest at nine-thirty, the Captain closed his telescope, divested himself of coat, waistcoat and cravat, kicked off his buckled shoes, and lay down upon his four-poster bed.

Meanwhile the secret stable had once more swallowed up the Vicar of Dymchurch and his Sexton, as well as both their animals. Here, while Jimmie Bone groomed the three horses, ready for business, Syn and Mipps perfected the code and committed it to memory. There then followed other affairs connected with the Scarecrow to be discussed and settled. The various gangs of men had to be allocated to their particular jobs for the next 'run.'

Doctor Syn, or rather the Scarecrow, had already received the names of the vessels expected for the landing on the following night, and each vessel had to have sufficient men for the unloading on the beach. The route to be taken from the coast to the hills way gone over carefully with the help of a large map that marked every twisting lane and dyke upon the Marsh. Doctor Syn had copied this from amongst the ordinance survey archives in the Court House.

He had made three copies secretly. One he kept at the Vicarage, another in the hidden stable, and a third in the little summer hut which the Squire had had built for him upon the sea wall, a place in which he very often worked out his sermons, so that he could keep an eye upon shipping in the fairway of the Channel, when needing a relaxation from divinity.

By the time Doctor Syn's plan of campaign had been settled in detail, it was dark outside upon the Marsh.

While Mipps helped his master to divest himself of clerical clothes and to put on the wild rags of the Scarecrow, the Highwayman painted the faces of the horses with phosphorus.

The three men then put on hideous masks, and mounting their spirited horses, rode from the stable into the dry dyke, while the old hag, who had been

watching from the opening of the door since darkness had settled in, was ready to close it quickly behind them. Telling her that they would return within the hour, they galloped away across the lonely Marsh towards the Oast House on double-dyke Farm.

2

THE TWO HEARTS

On arrival they were met by some thirty Nightriders, masked and cloaked, who had already tethered their horses in the large farmy ard. The leader's horses were taken to the stables, and as soon as the Scarecrow was satisfied that a lookout had been placed to guard against any surprise attack, he entered the Oast House, followed by his men. The interior was lighted by lanterns, and the three leaders sat upon barrels, facing the others who were ranged against the circular brick wall. The doors were safely barred, and then the Scarecrow addressed them, calling each man by the name he went by in the gang.

Indeed, for everyone's security, no one knew rightly just who his colleagues might be in the ordinary way of life upon the Marsh. This guarded against any personal betrayal, and gave to each the same feeling of security as the Scarecrow himself enjoyed. Certainly not one of them had any idea who the great leader was, and though they might have had a shrewd guess as to one or two identities, the only one they were sure about was Sexton Mipps, since whether he was dressed as Hellspite or himself, he was the voice of the scarecrow when the leader was not present.

With the utmost patience the Scarecrow explained the new code and put each man through a rigorous examination of it.

"Now, Curlew," he would say in his croaking voice which he always used when playing the Scarecrow, "suppose Percy carries a wooden diamond floating in his right bucket, and a club in the left, what will you know by that?"

"That the cargo is to be landed at Herring Hang. Scarecrow," came the answer in the singing tone used by the Night-riders to disguise their ordinary speech.

"Correct," replied the Scarecrow. "And now, Raven, if the signs were reversed, what then?"

"Littlestone Beach, Scarecrow," came the singsong answer from him who bore the title of the Raven.

It was a long and tedious business, since half of the Night-riders were more valuable in brawn and muscle than brains, but as Mipps remarked to his master later, Doctor Syn showed the same care in teaching his wild class as ever he did as the Vicar in the Sunday school.

At last, when satisfied that each of them knew every signal, including those who had been on guard outside whose places had been taken by those who had learned the code quickest, the Scarecrow warned his men that Captain Blain would be a real danger, since he was a man of ingenuity, but that if they kept rigidly to the orders he gave, they could feel confident that the 'runs' would be carried out in safety.

He then dismissed them with the order to be prepared for a big 'landing' on the following night, and to keep a weather-eye open for the watercarrier's buckets.

By ten o'clock Doctor Syn was supping pleasantly with the Captain, but though he gave his guest many details of the Scarecrow's past achievements, he was still unable to make the Captain communicative concerning his own plans, save that he intended to take his men for a night march in order to accustom them at once into the sort of night work they would be called upon to carry out till the Scarecrow was caught and placed in irons.

"We shall be setting out at midnight, Vicar," he said.

"Has I not a sermon to prepare against next Sunday, I might have offered you my services as a guide," replied Doctor Syn. "But I shall be working after midnight, I fear. My parish is so scattered, and I have so many of my flock down with the Marsh ague, that I get little time for study during the day, and even in the night hours I am no more free from being called from my bed than is our good physician Doctor Pepper."

"Ah well," said the Captain, "we shall steer a safe enough course I make no doubt, even though it may be taken by cutlass point. And if you will kindly loan me a key to your front door, I shall be able to let myself in without any disturbance."

Doctor Syn did not sit up long after midnight. He did not need to prepare a sermon. He could always depend upon his own ready tongue when the moment came. It amused him to preach dry-as-dust sermons, because no man in the Church had an easier facility for preaching good ones that gripped a congregation when he felt the occasion warranted it. He only became dry-as-dust, to prevent his own preferment in the Church. He did not seek publicity or popularity as a preacher because it would not have suited his book at all to be transferred from little Dymchurch.

Knowing the value of conserving his strength, he went to bed and to sleep directly the Captain had set out, knowing also that for that night at least the sea-dogs could do no harm upon the Marsh, which they would find utterly deserted.

He was awakened by Mrs. Fowey, the housekeeper, with a cup of chocolate at nine o'clock, and so good a host he was that he ordered her to let the Captain sleep."

"I have no idea when he came in from his duty," he said, "but I told him to ring when he woke and needed chocolate and shaving water. Did you hear him come in?"

Mrs. Fowey had not.

As it happened the Captain had let himself in very quietly about six o'clock, for Percy had seen the sailors return muddy and weary when he was working the windlass for his first pair of buckets, which he carried round to the Coffin Shop earlier than usual, since he was anxious to see the new pieces of wood which Mipps had told him about the night before.

He found the Sexton still in his hammock when he peeped through the open casement, and blew loudly upon his whistle.

"Belay there with that pipe," ordered Mipps, "while I lights up mine. Then I'll show a leg and let you abroad.

Mipps stretched and yawned, and then took a tinderbox from the oak beam above his head and lit his short clay pipe. He then gripped the beam with his fingers, and unhooked the head end of the hammock, then swinging himself along to the other end he let the hammock fall to the ground, dropping down lightly on the top of it. He then rolled it up in man-of-war's fashion, and stowed it away upon a shelf. All this time clouds of tobacco smoke surrounded his head. He went to the door and raised the bar, letting Percy in.

"There are your floats," said the Sexton, pointing to eight neatly chiselled pieces of wood which lay on the coffin lid.

While Percy lifted them carefully one by one, with many a gurgle of delight, Mipps went to another shelf and took down a tin which Percy knew of old contained snuff.

"You'll keep them signs here, my lad," announced the Sexton, " and each morning I'll tell you which ones we'll put in, eh? Sometimes we'll have hearts, and sometimes diamonds, clubs or spades, as the fancy strikes us, eh?: I'll wager the villagers will be wondering every journey you take which ones will be floating in them bucket. I shouldn't be surprised if it don't encourage betting more than a race-meeting."

"Will you chooses one and me choose one?" asked Percy, "or do we go turn and turn about?"

"We'll always ask Judy," replied the Sexton solemnly, "and I'll go and ask her now."

Judy was the mane of a wooden idol which Mipps had acquired in the east Indies. A female figure with large ears, sleepy-looking eyes, and elaborately carved necklace upon her naked breasts, a tall head-dress and a skirt with carved snakes all over it. Her hands were clasped upon her middle as she stood with bare feet upon her block of wood.

This brown figure, which was about a foot in height, possessed Percy with vague terrors for the soul of mister Mipps. He thought it misguided of a Christian sexton to posses an idol, until its owner had assured him solemnly that he had himself baptized the goddess into the Christian Faith, and given her the good name of Judy in place of a long heathenish title which he had never been able to pronounce.

Mipps held a piece of parchment in front of the idol and thrust his little finger through the crook of her arm.

'Now, Judy, my beauty," began the Sexton," we wants you to point out with the help of my finger, since you can't move your own off your belly, which floats will be lucky for Percy to place in his buckets. Take your time, my girl, and choose.

First which of these signs goes in the right one. Here they all be drawed out very nice. What do you say?" He put the idol up to his ear, as though it was whispering to him. "Oh, I see. Well certainly, having been a goddess you've every right to have you own say in it. You don't want to choose from the drawings, eh? You wants to choose the bits of wood yourself and give 'em to Percy into his own paws, eh? Well, then, we shan't be wanting the drawings any more then since the signs is all made ship-shape, so we'll throw it away? Certainly." He crumpled up the parchment and dropped it on the floor behind the coffin which served as his counter.

He then thrust his other little finger through the other crook in her arm and walked the idol up and down the coffin lid as though it was viewing the various pieces of wood. He then made the figure stoop, and with his fingers he lifted up one of the two aces of clubs.

"There you are, Percy," said Mipps solemnly. "Take it from her and hold it in your right hand while she considers the other one." This time he made the idol pick up one of the diamond shapes, which Percy accepted in his left hand, giving the idol an absurd little bob of respect.

"So that's settled all very amicable," went on the Sexton. "Put the club in you starboard bucket and the diamond in the port. And mind you, Percy, if you was to change them without Judy here telling you, she'd bring the most 'orrible disaster upon you, me and the village, not to mention Squire and the 'oly Vicar. So don't you change 'em for no one, see?"

Percy did as he was ordered, and stooped down to place the floats carefully at the bottom of the empty buckets, for he had poured the water into the cask as he had come into the door.

Mipps, thinking him to be occupied below the coffin with his buckets, very quickly picked up the parchment he had thrown down, but Percy saw him do this through the trestles on which the coffin rested, and he wondered why Mipps who had thrown away the paper should pick it up again, and place it with so much care and so furtively inside the old tin containing the snuff. He would have liked to have seen that parchment with the drawings, and was about to ask Mipps if he might do so, when there suddenly dashed through the open door a fisherman named Hart, who, seeing Percy, shouted out, " Where's Mipps?"

"Here he be," replied that worthy, looking round from the dark corner where the shelves were. "What do you want, mate? Something wrong?"

"Aye, big trouble, Sexton," explained the fisherman, who was almost out of breath with running.

"Trouble?" snapped Mipps, and Percy wondered why he put his finger to his lips, and glanced angrily first towards the fisherman and then in his direction.

"Personal trouble," replied Hart. "Nothing to do with King's men or wicked smugglers. No. It's that our boat has been washed up on the tide and badly holed. She's empty, too, and my young bother had her out last night. May I have the loan of yours to search for him?"

"Of course, mate," replied the Sexton, quickly pulling on his coat. "I'll come along and lend a hand. Poor young Fred. Not come back, eh? And his wife with a new-born kid."

"Aye, and what seems to make it worse," went on Hart, "is this day being the old folks' Golden Wedding. The only hope is that Fred may have got picked up, but it's slender."

"Aye, maybe, by some vessel that couldn't put him ashore immediate like, replied Mipps. "There's a good chance of that, I should say. Fred's a good swimmer and a strong enough lad, and there weren't a great sea running last night. Come along. We can pull round to Dungeness and see if we can hear nay news of him. Last night's tide ran that way."

As he hurried to the door he looked at back at Percy. "Stow them other floats on the shelf there, my lad," he ordered, "and don't go changing 'em from what we said whatever happens, mind."

Left alone, Percy's curiosity got the better of him, for as he placed the spare pieces of wood on the shelf his hand touched the tin of snuff. There could be no great harm in opening it, he thought, and having a look at the drawings from which Mipps had fashioned the floats.

When he took the lid off and peered inside, he could see nothing but the dark brown stuff, and no sign of the parchment. But he remembered that Mipps had given the tin a good shaking, and had thus covered it up with the snuff. Percy wondered whether he had done this on purpose. Why should Mipps want to hide a small piece of parchment which he had already crumpled up and thrown carelessly away and then picked up again? Percy put his ling fingers into the tin, and sure enough he found the parchment buried beneath the snuff. He drew it out very carefully, anxious not to spill any of the brown dust, which made Mipps sneeze so heartily. He somehow did not want Mipps to know that he was prying. The little sexton might not like it, he though, and he did not want to vex one who had shown him such kindness.

He looked at Judy, and was relived that her eyes appeared to be close shut beneath her heavy, languid lids. He hoped she wouldn't tell the Sexton what he was doing, but for the life of him he could not resist the temptation. He had meant to ask the Sexton if he might see it when all was said and done, and this though weighed with him and gave him a little comfort.

Now although Percy had done little good for himself at school, partly because he hated the master, Mister Rash, who had no patience with him, and made him a butt upon all occasions, and partly because everyone calling him the Village Idiot, he took no pains to make them think otherwise, he had at least mastered the alphabet, and could spell a few words of one syllable. In spite of this limitation he yet knew all the names on the local signposts, and no sooner had he spread out the piece of parchment, than he recognized that here was a list of familiar places, against which were sketches of his bits of wood. There, for instance, was the starboard club and the port diamond, commanded by Judy, and against them was the name Littlestone Beach. After some difficulty he made out the word at the top of the list to be LANDINGS. Two hearts together against 'Dungeness, Sou' west', made him think of this sudden trouble to the Hart family.

He not only liked Fred, who had always been kind to him, but he knew how much the old people had looked forward to the golden Wedding, which was to be a day of great rejoicing, and now it seemed all was spoiled. As he stowed away the list into the tin and covered it once more with the snuff, his eyes filled with tears of sorrow for the Harts, so to clear his snivelling, which he had no wish for the parish to see upon his first day of rounds with his new floats, he stole a good pinch of snuff, had a prodigious sneeze and felt better.

Then with the ace of clubs in his right bucket and the diamond ace in his left, he went back to the well to refill.

Now although the Hart tragedy was the source of village gossip, he could not fail to notice that at each cottage particular interest was taken in his bits of wood.

Some folk said how good it was of the Sexton to have taken so much pains, and others praised the workmanship and quaint design. As the interest continued throughout his round, Percy thought of that piece of parchment in the tin of snuff, and quite suddenly, from one of the livelier cells in his queer and generally sluggish brain, he became aware of a startling fact which he realized was true, namely, that he was being used to carry these signs at the Scarecrow's orders. He knew well enough what the word LANDINGS signified at the head of the mysterious list. He knew that there were no landings carried out upon the neighbouring coastline that were not the work of the Scarecrow. The signs in his buckets meant Littlestone Beach. In spite of the utmost care exerted by all concerned not to give themselves away when a landing and a run was contemplated, there was a something in the air that made Percy suspicious. On such nights he would never go out late to dig lug for his patron, Mipps. In fact, Mipps would generally tell him that he was not in need of lug upon such occasion.

The more Percy thought about it, the more he was convinced that he was being used by the dreaded Scarecrow, and frightened as he was of the gallows permanently standing so close to his well, he was more scared of the Phantom Rider of the Marsh and his followers of whom such dreadful tales were told.

It was this terror that persuaded him at all costs to keep his dreadful discovery to himself, and not to mention it even to his mother.

He tried hard to forget what he had guessed, but found it impossible, and to make matters even more frightening he made another discovery that very evening at the start of his last water-round, which set his heart thumping with fear.

He was about to enter the open door of the dark barn in which the sailors were billeted when he heard a moan as of a man in pain. Now Percy had a hatred of pain which made him almost hysterical. He could not bear pain himself nor to see it in others, and this pitiful moaning coming from the darkness frightened him, and he wished that there had been a sailor mounting guard outside the barn as there had been in the morning when he had delivered the water. He then realized that in the morning he had approached the barn from the other side which was the main entrance. The open door faced the Marsh and not the village. The guard would therefore be outside the closed door on the opposite side.

Percy stood still and listened. He could hear nothing but those whimpering moans, and thought it must be some sick sailor left by himself in the barn while his fellows had gone out on duty. He tried to make up his mind what was best to be done. In the morning the sailor on guard had taken in the buckets of water, saying that Percy was not allowed abroad. The water cask was inside the barn, and it sounded as though the sick sailor would not have the strength to take in the buckets, which Percy had no intention of leaving.

It looked therefore as though he must disobey the orders of the morning sentry, and go boldly in himself. It never occurred to him to go round to the other side of the barn and find the sentry. But there was so much to be afraid of.

The Scarecrow, who was using him to carry messages, without asking his consent, and the sailors themselves. He was water-carrier to the dragoons, too, and would it infuriate the Scarecrow that he was thus doing service to the enemies of the Night-riders?

It was then that the groans rose into a pathetic squeal, like that of a trapped animal. Percy suddenly thought about the story of the Good Samaritan which Doctor Syn had told them about in Sunday school. Christian charity told him it was his duty to go and see if he could help this sufferer. Perhaps a drink of water would do him good.

He was just going in, on this resolve, when he was pulled up sharp by a voice which he recognized at once as Captain Blain's, and its very first sentence made him go weak at the knees.

"That's enough for the moment, men, or he'll faint, and an unconscious man cannot give information, and that we have got to get."

The relentless tone of that deep husky voice frightened Percy enough, but the words that followed brought a sweat of panic on to his brow.

"Now, Fred Hart, if that's your name as I understand, think well. The village thinks you dead. Why? Because we stoved in your boat. If you persist in refusing to tell me what I wish to know, in the King's name, I'll have you shipped aboard a man-of-war quicker than the Press gang, and no one here will be any wiser. Your conscience tells you not to be disloyal to your fellows, eh? Well, it is better that you should be when is comes to proving yourself loyal to your Kung. No man can be blamed for obeying the law of his country, and you have the fortunate opportunity of being able to atone for your law-breaking by a full confession. If you do the right thing and follow now the straight path of your duty, you will be accorded safety and reward. If you do not, I can either ship you to sea, sell you to the Plantations, or, to save a lot of trouble, string you up to the yardarms as a member of this Scarecrow's gang. I'll pledge you my word not to ask awkward questions concerning your own relations. That bother of yours for instance, who is no doubt as implicated as you are. Blood is thicker than water as the saying goes, and you should think of your wife and kid. Now then, am I to extract this

information by ordering my men to give you another dose of pain, or do you want to go home with money for your wife and kid? If it's information got from torture I warn you there will be no reward and no pardon. If you tell me now with freewill, I'll see that no one knows from whom I gained information."

"The Scarecrow knows everything," replied Hart's voice, which, though very weak, Percy recognized.

"And you're afraid of what he'll do to you, eh?" retorted the Captain. "Well, I give you my word, he'll not be able to do a thing, for he'll be swinging before he knows a thing against you. Now come along, Hart. You've shown yourself a brave man, according to your lights, and I've no wish to duty, and I must do mine. No? Well your damned obstinacy means good-bye to your wife, kid and home. Give him another, men."

Whether they did nor not, Percy was not sure. The sharp squeal which Hart let out may have been due to a horrible anticipation. But the squeal was short -lived and tailed into the sentence of, "I'll speak and god help me."

"Sensible fellow," came the Captain's voice in a kinder tone. "Now then, Hart, I must know first when and where the next contraband is going to be landed."

Percy listened to the weak voice almost whispering: "Tonight, sir, on Littlestone Beach at the low tide. The Scarecrow will be there, and if you can discover who or what he is you'll be wiser than any of his followers. Now set me free in God's name and let me go home."

"When I know that your information is correct you will be let go," replied the Captain's voice in a tone of triumph.

Just then Percy had a narrow escape.

A sailor swung out of the darkness and pulled up quickly in the doorway s he saw the unexpected water-carrier.

Percy knew that the agitation he had gone through over what he had overheard must show clearly on his face.

The sailor had every reason to suspect that he had been listening to the Captain interviewing Hart. But Percy was too quick for him by doing nothing quickly. Very slowly he set the buckets down and unhooked the yoke, allowing the pain written upon his face to appear as though it had been written there by fatigue.

"Water, sir," he said wearily.

The whole bearing of the lad convinced the sailor that he had only just got to the door, but to make quite sure he asked, "Been waiting long, lad?"

"You saw me put them down," replied Percy, indicating the filled buckets. "P'raps some 'ud hold 'em standing still, but I has enough of 'em when walking. Shall I bring 'em in?"

"You stay here." Ordered the sailor. "I'll take 'em and show our Captain your clever dodge with them bits o' wood. I was telling him how you prevent your legs from being splashed, but he didn't see the buckets come abroad this morning same as t he rest, and he'll be interested."

While waiting for his buckets to be returned empty, that live cell in Percy's brain worked clearly for the good of the parish. It told Percy that it had been the bits of wood that had enabled poor Fred to turn traitor against the Scarecrow, and Percy knew that would mean the rope for anyone caught that night upon Littlestone Beach.

Now is the 'landing' was changed to the far side of Dungeness, thought Percy, the smugglers would be hidden by the promontory. He remembered that two hearts stood for Dungeness Sou'west on the list. If he changed the signs it would at least be a warning to those concerned.

When Percy got an idea into his head he would carry it out with a stubbornness that showed grit, and so directly he received back the buckets he hurried off to the Coffin Shop to find Mipps and to change the signs.

It so happened that Mipps was at the Vicarage, but the door of his store being open, Percy entered and went straight to the shelf upon which stood Judy, the idol.

"Got to change 'em, Miss Judy," said Percy, as he picked up the two hearts in place of the club and diamond. "If the Sexton was here I'd ask him, but as he ain't, I asks you. As you're a good Christian idol, please make the Sexton know that I done it for the best. I'll be glad of your good word, Miss Judy, and thankee."

Percy continued his round to the cottages, and when he saw what a deal of surprise and runnings and whisperings the two hearts in the buckets caused, he knew that his theory was right. But for his own inner satisfaction he determined to prove it in his own defense, and if possible do something more to save the village from disaster, and so, since he had not met Mipps anywhere during the evening, and therefore had to continue to work on his own initiative, such as it was, he informed his mother at supper that since the Sexton had been so kind to him he was going to give him a surprise by digging him some lug.

He set out with his spade and tin, digging along just above the water line. He took no lantern, for the moon was full, and he worked his way towards Littlestone. He met no one on the way, and no one could see him from any distance, as the flat sands were swept by low-lying wreaths of mist. This made it an ideal night for the King's men, who lay in ambush behind one of the great wooden breakwaters.

Percy first sensed their presence by hearing a horse neigh, and as he crept towards the shadow of the sea-wall, the moon caught the glint of a Dragoon's helmet on the beach beyond.

As he crouched listening, the only sound that reached him above the continual swish and grinding of the waves, was an occasional creak of leather, or the champing of a bit.

He wondered whether the sailors were on the same section of beach, or somewhere hidden on the Marsh behind the sea-wall. He realized that any Dymchurch man who had not received his warning would walk into a trap here, and so he retraced his steps and on the smooth sand drew with his spade two large hearts side by side.

He then made his way back to the village and went to bed. He was fast asleep long before the scarecrow and his lieutenant, Hellspite, galloped along the sands towards Littlestone.

Suddenly the Scarecrow pulled up his fierce black horse and pointed. The moon shone upon Percy's hearts.

The Scarecrow's companion had pulled up as suddenly as his master, and from behind the hideous mask of Hellspite came Mipp's whisper: "Dungeness, Sou'west. Someone has altered our plan."

"Hold Gehenna," ordered doctor Syn from behind the Scarecrow's mask. Hellspite took the bridle while his master dismounted and crawled forward toward the breakwater, listening.

He returned with the news that the Navy men were entrenched behind the breakwater and the squadron of Dragoons were beneath the sea-wall.

"So the rival forces are working together against us after all," he whispered, as he silently remounted. "Someone has betrayed us, and someone has altered our plans, as you say. I would sooner have risked a brush with the enemy than that anyone should dare to cancel the Scarecrow's orders. On to Dungeness, by way of the Marsh."

The mist concealed them as they rode up a sandy path that ran from the beach over the high sea-wall, and down again upon the other side to the Marsh.

On reaching the far side of the Ness, after a wild gallop, they found everything ready for the landing, just as it had been arranged for Littlestone. The gangs were set in parties of eight to a boat, and only waited the Scarecrow's arrival to begin operations. The beach was guarded by a cordon of thirty mounted Night-riders, and as Doctor Syn rode down the beach, their leader rode up to meet him.

"In contact with the ships yet?" asked the Scarecrow.

"Aye, aye, Scarecrow," replied the leader, whom Doctor Syn and Mipps knew to be the Highwayman, "and the boats are ready loaded and waiting to pull in."

The Scarecrow raised his right arm above his head, and immediately the thirty wheeled their horses and galloped down to the water-line. The signal was given: three hoots of an owl, three cries of a curlew, and four screams of a gull.

With muffled oars some twenty boats pulled in out of the mist and the waiting gangs waded into the water to unload.

Doctor Syn watched the tubs coming ashore to be lifted upon the pack-ponies. Not only were the boats well loaded, but great rafts of lashed barrels were floated in their wake and dragged ashore by ropes.

"A good landing," whispered the Scarecrow.

"Aye, and thanks to the new code, every man got the warning of your changed plan." Replied the Highwayman.

"They guessed you had some good reason for the change, and worked with a will to get here in time."

"Aye, we would have had a rougher landing on Littlestone Beach, with a full ambush of soldiers and sailors to contend with," said the Scarecrow. "We must find out how they got information."

"The two hearts in Percy's buckets did the trick," went on the Highwayman, "and we gave Littlestone a wide berth."

The Scarecrow looked at Mipps and whispered, "So that was it."

"Aye," replied the Highwayman, "and the boys have done nothing but whisper admiration for the Scarecrow's cleverness. Them signs in the buckets is certainly a master-stroke."

"I marvel that I never thought of it before," said the Scarecrow.

When the last barrel was ashore, and the packponies loaded, the carriers slung tubs on their shoulders, and guided by the thirty riders, the long trek across the March began. Doctor Syn waited till the last boat had pulled back to the ships that were hidden in the mist. He heard the anchors shipped, and then across the water came the same signal as had been given from the beach.

"All's well and away," he chuckled to Mipps, "and the worth of some three thousand pounds crossing the Marsh already. I think our lads will all be a-bed before the King's men realize they have been fooled. I fancy my guest will not be in the best of tempers in the morning."

"And not a smell of powder from the revenue cutter, neither," replied Mipps. 'And to think it were all through that looney Percy disobeying my orders. But you know, sir," he added, "although the idiot has saved us from a pitched battle on Littlestone Beach, and without knowing it kept many a tough skull uncracked, I'll have to belt him for all that."

"For my part," said Doctor Syn, "I am glad to find that it was but the work of an idiot, and not the clever officiousness of one of our own men. I should deal gently with him and not give him the chance to do such a thing again. I would be highly dangerous. You must keep that set of signs away from his fingers in future."

"You mean I'm not to belt him?" asked Mipps.

"You can discover if you can what induced him to do it," went on Syn. "But I doubt whether he'll know by tomorrow. We must bear in mind that the poor lad is simple."

As they galloped after the cavalcade across the Marsh, Syn instructed Mipps to find out whether any of the Night-riders had heard news of the missing fisherman, Hart. "We must remember, Mipps, that he is not only one of my parishioners, but also a Scarecrow's man, and the more I think of that stove boat, the more I suspect foul play.

Now Fred had no enemies. He was a good companion to all. But the Scarecrow has plenty, and there is always the possibility that one or more of them, unable to get at the scarecrow, are trying to do so through one of his followers.

It is significant that it should happen immediately upon the arrival of Captain Blain. If my guest knows anything of the matter he'll be hard put to it to conceal his knowledge from me. That is the advantage of having him at the vicarage.

"We'll get Jimmie Bone to keep his ears open," returned Mipps. "He has a rare knack of picking up information. His 'orrid trade of a robber has taught him
    that."

"Aye, tell him we must know what has happened to Fred Hart," said Syn. "Until we can question him alive, or examine his dead body, we shall not know who has done this thing, and we have enough dangers to cope with, without the greatest one, which is Uncertainty. Find out what you can."

In spite of the added forces against them, with the coming of the Navy men, all concerned congratulated themselves that there had never been a landing run to the hills more smoothly, for by the time the goods had been dispersed amongst the 'hides,' and horses and pack-ponies had been returned to their various stables there was not a sore head that sought its pillow, two hours before the dawn. Not a blow had been struck, except a mighty one against the pride of Captain Blain, who did not reach his bed without an unpleasant storm of derision from the soldiery.

"I think in future, sir," Major Faunce had remarked icily, "that we had better work separately, or with a fuller confidence together. How you got your information of a landing upon

Littlestone Beach I do not know. Had you thought fit to tell me I might have been able to see that it was but a red herring drawn across the trail by the Scarecrow's order. You forget, sir, that I have had a pretty good experience of his cleverness, and as you can now see for yourself, the clue that lured you to Littlestone was just to ensure that you were there, wasting your time.

Until we realize that the Scarecrow is a good deal cleverer than we are, we shall get nowhere."

"It will not be very long, Major Faunce," retorted the captain, "before I invite you to attend the Scarecrow's hanging. I have never been the man to give up a fight because my opponent has the advantage of me in the first round, and I have not yet begun to fight the Scarecrow. I promise you that he will not fool the senior service while I represent it, as he has fooled the junior one."

"Your manner, Captain Blain," retorted the Major, "suggests a challenge, which I am perfectly willing to take up.

You say that you will invite me to the scarecrow's hanging. Personally I confess that I have no great faith that either of us will catch him, much less hang him. You forget that we are dealing with a person who was once imprisoned in a cell at the top of Dover Castle, and yet managed to fly out of the window and float through the air like a witch on a broomstick. At least this was vouched for by members of the Castle staff and the sentries. However, hopeless as I take our task to be, I'll yet wager you a hundred guineas that I will catch this criminal before you do. Let it be a rivalry between us. If one of us succeeds, well, it will be all the better for the Marsh."

"I doubt that indeed," responded the Captain. "The prosperity of this little village is not due to the munificence of the Squire, with whom you lodge, but to the good money which is slipping through the fingers of the Revenue."

When the village woke to work the following morning, everybody seemed to know that there was open friction between the two camps ranged against the scarecrow.

But the same capacity for gleaning information which Dymchurch seemed to possess, had as yet no news concerning the missing Fred Hart, for Percy

was late at the Coffin Shop, fearing to tell Mipps that he had changed the signs, and when he eventually did so, Mipps kept the information for only the ears of Doctor Syn.

When Percy sheepishly entered the Coffin Shop with the two hearts in his buckets, he saw to his horror that Judy was standing upon the coffin lid, and as he blinked guiltily at the idol he was aware that the Sexton was unstrapping the thick belt that held his breeches. He shuddered as he saw the great brass buckle, and imagined it cutting into his flesh, especially as Mipps was demanding sharply what he meant by changing the floats without permission.

Fear made him drawl out a lie which his simple brain told him might be a good excuse.

"I asked her about it," he stammered. "You was out, or I'd have asked you, Mister Mipps. I wanted to."

"But why did you do it?" demanded the angry Sexton.

"I done it out of respect to the old Harts," he drawled. "They was always good to me, same as you, and I thought s how it would please 'em what with their Golden Wedding, and them not having lost poor Fred after all, as yet."

"What's that?" snapped Mipps. "As yet? What do you mean by, 'As yet'?"

Thereupon Percy recounted what he had overheard outside the barn, and all he had done after it, adding as a great confession of guilt: "And I stole a pinch of snuff from your tin up yonder. I done that to cure myself of the snivels, what come when I heard about the Hart boat, I come back here as I told you to get the two hearts, I did. I was wrong about the snuff. I didn't mean to be a thief, but you can belt me for that if you please."

"You keep your mouth shut, now," replied Mipps, "and don't tell no one what you've told me, and then no one won't be the wiser. I don't think I'll have to belt you, seeing as how you did what you thought best, but I'll have to go and ask the Vicar what he thinks."

Doctor Syn had an amusing breakfast watching the disgruntled Captain, who was in the worst of tempers, and could not be led into conversation.

It was while preparing to read Matins that he met Mipps in the vestry, and heard the news dragged out of Percy.

He took a serious view of the fact that Fred Hart had betrayed them and was still a prisoner.

"He'll get no mercy now from Captain Blain," he said. "But we cannot see him hang, for the sake of his wife and him, and then deal with his case. As to Percy, I agree with you, Mipps, that your belt would be a scurvy thanks, and it occurs to me that anyone who can look such a fool and yet act so promptly should be enrolled on the scarecrow's pay list. I'll leave you to deal with him, while I devise a scheme for snatching Fred Hart from the Captain's guard."

3

THE SCARECROW RUNS UP HIS FLAG

In the bedroom of a little white-washed cottage tucked away under the sea-wall, Doctor Syn sat one morning reading the Scriptures to a young mother propped up with pillows nursing her newborn son. Her beautiful face was stained with tears, for despite the fact of the comforting presence of the Vicar, whom all the parish of Dymchurch knew as the holiest of men, she had black despair in her heart. For three days she had received no news of her husband, alive or dead.

The boat in which he had been fishing had been washed into Dymchurch Bay, capsized and badly holed.

Mrs. Hart could not believe that her Fred had been picked up by some ship outward bound, which was the only comfort held out to her by sympathetic villagers. Four Dymchurch men, however, knew that he was alive and near at hand: the Vicar, the Sexton, the Highwayman and the water-carrier. Captain Blain from the guard Ship at Dover knew it too, and so did his sea-dogs who were billeted for the time being in the Tythe Barn during their search for smugglers. But Blain saw to it that his men kept the knowledge to themselves when talking to the villagers.

He had kept Fred Hart a close prisoner in the barn and had by mental and physical torture compelled him to confess that he had not only worked for the scarecrow and his gang of smugglers, but had made him betray the place of landing for the next cargo. Unfortunately for the traitor, the scarecrow had been warned in time by Percy, the half-witted water-carrier, and so it appeared to the Captain that Hart had deliberately lied, and he determined to show him no mercy.

Neither had he any intention of putting his young wife out of her misery.

Doctor Syn was more merciful, and although he could not impart knowledge that he had gained as the Scarecrow, he resolved to drop a hint to the wife that she was not yet a widow.

With this end in view, he selected for his reading such passages from Holy Writ, that dealt with God visiting mankind in dreams as a means of giving warnings, orders or comfort.

"And now, my daughter," he said kindly as he closed his bible, "perhaps you are wondering why I have read about so many

God-sent dreams. I will tell you. The age of such miracles is not yet over, for last night I dreamed a dream, which may be full of comfort to you. I seemed to see your husband riding with the Scarecrow's men, and when I upbraided him for thus breaking the law, he told me that he had done so in order to make more money for your happiness. The scene then changed and I saw him fishing in the Hart boat. Captain blain and his men hailed him from the beach, and when he rowed ashore they fell upon him and then until he betrayed the Scarecrow. I awoke with the feeling that this was true, and while we keep this to ourselves I will try to find out the truth. Perhaps this very day I may discover where he is, and then I will do what I can to restore him to you."

Leaving the young woman with this ray of hope, Doctor Syn proceeded to the Coffin Shop for a word with Mipps, whom he found busy at his bench.

"Any more news about Hart, my good Mipps?" he asked.

"Only a bit of guesswork, Vicar," replied the Sexton, "which I takes to be as good as news. If Hart was ever in the Tythe Barn as a prisoner, which according to Percy is a fact, well then, there he is still, 'cos I've had both doors watched as you ordered, and no one but the King's men have gone out or in. Even Percy ain't allowed inside when he carries round the water-buckets from the well. Why? 'Cos they don't wish him to know that Hart's alive and in their power. One comfort is that he don't know nothing that can harm the Scarecrow, and if you was to leave him to his fate, well it might be hard on his wife, but no more than he deserves for having tried to betray us."

"If we leave him to his fate, my good Mipps," said the Vicar quietly, "he'll be shipped to the Plantations, and his wife will never hear of him again. We must be merciful to her, and thwart this Captain Blain. Besides, it touches the reputation of the scarecrow. Anyone betraying him must be judged by him. I have settled how to punish Fred Hart, but to carry out the punishment he must first be rescued from the Captain. And for that end, my friend, I want you to cut me a strong wooden wedge from the outside of the Captain'' room at the Vicarage."

"I was wondering when you was going to batten him down," chuckled the sexton. "Been a bit awkward having had him on top of us, so to speak."

"It had had its advantages, too," replied the Vicar. "I billeted him at the Vicarage for two reasons. First that he would have no suspicions that I could be connected with the scarecrow, and secondly, so that I could keep an eye on him, and an ear, too. I confess that he" s close an oyster as ever I met, for not even in his cups can I make him talk about his plans. He confines his conversation to naval gossip concerning our old friend Admiral Troubridge, and to the family history and qualities of his junior officers abroad the Dover Guard ship. I know all about them, but of his plans, nothing."

By this time Mipps had fashioned a neat wedge which he handed to his master, saying, "Whether the Captain snores or no, I should put that in his door whenever things move at night on the Marsh."

Doctor Syn put it in his pocket. "Thank you, I will, for the Captain's snores are no longer reassuring to me.

They sound convincing enough, but last night during his nasal trumpetings I heard the squeak of his shutter's hinge as he crept to look out of the casement. I know now that the Captain does not snore when asleep, but only when he's very much awake. I shall therefore wedge his door when I am ready to join the Night-riders at the Oast House at Doubledyke's. You have passed the word for arms and horses?"

Mipps nodded. "thirty, s you ordered, with a spare horse. I suppose now that the extra mount is for Fred hart, and that we attack the barn."

Doctor Syn nodded back. "In the meantime continue the watch on the doors, although I think the Captain will not attempt to move his prisoner in daylight, since it is against his interest to let anyone know that hart is alive. Keep watch though, all the same."

Later, at dinner, Doctor Syn tested Captain Blain by asking whether he would be attending the memorial service to Fred Hart which would be held for the parish if no one brought news that he was alive.

"I think, Vicar, that there can be no doubt as to his death, and that it is quite right to hold the service. I dare say some of my men would like to attend. I shall come myself out of respect to his widow."

For which piece of hypocrisy Doctor Syn scored up another mental black mark against his guest.

Earlier than usual that night Doctor Syn suggested retiring to bed. "One of my flock is very ill," he explained. "and Doctor Pepper tells me the crisis is at hand, so I must hold myself in readiness for being awakened in the night. I have also told the Hart family to summon me should poor Fred's wife need spiritual comfort.

We must do what little we can."

"I applaud you for taking your duties so seriously, Parson," replied the Captain.

"I suppose you are right, and that Hart is dead," went on Doctor Syn, "but what mystifies me is not that such a good fisherman should be capsized, which might happen to the best, but that the boat should have been so savagely holed when there is but sand in Dymchurch Bay. The nearest rocks, and they are not dangerous , are Sandgate one way and Littlestone the other. As you must know, they are flat shelves and amply covered at high tide for a fishing boat. Neither was there a high sea running that night, they tell me."

"The revenue cutter reported a high wind and something of a swell," explained the Captain. "His boat may have been dropped on to some ugly piece of wreckage."

"I think that unlikely," returned the Vicar. "Do you know, I have been wondering whether there was any foul play, though I can find no reason to suppose that the young man had enemies." The Vicar sighed. "I would give a lot to be able to hold out some hope to that poor girl."

"Your suggestion of foul play, Parson has made me wonder whether he might not have been murdered by this Scarecrow's orders, for we know him as an unscrupulous rascal."

Doctor Syn looked shocked. "Surely you have no grounds for any suspicion against young Hart? You do not suggest that he has been a law-breaker? I have always looked upon him as loyal to both Church and Government."

"I am glad to hear you say so, since he has gone to his account," replied the Captain. "After all, you knew the man, and I did not." And for this lie Doctor Syn registered another black mark to be dealt with in his dealings with the Captain.

That night the sailors in the Tythe Barn turned in sooner than usual, for Mipps had taken round two barrels of rum with the compliments of Mrs. Waggetts, landlady of the Ship Inn, and with their own allowance the Bos'n and his men were drunker than ever. Even the man on watch allowed himself to sit down, and was soon nodding over his drawn cutlass that rested on his knees.

Their awakening was surprising and alarming. A clattering of hooves; the cry of the awakened sentry as his cutlass was struck from his grasp; and then the sharp orders from a terrible figure who had ridden a great black horse into the barn. Behind him were a score of other mounted figures masked hideously and carrying Jack-o'-Lanterns.

These devils on horseback were all armed, and their leader was crying out to the Bos'n to get out of his hammock, while all the rest were to remain where they were, or be shot as the Scarecrow's enemies.

"We are here, Master Bos'n," said the Scarecrow, "to take from you the person of one Fred Hart, held here as your prisoner. Deliver him over to us at once."

"He ain't 'ere," replied the sea-dog, with what courage he could muster.

"Search the barn, some of you," ordered the Scarecrow. "He was here and must be still since I have had the barn watched day and night. Unless you tell me where he is within the next thirty seconds I shall employ the other half minute in hanging you from the rafters."

"There's no harm in telling you," faltered the Bos'n. "The prisoner is abroad the Revenue cutter. He was took under escort some three hours back. And that's truth, so 'elp me."

"Who watched the barn three hours back?" demanded the Scarecrow of his men.

"I and Curlew," came the prompt answer from one of them. "And so 'elp me none come out but four of these dirty king's men. One had a drawed cutlass and the rest carried bundles."

"And 'cordin' to Captain's orders, one of 'em was this Fred 'Art, dressed up in poor Joe's kit, and there's Joe been shiverin' ever since in a blanket."

"There's no signs of the prisoner here, Scarecrow," said one of the search party. "We've turned over the straw, and the barrels are all empty."

"Very well, replied the Scarecrow. "Then we'll tear a leaf from the clever Captain's book.

Collect all these men's clothes and bring 'em along, and you, Hellspite, put a dozen or so six-inch nails through the door bars when we've closed these rascals in for the night."

The Scarecrow's men worked quickly, and within a few minutes the captured piled arms of the King's men had been thrown into the Glebe Field Dyke, and behind nailed-up doors in the dark the party of disconsolate sailors shivered and cursed, as they listened to the departing horsemen who had taken their clothes and were galloping back to the Oast House, from which they had set out.

The Scarecrow and Hellspite remained behind, promising to rejoin the Night-riders within a few minutes.

"What now?" asked Hellspite in a whisper.

"Hold Gehenna, Mipps," replied the Scarecrow. "I have no time to ride to the Mother Handaway's to change my clothes to Doctor Syn, so I must leave them for the moment in the hidden stables. Fortunately for my plan, Captain Blain is a careless drinker when in cups, and slops his wine upon his uniform. Mrs. Fowey, taking it as her duty to clean them, insists that he leaves them outside his door at night for here collection early in the morning. So, my good Mipps, I can collect a uniform which will fit me. Despite slopping his wine, he is a man who likes to be trim on duty, so he also leaves his wig to be freshly powered. I venture to think that I can close my left eye and stare with the right as he does. We are of a height, too, and it will be dark enough aboard the cutter. We may take our prisoner therefore without bloodshed."

Thus it was that Doctor Syn entered his Vicarage quietly as the Scarecrow and in ten minutes emerged in the uniform of Captain Blain. Luck had been on his side, since his guest had left his sword in the hall with his cloak and hat, and every other night he had taken his sword to his room. He had also listened at the Captain's door and had heard deep breathing, but no snores.

On rejoining Mipps, the little Sexton grinned. "I knows you better than most," he whispered, "but you ain't the Vicar, you ain't the Scarecrow, but you are Captain Blain, one eye and all."

On reaching the Oast House, Mipps superintended the Scarecrow's orders being carried out, picking twenty to dress in the sailor's kits they had stolen. The Bos'n uniform gave him an extra one for himself. "The Revenue cutter carries a crew of twenty men, a petty officer, and a captain. Well, the Scarecrow is the Captain, I'll be petty officer, and you the crew. The ten who remain as Night-riders will see to the horses getting back to stables from the beach at Littlestone, where we shall board the lugger and sail for the Revenue cutter to capture the traitor, Fred Hart."

An hour later, Mipps entered the cabin of the lugger where Doctor Syn sat alone, and reported that they were half-way between Sandgate and Dover and that the cutter lay ahead anchored.

"Run us alongside, Mister Bos'n," ordered Syn, "and Captain Blain will speak to the officer of the watch."

Doctor Syn climbed out of the cabin and strode along the dark deck, till level with the companion ladder. "Is Mister Swinnerton in charge?" he demanded in Blain's deep and husky voice. He had got the name from Blain himself.

"Speaking, sir," came the answer promptly.

"Plans are changed, Mister Swinnerton," went on Doctor Syn. "The prisoner, hart, is to be tried at the Dymchurch Court House, and I have come to escort him back on this lugger which I have requisitioned. Put him abroad."

"Sorry, sir," replied the officer, "but your orders have been carried out. Hart is in irons abroad the Guard Ship in Dover harbour. We have only just returned and piped the men below."

"I was afraid of that," went on Doctor Syn. "Well, my men are fresh and the cutter is faster than this old tub. We'll change over crews and you may lie anchored aboard here, while I go and fetch Hart from the Guard Ship. I'll come aboard."

"Aye, aye, sir," replied the unsuspecting officer, and as Syn climbed on to the cutter's deck, he sang out the necessary orders.

"Make fast, Bos'n, and send our men aboard," growled Syn.

"Aye, aye, sir," sang out Mipps.

Before the first man rolled out of the fo'c'sle curing, Syn's men were at the ropes. Canvas was spread and anchor weighed, while the workers kept sullen backs to the awakened sleepers. Keeping away from the ship's lanterns Syn strode the deck, curing Swinnerton for not driving his men harder, so that in a few minutes the last of the cutter's crew was aboard the lugger, and Syn gave a curt good night to the officer as he followed his crew aboard the unsavoury lugger. As he went over the side with a salute, Swinnerton said, "We'll stand by you at anchor here, sir."

"Right. And between ourselves, Mister Swinnerton, was mister Rowton drunk as usual when you reported aboard the Guard Ship?"

"Well, sir," replied the young officer diffidently, "he was not altogether pleasant, but he seemed put out that the Admiralty have superseded Admiral Troubridge for Admiral Chesham, who I believe is to take over the command."

"I know Chesham well," chuckled Syn. 'He'll make us jump for him."

As the cutter drew away into the fairway they heard the anchor being dropped aboard the lugger.

On the way to Dover, Mipps and two others who had served aboard a man-o-war trained the crew as to their bearing, and in the meanwhile Syn having sent for white paint and tar, and procuring a flag from the locker, bedaubed a white scarecrow on a black ground. "The adventure has so far been a joke with no bloodshed. With luck it may so continue, Mipps," he laughed, "and I have a mind to run this flag up on the guard Ship peak-head."

The cutter entered the harbour and came alongside the guard Ship without suspicion. The officer of the watch saluted Syn. "I was appointed here, sir, since you left for shore duty."

"Name?" growled Syn.

"Osmund, sir."

"Mister Rowton below?"

"Yes sir."

"In his cups, too, I'll be bound."

"I couldn't say, sir," replied the tactful midshipman.

"Order two men to put the prisoner Hart aboard the cutter. I am taking him ashore for trial."

"Yes sir. Shall I take the order to Mister Rowton, sir?"

"No. Take me to him. I'll make it clear to him. Have the prisoner put aboard at once. Rowton's in my cabin?"

"No, Captain Blain. Admiral Troubridge has been ashore for two nights and Mister Rowton is preparing the quarters for Admiral Chesham."

"Very well. Get the prisoner aboard."

Syn closed the door of the Admiral's cabin behind him, and called a very drunk officer

asprawl across a chart table to attention.

"Mister Rowton," he said sharply, "I shall have you suspended for this. I come unexpectedly to escort the prisoner Hart back to shore trial, and I find you drunk on Admiral's liquor. Get to bed and you'll hear that tomorrow which will surprise you."

Suddenly the drink seemed to drop from Rowton's eyes. "What's all this? "Just a minute. Who the hell are you? You're like Blain, but I've served under that devil for years, and you ain't him. Who are you?"

Syn strode towards him, saying, "An officer whom no subordinate shall insult."

With a terrific blow on his chin Rowton went down on the cabin floor. There was a knock at the door and young Osmund announced, "Prisoner's being taken aboard, sir."

"Mister Rowton has fallen over drunk. When I've sailed come back here, pour a bucket of water over him and let him sleep. And take example. Don't drink on duty if you wish to get on in the Service."

"Yes sir. Thank you, sir," replied Osmund.

On deck Syn saw Hart being hustled below on the cutter. Leaning over the side he called, "Got the Admiral's flag there?"

"Yes sir," replied Mipps. "Shall I bring it aboard."

"Throw her up."

The rolled flag fell on the deck. "Do you know how to break a flag, Mister Osmund?"

"Yes sir."

"Then let's see you run up Admiral Chesham's."

"He's not aboard, you know, sir."

"Obey orders, and don't try to teach me regulations," snarled Syn. "If the new Admiral wishes his colours to be seen in the morning as though he were aboard, that's his look-out and mine, not yours."

As Syn stood once more on the cutter he saw the black bundle mounting to the peak, and then with a convulsive twitch break out into t he breeze. "You strike that at Admiral Chesham's orders, and see that Mister Rowton does not tamper with it."

The next morning there was fine to-do when the Scarecrow's flag was seen waving above the flagship. There was more to-do when the cutter was discovered run on Dymchurch sands with all her brass guns, fourteen in all, shining below the water, and a hue and cry for Fred Hart who was shipped over to France that night for internment in the Scarecrow's secret port.

Meanwhile the Captain's uniform and wig were brought to his room neatly brushed and powdered, and doctor Syn, in the clothes that Mipps had brought to him from the hidden stable, went out before breakfast to give comfort to Mrs. Hart.

"I will see that you join your husband as soon as you are well enough to cross the Channel," he said. "He is alive and well, having escaped from the jaws of death through the skill of the mysterious Scarecrow. How I came to this information I may not say, and for the sake of your husband's safety we must not speak of it. But you see, my daughter, it was as I thought. My dream was a visitation from God."

As to Captain Blain, he had a lot to puzzle him, and he vowed to be revenged upon the Scarecrow.

4

THE SCARECROW RIDES TO THE HOUNDS

That the Prince of Wales should invite himself to reside for a day or so at Lympne Castle was a great feather in the cap of Sir Henry Pembury, Lord of Lympne. That His Royal Highness should express the wish to hunt with the Romney Marsh Pack was perhaps a greater feather in the cap of Sir Antony Cobtree, Squire of Dymchurch-underthe-Wall. Chief Magistrate of the Marshes, and Master of the Hounds. That Doctor Syn should be invited to meet the Prince in order to pronounce grace at the Hunt Dinner, was only right and proper, since he was Dean of Peculiars, and consequently the head cleric of the district.

On his fat white pony the reverend gentleman jogged his way from Dymchurch Vicarage, and mounted the hill to the castle, in order to accept the invitation personally, and to learn details of the Royal visit. He was attended as usual by his henchman, sexton Mipps, perched upon the donkey that pulled the churchyard roller. Although the

stone roller was not on this occasion attached to the sexton's mount, they could not have proceeded slower if it had been, for it was never the custom of the Vicar to urge his lazy pony to any speed beyond a walk. Besides, Lympne hill is a steep climb for a man or beast.

As Doctor Syn gazed at the majestic walls he began to chuckle.

Mipps, wishing to know what was passing in his master's mind, asked, "Notice something funny, sir?"

"No, my good Mipps," replied the Vicar. "Do you?"

Mipps shook his head. "No, sir. Not me. This 'venerable pile', as the guide-book calls it, always gives me the dejections."

"Then why did you ask if I noticed something funny?"

"'Cos you let out a out-loud sort of giggle," explained Mipps.

The Vicar smiled. "Did I? Well, perhaps I did. A certain thought amused me, that's all."

"I don't think it will be all at all," contradicted the Sexton. "In all the long years I've served you, sir, it generally means disaster to someone when you starts chuckling to yourself."

"My thoughts were comparatively harmless, Mipps, I assure you. I was thinking ahead a day or so, and of the great doings there will be when the Prince arrives. I'll wager the gentry for miles around are agog to know whether old Pembury will remember to invite them to the festivities."

"Aye, sir," nodded Mipps, "and from what one hears tell of the first gentleman of Europe, old Pembury would do well to leave out most of 'em. The Prince don't like nothing dull. If it was me giving the party to him, so to speak, I'd beat up the countryside for buxom wenches, and fill the old place with laughing chambermaids."

"I fear, Mipps, that Sir Henry has neither your daring nor quick appreciation of humanity. Indeed I do not envy him his task of selection. He is bound to make enemies. Indeed to my knowledge he has made a very formidable one already. A man of some standing, too, who will no doubt be giving Sir Henry a rap over the knuckles for his neglect. As a matter of fact it was the thought of that coming rap that made me chuckle but now."

Mipps pulled up his donkey with a jerk. Doctor Syn's pony stopped walking, too. Doctor Syn was smiling, but a look of horror had spread over the Sexton's face. "You don't never mean-----?"

The unfinished question was checked by the Vicar's nod.

"But it's madness," explained the sexton. "It's worse than madness. It's—well, it's..."

"Impertinent audacity," completed Doctor Syn.

"Now come, Mipps, when during our long association have you begrudged me a little harmless amusement? Let me put my case to you before I enter the castle. You know the policy I have followed when the Hunt meets at Dymchurch? I attend on this ridiculous but charming pony. I am an old parson, is it not so? I must play the part I am. And yet all the time can you tell me of a better horseman on Romney Marsh? Include my good Squire Tony Cobtree, and the youngest of the hunting gentry, and add our good friend Jimmie Bone, whose good riding has saved his neck for years when holding up His Majesty's mails on the highway. Cannot Doctor Syn ride harder than them all? You know he can. But no. If I am seen outstripping and overjumping them all it is possible that my horsemanship will be compared to the best rider of the Marsh. The Scarecrow. I must not risk even comparison with him, for the safety of his followers depends upon the safety of the Vicar of Dymchurch. But, Mipps, I have heard

Tony preparing this meet with all his skill. The Prince is to have a good day, and he will get it, thanks to Tony's knowledge. He knows where every fox is earthed, and the riding will be soft or hard according to the Prince's whim. Do you blame me for being envious? I must be left behind with the children upon this dear old creature, when my whole blood calls to be behind the pack. So, Mipps, since Doctor Syn must not show the First

Gentleman of Europe what riding is, the Scarecrow shall. It is not conceit. At least not personal conceit. It is the pride I have for our Marshland. I would have the Prince own that he has never seen such riding as from one he met on Romney Marsh. I must have him say so for our credit. Trust me to carry this through without endangering our friends, but the Scarecrow must ride to hounds beside the Prince of Wales."

Mipps sighed, and kicked upon his donkey to approach the castle gate, muttering: "Well, if he must, he must and will, and not even old Pembury can hinder him. But I might remind you, Vicar, that the night before the Meet, there is a landing planned."

"I know, my good Mipps," whispered Syn. "And that will be the greatest help to the scheme I have in mid, and if all goes as I mean it there will be two men who will enjoy the hunt. The Scarecrow and the Prince. The rest will I fear be disappointed with their day. I'll risk a hundred hangings to carry this through well."

"But no man has a hundred necks," replied Mipps.

"I know of two to prove the lie to that, Mipps. A cat has nine lives they say." Then, looking back, "How many in the devil's name have we?"

"Oh, we've done pretty well," nodded Mipps. "I'll say no more, except to assure you that if the Scarecrow wants to hunt, with Royalty, well so he shall if Mipps can help him to it."

Dismounting before the great entrance Doctor Syn entered Lympne Castle, while Mipps led the pony and his own donkey to the stables in order to gossip with the grooms while waiting for his master.

Thinking that any information he could pick up concerning the hunt might prove useful to his master, he entered the stable where the hunters were stalled. In a loose box he saw the magnificent chestnut that had been reserved for the Prince.

"As fast as anything we've got," exclaimed the groom to Mipps. "Easily the best jumper, and there's nothing Colindale won't take, and add to that no vices. Sweet on the mouth and comfortable. Anyone astride Colindale would think they was the best horseman in the field. But it ain't the rider: it's the horse."

"Very tactful of Sir Henry to put the Prince up on him," said Mipps with a wink.

Meanwhile Doctor Syn waited in the library while a servant went in search of Sir Henry. He returned to say that his master would be with him in a few minutes, and would the reverend Doctor take a glass of wine. The ancient butler brought in a bottle and two glasses, followed by the same servant carrying a pile of letters, which he placed on the oak table in the centre of the room.

"Each mail brings us in a larger collection, sir," said the butler. "Since this business of the Prince's visit became known, we can hardly cope with Sir Henry's correspondence."

"Invitations accepted and asked for, I suppose," laughed Doctor Syn.

"That is so, sir," replied the butler. "Buckingham Palace wouldn't hold the applications we have had. And everyone expects us to accommodate his family and servants. Sir

Henry is now inspecting the roof rooms, a thing he has not done to my knowledge in the past thirty years. Most unusual and upsetting for a gentleman of his years.

"Your wine, sir."

No sooner had the butler closed the door behind him, than Doctor Syn drew a letter from his side-pocket with a glance of appreciation at the scrawled address on one side and the seal of black wax on the other. For a second or so he listened, then crossing quickly on tiptoe to the centre table he placed the letter beneath the top one of the pile.

He then returned to his seat and sipped his wine.

At last the door opened and Sir Henry, corpulent but dandified, entered to greet his guest. But at the sight of the further pile of correspondence his smile changed to a scowl. "More, by gad. I trust, Doctor, that you have come to say you will pronounce grace at the Hunt Dinner, but I hope you do not want a bedchamber. I'll wager that these are all letters reminding me that I have forgotten to invite them to meet His Royal Highness. Let us see now. Pour me out a glass of wine, Doctor, and I'll open the top one. By the way, I trust your Squire, Sir Antony, sees reason and will call the Meet here rather than at his Court House. We can hardly expect the Prince to ride to meet the Meet."

Doctor Syn laughed. "My dear Sir Henry, no. the Master of the foxhounds agrees with you that the Meet must meet the Prince.

We shall bring the pack with the Marsh Field up to Lympne at whatever time convenient."

"Good," exclaimed Sir Henry, as he perused the first letter. His mind was at rest on one point at least, for he had feared Sir Antony would claim the right to call the Meet at Dymchurch. The contents of the letter, however, brought the scowl back to his face.

"Just as I said," he snapped. "Same thing again. Listen, 'Colonel Buckshaft presents his

compliments to the Lord of Lympne and while thanking him for his kind invitation to meet the Prince of Wales, respectfully points out that although the said invitation includes Mrs. Buckshaft, there is no mention of Mis s Buckshaft. Feeling sure that this is but an oversight, since our little Fan has been presented for attractive young ladies, I shall be glad to receive an emendation at your early convenience.'"

Doctor Syn laughed. No so Sir Henry. "Calls her 'little' when she's six foot in her socks, and her only resemblance to a 'fan' is that she has a neck like an ostrich. One glimpse of that dragoon in skirts would send His Royal Highness posthaste back to Town. I shall write regrets that Lympne ceilings are not lofty enough to accommodate her."

Tossing the letter aside, he stared at the next one. "And who in thunder writes to Lympne with and up-and-down fist like this? I seem to remember this scrawl. Now whose is it?"

"Perhaps you would know by unsealing is, Sir Henry," laughed the Doctor.

The old gentleman turned the letter over. "Black wax," he ejaculated. "This is hardly the time to exploit a private mourning."

Sir Henry's podgy cheeks, already red with the Buckshaft irritation, suddenly turned to vivid purple. "Look! Look! Look!" he screamed.

To Doctor Syn's quiet query for explanation of this further rage, his host could do nothing but choke out another, "Look!"

Doctor Syn rose and crossed behind the Squire, who was pointing to a crude device stamped upon the black wax.

A soft whistle of astonishment came from the Vicar's lips, and then he added, "A scarecrow. The Scarecrow's writing, too. We should know, since this had has victimized us both. A letter of warning to me, on the day of the Exciseman's funeral, and..."

"I know. I know," interrupted the testy Squire. "The inscription over my head when the rascal lashed me to the

Dymchurch gibbet post. 'A laughing-stock, by order of the Scarecrow.' What further blackmail is here, I wonder."

The contents were worse than he imagined. The words were gasped out in a tragic duet.

Sir Henry read, "*The Scarecrow salutes his old laughingstock of Lymphne.*" Rage choked his voice, so Doctor Syn read on," *to remind him that he has not sent me an invitation to meet the Prince of Wales. Of all your guests I am probably the only one he has ever heard of or would care to meet. As the best rider of Romney Marsh and the best mounted, I shall be a credit to you. Nail my invitation to the gibbet post of Dymchurch. I will collect it. If you fail to do so, the worst will happen, and in any case I am determined to ride in your Royal Hunt.*"

The signature was a crude drawing of a scarecrow, and by the time Doctor Syn had reached it, Sir Henry was repeating his words like a bewildered schoolboy.

"And now what am I to do?" he asked pathetically.

"Knowing the Scarecrow to be a creature of his word," replied Syn, "I can only suggest that you do what he asks."

"You mean invite him?" gasped the Squire.

"I think he will come if you don't," said the Vicar.

"But he would be walking into a trap," said the Squire. "He would not dare."

"He has dared a good deal, as we know to our coast," went on the vicar. "Are all your invitation sent out?"

Sir Henry went to a bureau and handed Doctor Syn a list of names. "I have sent all these that are marked, and the others will be sent today."

"Has it occurred to you sir, that the Scarecrow may be one of these gentlemen not yet asked? Since none of us know who he is, it is obvious we would not recognize him if he comes." Doctor Syn looked at the list and then added: "May I have a copy of these guests? I would like to consider them one by one at leisure."

The Squire of Lympne assenting, doctor Syn sat down and made a copy of the list, and then under his host's direction, marking off those who were to follow the hounds.

On the ride back to Dymchurch, Doctor Syn gave this list to Mipps saying, "Our next 'run' is on the night of the Prince's arrival. The Meet is on the following morning. The scarecrow will borrow all horses from these stables, with the exception of the Prince's chestnut. I only wish that animal to be fresh, so let the warning go out as usual to open all stable doors, especially these. Warn all grooms in our power, for I know they would rather fail their masters for the hunt than the Scarecrow. They will remember that those who have failed us in the past have disappeared into the mist."

Whatever may be said about the Scarecrow's secrecy, in that not one of his followers save tow, Mipps and Highwayman, knew who he was, his methods of challenge were always in the open. The night before the Prince's arrival at Lympne Castle, the Scarecrow's chalk effigy was scrawled upon all the stable doors, including those of the gentry who were providing mounts for the Royal Hunt.

The grooms concerned knew that it was to their advantage to betray their masters rather than to play false with the mysterious being who could put many guineas in their purses by borrowing their masters' cattle. He never stole the horses. No. They were all returned before the dawn, sweated and muddy maybe, but with a secret bag of money

in their mangers. Such head stablemen who had defied the chalk order to open the stable doors, had mysteriously disappeared, so their philosophy was rather to make suck monies as they could instead of wreaking their humble homes. That this particular hunt was a Royal one weighed not a jot with them. They were loyal to the master they dreaded. The master who was the most good to them and their families, for the Scarecrow never failed those who were faithful, and gave them higher payment than the squires they served. And they were more than well paid for the extra grooming they were bound to do.

Unfortunately no amount of horse-care could make the animals fresh after the gruelling riding of a Scarecrow's 'run'. And the scarecrow had seen to it that this particular 'run' was harder than ever on the horses.

Every member of the Hunt was furious to find after the first gallop that all the ginger had gone out of his mount.

Not so the Prince. Three miles hard riding showed His Royal Highness that he had a mount in Colindale that could out-strip them all.

Sir Antony had shown the greatest skill in arranging the course. Two kills, which saw the

pack still fresh but the horses tired, and then the third fox broke cover, and it was from this cunning fellow that the master planned to get the run of the day; a fox that could be depended on to give the pack a long, long course. For the first time in his life the Prince found that his riding and his alone could hold the pack. For the first time, too, he found himself riding alone, unattended. One by one the others had dropped out, either worn with terrific pace or come to grief at the stretched jumps over the countless dykes. Twice the old fox led them to the hills and down again, and then once more in and out, doubling the dyke-cut fields.

When dusk fell the Prince was far out of sight from his followers, and the old fox still led the pace, but it was across the Kent Ditch and away into Sussex that he showed first signs of exhaustion. The Prince's excitement was then redoubled, for he saw the kill in sight, and the honour of being alone. He had shown these Kent squires what riding was. His voice was hoarse with halloing when he heard that at first he thought was his own echo. Whenever he cried out to the hounds, a derisive answer came from the mist behind him. And then he heard above the tongue of the pack, and thundering of hooves that did not belong to Colindale, and he realized that another huntsman was pressing up behind him.

Determined not to be cheated at the last moment of the honour for which he had striven so hard, His Royal Highness pricked Colindale forward desperately. As a huntsman he resented being robbed of his line kill, and as Heir Apparent he was exceedingly displeased at the derisive laughter coming nearer and nearer from his pursuer.

In full cry the pack was hidden in the mist ahead, and the Prince kept glancing back for a sight of his rival.

Catching a glimpse of a magnificent wild head of a coal-black horse, he shouted haughtily to the rider to rein back.

With another scornful laugh the rider's answer was to press alongside Colindale, and the Prince saw the rider's face, which gave him such a shock that he all but lost his seat. It was a demon horseman with a hideous face that shone like phosphorus in the mist, and his clothes were wild black rags that streamed behind him as he rode.

Keeping pace easily beside him, the figure croaked out: "The fox ahead has been named the Devil Fox of Romney Marsh, and no one shall take his brush but I the scarecrow. You may tell the Lord of Lympne that you have had the honour of riding neck to neck with the best horseman of the county. Farewell."

The aspiration streaked forwards, and as Colindale screamed with terror, disappeared in the mist ahead.

After the scream the Prince found that the spirit had gone out of Colindale, and he had the greatest difficulty in urging the poor beast forward. Ahead in the mist could be heard the cries of the kill, and the Prince guesses rightly that it was taking place on the summit of a grassy knoll confronting him. Dismounting he led the unwilling Colindale up the slope, and in doing so climbed out of the low-lying mist.

It was a strange sight for the Heir Apparent. Above the pack who were fighting for their share of the hard -won spoil stood the terrible figure of the Scarecrow, with a blooded hunting-knife in one hand and a whip and the brush in the other. Behind him stood his great black horse, Gehenna.

On seeing the Prince, the Scarecrow bowed, and said in a deep, croaking voice: "I am desolated to rob Your Royal highness of the honour he so richly deserved, but I am forced to take the brush in order to settle scores with Sir Henry Pembury. If you ride some five hundred yards to9 your right, you will come out upon the main road leading you direct to the Lympne hills and the castle, where no doubt the Reverend Doctor Syn is awaiting your arrival to say the dinner grace. Since he has met the scarecrow in the past, and to his cost, you will have an opportunity of comparing notes upon the Leader of the Marsh. I bid you farewell again, and a most Royal appetite."

With a leap which the heavy Prince envied, the figure mounted and waving the brush above his head, dashed down the knoll into the mist.

On reaching the main road indicated by the Scarecrow, the Prince encountered a search-party headed by Sir Antony Cobtree, who escorted him to the castle, where most of the disgruntled huntsmen had been congregated for hours. While the Prince dressed for dinner, doctor Syn jogged unobtrusively into the courtyard upon his white

pony, explaining to the grooms that he had been unsuccessfully seeking for the missing Prince.

During dinner the Prince was full of his adventure, and he found that his encounter with the Scarecrow gave him more credit with the ladies than had be brought back the brush. The gentlemen, however, secretly discredited the story, whispering that the Prince had no doubt spent the evening in some inn, ogling the barmaids. Doctor Syn seemed the only one who was convinced by the account, till something happened which showed the whole company that the Prince was not boasting.

The old butler whispered to Sir Henry that one of the footmen opening the castle doors to a ring, had found a wooden box marked 'urgent' and addressed to His Royal Highness. At the Prince's command it was brought in. A narrow oblong box, well made and hinged. No one knew that it had been fashioned for the purpose in Mipps' Coffin Shop. Throwing back the lid his Royal Highness lifted out a fox's brush with the following message attached to it:

The Scarecrow presents his compliments to the Prince of Wales, and returns the accompanying brush which he unfairly robbed from him at the last moment of a splendid run. If any man deserved this brush it is Your Royal Highness.

"By heavens!" cried the Prince, "but the rascal's a sportsman after all, and should he ever be taken I shall ask my royal father to pardon him. What do you say, Doctor Syn?"

"That the Scarecrow would appreciate your sentiment, sir," replied the Vicar, "though I think it is a wasted one, for in spite of the vigorous drive against him by the authorities, I fancy the rascal will never be laid by the heels."

"Then I give him a toast," cried the Prince. "Ladies and gentlemen, you will drink with me to the scarecrow."

After dinner His Royal Highness remarked slyly to Doctor Syn that he feared he had shocked not only his host but many of the gentry by his toast, adding, "I hope my good Doctor, that you who have so vigorously opposed this rascal from the pulpit will not condemn me for being too unorthodox?"

"Your Royal Highness places me in a difficult position." Replied Doctor Syn, with a smile. "I had every excuse to drink the toast, since it was a Royal command, just as it is my bounden duty to condemn him from the pulpit, while I hold Orders under your Royal Father as Defender of the Faith. But I will confess that I drank the toast willingly enough because I admire the rascally Scarecrow prodigiously."

"And so do I, Parson," laughed the Prince. "I can take a beating with the best, and the fellow out-rode me at the kill."

"Your Royal Highness is perhaps too modest," said the Doctor. "No doubt he outrode you because he and his horse were fresh."

"And what a horse," exclaimed the Prince. "I should like to know where the devil he got it from."

"Men say that he got it from the Devil at the price of his soul," explained the Doctor. "There are many who can vouch that he calls it Gehenna, which certainly suggests hell's stables."

"I'd give him a thousand guineas for it tomorrow," laughed the Prince. "It beats anything in my stables, and in the King's too.

If you sermons are half as good as those humorous stories that you told us over the port, I'll make you my spiritual adviser when I become Defender of the Faith."

"As I believe your Royal Highness has expressed his willingness to attend Divine Service at the Castle Church on Sunday," remarked the Doctor, "Your Royal Highness will be able to judge, since I have been ordered to preach."

"Well, if you keep me awake, Doctor, I'll get you a pair of lawn sleeves," laughed the Prince.

The sermon in question pleased the Prince so well that the Doctor was summoned to bid His Royal Highness farewell.

"And see here, Doctor," he said. " I have made two promises in this neighbourhood. One concerns you and the other the Scarecrow. I have told that human bloodhound, Blain, that if he catches the Scarecrow I shall see to it that the rascal does not hang. The other is what I said about your lawn sleeves. You say you are content to stay on

Romney Marsh for the rest of your ministry. If you should at any time change your mind, come to me in London, and ask for what promotion you like, and I'll see that you get it at once."

Although Doctor Syn thought little of these promises at the time, the day came when he claimed them both.

5

THE SCARECROW FACES MUTINY

Although the revenue authorities were perfectly aware that the Romney Marsh Night-riders owed their continued success to the amazing audacity of their leader, the Scarecrow, they did not know that this Phantom horseman, as many supposed him to

be, owed his safety to the extreme caution he displayed when moving amongst his parishioners as Doctor Syn. The Vicar of Dymchurch could go out upon the Marsh by night as well as by day without suspicion.

It was generally accepted that this Parson was a man who took his cure of souls very seriously, and to be seen riding slowly back to his Vicarage in the early hours of the morning, was to him but an occasion for having further blessings poured upon his head. A good man who claimed the sorrows of the humblest cottager as his own, and regarded the lowest hovel with the same importance as he did the Court House where the Squire resided. His genuine affection for young and old, his geniality, wisdom and uprightness, had created in the minds of all a saint who has as great an influence upon

the Marsh for good as the scarecrow had, in the same district, for evil. Even those secret ones who were made rich by the dark activities of the Night-riders were fearful that their mysterious leader might one day seek revenge upon their good old vicar, who considered it his duty to attack the crime smuggling from the pulpit. But for all the

Parson's exhortations, greed, fear, and amongst the younger a love of adventure, prevented any of the contraband runners from betraying their leader to the fearless old Doctor of Divinity they loved.

Little did they know that all these admirable qualities in Doctor Syn ensured the safety of the Scarecrow. Only the Sexton and the Highwayman, his close lieutenants, knew with what careful foresight the Parson proceeded to keep his double identity secure.

His strictest rule was a complete separation of his two personalities, both so strong in their own way. And to this end it was only in a state of great emergency that he allowed the figure of the Scarecrow to darken even secretly the closeness of the Vicarage. As Doctor Syn he would leave his home, and as Doctor Syn he would return. What happened to him during those absences was his own good business, and not questioned.

In their admiration, begrudged and yet sincere, the authorities in London wondered how the Scarecrow, with the vast organization of hides and runners on the London road, was able to control the vaster plotting necessary across the channel with the hated French. The luggers left some destination unknown except to him, on time and tide which he ordained.

With French spies rife in London the Admiralty commissioned Bow Street Runners to obtain information from these agents, not on political questions, but for some clue to lead them to the French headquarters of the scarecrow's shipping. That the Scarecrow had to visit France from time to time they guessed, and the packet-boats were watched for anyone who might be him. They were cute enough to guess right. The Scarecrow did have to visit France, and on those occasions Doctor Syn was forced to find an alibi for his clerical absence. This was simple. The Vicar of Dymchurch was also the Dean of Peculiars, and in that capacity had to journey like bishops and archdeacons amongst the clergy under him.

As the clergy of the Marshes affirmed in his praise, the good and generous cleric over them never grudged spending some days in an endeavour to assist some remote parish. Therefore, when it became necessary for the Scarecrow to visit France, Doctor Syn arranged a temporary leave from his parish in order to undertake some remote visitation. On such occasion, Mipps accompanied him as his servant.

Doctor Syn's parochial visitations took him frequently across the Sussex border to occupy the pulpit in the picturesque town of Rye, in which resided many French families, descended from the Huguenot refugees, who had never returned across the Channel. A thriving trade was done with these exiles by the onion boys, who with their long poles and French blouses were a familiar sight to the townsfolk.

In Dymchurch, however, the onion boy was as rare a sight as an American Indian, so one day when an onion bearer came slouching along the sea-wall and asked for the house of Monsieur Mipps, a crowd of laughing and inquisitive school children accompanied him to the Coffin Shop, where Mipps soon sent them about their business.

Along with the sexton the boy asked, "Monsieur Mipps?" To which Mipps answered,

"Monsieur Mipps, moi, but I don't want no onions." From the string the boy detached one onion and handed it to the Sexton, who shook his head emphatically.

The boy nodded vigorously and said, "*Regardez.*" With his little finger he pushed the on

ion from the bottom, peeled off the outer skin, and Mipps saw a small row of parchment sticking out from the top of the bulb. As he drew it out the boy said, "L'Epouvantail."

"And that's Froggy for Scarecrow," said Mipps. "A message, eh? That's queer. Well, I'll see it gets to him, and find you a penny for your pains.

To make his promise good, Mipps retired to the back of the shop and found a penny from his secret store, but on returning the onion boy had gone, and Mipps realized that he had not understood a word he had said. So with a penny to the good he unrolled the parchment, only to find it was French writing. Curious to know what it was all about, he decided to seek out the Vicar at once, knowing that the writing would not trouble Doctor

Syn who could write and speak French as well as English.

The Sexton found the Vicar in his study at work on a sermon, which he interrupted by telling the adventure of the onion.

"To write letters is not encouraged in the Scarecrow's legion." Whispered Syn when he had signed to Mipps to lock the door. "It must be something serious. Give it to me."

The note was written in print hand, and Doctor Syn translated it to Mipps as he read.

"THE SCARECROW'S ORDERS FOR NEXT RUN MUST BE CANCELLED. OUR PRISONERS HAVE MUTINIED AND SEIZED BOTH STORES AND ARMOURY. THEY DEMAND A LUGGER IN WHICH TO RETURN TO ENGLAND AND FREEDOM. OTHERWISE THEY HOLD OUT, WHICH THEY CAN WEE DO FOR SIX MONTHS OR MORE. THEIR ARMS COMMAND THE QUAY. THEY FIRE ON ANY MAN WHO CROSSES IT. ANY COMMUNICATION IS MADE THROUGH THEIR WOMEN-FOLK. BY THE WAY THE LAST PRISONER, HART, IS WITH THEM, AND HIS WIFE AND BABY REACHED HERE SAFELY. WE CANNOT LOAD OUR CARGO. WE ARE SHORTHANDED AND UNDER THREATENED ATTACK. WE HAVE GREAT NEED OF L'EPOUVANTAIL. YOUR SERVANT, DULOGE."

Doctor Syn looked at Mipps and said quietly, "It is the first time that our prisoners have taken concerted action against us."

"Do you think it's young Hart that's put fight into 'em?" asked Mipps. "The rest have all been there a long time.

Some of 'em a very long time. Broken men with no hope and no spirit."

Doctor Syn nodded. "Aye, Mipps. When I last saw them I thought of them as ghosts. Ghosts of their former selves. But what could we do other than what we did? They were traitors all. As each one was tried by the Night-riders, he knew they deserved death, too. They were given their choice. Each man chose exile. Their lot might have been far worse. Their wives and in some cases their children were kidnapped and sent after them, and those who repented and promised loyal service in the future, were allowed married quarters. There was never complaint against their rations. They live better than they would on Romney Marsh. True they have to work, and work harder than they might have had to do at home, but they must never forget that they are working out their own salvation, for I think the sin of treachery will be the most grievous count against a sinner in the Latter Day. There is something behind this mutiny. I cannot think it is Hart. He expected to be sent to the Plantations by Captain Blain, when we rescued him. He then expected death at our hands. Instead of which the wife and child he loved have been sent to him in safety. At his trial at the Oast House he was penitent and grateful for the mercy shown him. Well, we must go to France and look into it."

"Let's see," said Mipps, "there's eighteen prisoners besides hart, and all able-bodied men. That means we must take our biggest boat, for we'll need some thirty of our men to raise this 'ere siege."

Doctor Syn smiled and shook his head. "You and I, with the help of Duloge, will be enough to raise 'this 'ere siege, as you call it."

"I meant 'that there siege,' Vicar. Sorry," replied Mipps, grinning. "But what about Jimmie Bone? He speaks French same as you only not so good, and he knows the place well. He'll want to come with us, too."

"But I want him here, Mipps. He is the only one we can trust to take the Scarecrow's place. Remember, Captain Blain is still here, and we must not let him think that his presence has scared the Scarecrow. We will sail for France tonight. I'll go to the Squire now and tell him I am bound for Rye, and may not be back for a day or so."

"And what are we going to Rye for this time?" asked Mipps. "We ain't due to preach there, you know, till next month."

"You forget the confirmation candidates," replied Syn. "The young people are so important. The future pillars of the parishes, my good Mipps. I think I should tell them myself what a privilege it is for them to have the Archbishop himself willing to lay his hands upon their heads."

"All right, sir," grinned Mipps. "Just so long as I know. I'll tell Dymchurch that I has to go along with you all the way to Sussex to tell the young 'uns that the Aggerbagger is coming along to tap 'em on the skulls hisself."

"Aye, Mipps," laughed Syn, "a little grumbling on your part will not be amiss. Neither will it be amiss if Jimmie Bone dressed as the Scarecrow is seen by Captain Blain riding the Marsh while we're away. We must be in the mouth of the Somme by daybreak, and for that the wind sets fair. Name ten men for the lugger, with you and I to navigate. We will not waste time and tide, but come back with a run of good cargo. I'll instruct Jimmie Bone in the hidden stable tonight before we set out for France."

That night a lugger went out with the tide from Littlestone Beach. Five of the ten Night-riders aboard took the first watch while their fellows rested in the fo'c'sle. The Scarecrow himself set the course, and kept the helm till three in the morning when he called Mipps from the aft cabin.

"Hellspite, you will wake me at dawn," he ordered, "when we shall be within the mouth of the Somme."

"Aye, aye, Scarecrow," replied Mipps beneath the hideous devil's mask, which every Night-rider wore when on the Scarecrow's business.

The night was pitch dark, and the lugger showed no lights, so that she was hailed neither by ship not boat until just as dawn was breaking in the river-mouth a throaty tenor voice echoed across the calm water with the cry of "L'Epouvantail."

Although the water on the shelter of the rivermouth was smooth, there was a breeze stirring which rapidly brought the two vessels closer, the lugger and a fishing boat carrying a lug sail.

Through his mask, which looked more than ever hideous in the fair growing light, Mipps hailed back, and then gave orders for heaving to so that the smaller boat could fetch up alongside. He then went to the cabin and roused Doctor Syn.

"If I know Duloge, he will be in this boat that's hailed us," said the doctor, adjusting his

Scarecrow mask. "And what is more, I know why he is there. In all the years I've worked with him I find I can admire him more and more.

Perhaps this is conceit, but his brain always works in accord with mine own. What he does under certain emergencies, why, so do I, and vice versa. We think along the same courses. Duloge is in that boat because he wants to head us off before we enter our harbour. He has evidently something important to tell us, and he has timed our arrival with his usual skill. Help him aboard and bring him here, where we can talk in private, for we must know the situation before we land."

Duloge was a colossal creature, who on rare occasions of necessity looked magnificent in rough clothes, when he would shame his servants' manhood by lifting casks and stowing them, while four men working on one cask at a time took longer.

His appearance in more normal times, however, was marred by his love of effeminate finery. Descended from a long line of ancestors who owed their name to the sea fortress which they had held for centuries, the present master of castle and harbour liked to dress in the latest mode from Court, which, as Doctor Syn told Mipps, illbecame the grand old bull. Even his booming voice he trained to a languid tenor in order to show his fellows an aristocratic superiority. He was rich, because his ancestors had been sea rovers, which was a gentlemanly term for pirates, and since casting in his valuable lot with the Scarecrow, he had become much richer. His vanity in clothes had persuaded him to spend most of the night in an open boat dressed as thought he might have been attending a Royal levee. A contrast indeed to the fantastic rags of the Scarecrow who received him in the dirty aft cabin of the lugger.

Their meeting was cordial, and while Mipps served them with brandy their conversation was carried out in French, Doctor Syn explaining in English the vital points to his lieutenant.

The Frenchman concluded with: "My dear L'epouvantail, although the situation is annoying and the rascals think they have the whip hand, this is not so. True they hold the stores of liquor and food, and with the weapons from the armoury could sustain a siege, but against that they are also houses with the powder magazine, and if I chose to jeopardize the safety of my chateau, I can blow them to their Kingdom Come whenever I feel disposed. As you know, the store-house was at one time the kitchen of the old castle, before the present chateau was built. In the roof there is a secret door which opens into the great chimney. The disused hearth is stacked with powder down,

which they would think surely to drop loose powder down, which they would think but soot, and at our convenience lay a train across the roof and through the door. I think the chateau walls would bear the shock somewhat easier than they could. Since the rascals watch the windows I thought of letting myself down into the fireplace and surprising the vermin from the back. With my back to the powder barrels they would dread to fire, and my long sword would have been a match against their cutlasses. That was an alternative against the powder train."

"I should have thought of that myself," replied Doctor Syn.

"But I couldn't put it into practice," explained the Frenchman, "by reason of my cursed girth. I found I should need more powder than I had to blow me through the secret door. It's small, quite small."

"But Mipps and I could do it," said Doctor Syn, "and when we spring our surprise, you could attack them from the front with my ten Nightriders."

Duloge nodded. "I envy you your part in it. Surprises are enchanting, but fat men find them difficult. With a rope a thin man could be lowered without noise."

Duloge then explained that his chief reason for meeting the lugger was to prevent them from steering into the harbour, which would have put them under the direct fire of the mutineers, and he now proposed that they should stand in as near as possible and then land the crew from his own boat upon a beach protected from the store-house by the harbour wall, adding that this could be done the quicker by using another fishing boat which was beached close to the spot where he proposed to land them.

Since time was important in order that if all went well Doctor Syn and his men could make their return voyage that night, both vessels were headed towards the distant harbour of Duloge. While Mipps looked after this, the two leaders remained in the cabin and elaborated their plan of attack.

As it was broad daylight when the first boatload touched the beach, it was useless to attempt concealment, since the windows of the row of white cottages set aside for the prisoners' married quarters faced the sea, and despite the early hour a crowd of women and children were discussing the arrival of the Kent lugger.

This fact, however, Doctor Syn turned to his own advantage, and only waited till all his men were landed before putting it into execution. The landing took longer than Duloge had hoped because the other fishing boat he had counted on was nowhere to be seen. He conjectured that his own servants must have taken her out to catch fish for his table.

At the head of his men the Scarecrow strode up the beach and confronted the women, while Duloge went to the chateau to find a rope. In a stern voice he addressed them. "I am sorry you have allowed your men to mutiny, when I have treated them with mercy. Well, my punishment will be as sudden as their revolt. You may think I have brought my

Night-riders here for the purpose of attack. That would be foolish, since we have but to show ourselves upon the quay to be fired at from the cover of the store-house. I am too fond of my faithful followers for that. No.

They are here to remove you all, women and children, from your comfortable cottages. You will be taken aboard the lugger to a destination unknown to you menfolk. It is a fitting punishment that they shall never set eyes on you again. You will be prisoners in another chateau belonging to Monsieur Duloge. It is far from here, and guarded by rough and desperate men. There will be no comfort there. Nothing but prison walls, hard work, scanty food, and no husbands or fathers."

"That they may know your fate and theirs I will allow you half an hour to visit them and say farewell for ever.

You will go to them now, and when I fire a pistol as a signal, you will take immediate leave in order to get aboard with your children. Any by the way, you can add this for their comfort. With great care and upon the shortest commons they may hold the siege for six months. Then they may starve for all we care, since other arrangements have been made to keep our cargo trade alive. But tell them that although they successfully surprised Monsiuer Duloge, that clever French gentleman is no fool, and can turn the tables any time we think fitting, since beneath the cobble-stones of the store-house floor there is a powerful mine of gunpowder ready trained to prevent our valuable consignments from falling into enemy hands. Go now. You have but half an hour."

When the women and children, including Fred Hart's wife carrying her baby, had disappeared round the corner of the quay, the Scarecrow ordered his men to await the command of Duloge, and signing Hellspite to accompany him, he strode towards the chateau. Here they met Duloge carrying a length of rope, who led them by way of the stables and cowsheds to an outside staircase which brought them on to the roof of the storehouse.

As he pointed to a small oak door, concealed behind a flying buttress of the great chimney, doctor Syn whispered to Mipps: "Do you hear their chattering panic? Of course the women will never leave their men, but they'll be mightily in their way when we surprise them."

Duloge unlocked the little door, which let out a babel of voices from beneath. Peering down into the chimney he let down one end of the rope to the required length, making fast the other round the buttress, for Doctor Syn preferred to climb down rather than be lowered, and the deep embrasure of the chimney corner hid the rope.

Taking a silent farewell to Duloge they watched him go down the staircase and meet half a dozen of his servants armed with muskets. Giving him time to join the Night-riders, they waited, peering down into the chimney. They could not see any of the mutineers, for, ignorant of the small door, they had not considered placing a watch in the hearth. Slowly and silently Doctor Syn lowered himself through the little door, gripped the rope and slid down behind the powder barrels. Mipps followed. They had landed safely and without attracting attention, for the noise in the store-house was deafening.

All were talking at once. Some arguing that they would do well to keep the women and children with them and save them from the voyage on the lugger, and others saying that it was better to let them go in case the Scarecrow ordered the store-house to be blown up. This set some of them to work upon the floor in order to discover if possible where the mine was hid.

When Syn slipped round the barrels and stood behind them in the centre of the hearth, he saw several of them trying to dig up cobbles with their cutlass points. The married ones were fondling their wives and children. He noticed Fred Hart with tears streaming down his face as his wife was showing him their baby. One of the window guards had left his musket against the wall and was stroking the hair of his ten-year-old daughter. The other guard was more zealous to his duty, and was watching the quay with his barrel resting on the window-sill and his finger on the trigger. He at least was prepared for a sudden attack. But not from behind, and no one was more surprised than he when he knew that the Scarecrow's pistol had picked his trigger hand for his target. A sharp pain which made him cry out above the deafening reports of the Scarecrow's pistol and his own musket, which he fired spasmodically.

The terrified cries of 'The Scarecrow,' as men and women turned to see the Avenger in their midst, were allowed by his hard voice.

"We shoot to kill the first man who moves!"

Had any man been brave enough to take him at his threat, he would not have been able to, for the women saw the two figures with pistols in each hand, and they clung to their husbands desperately, while the children huddled to them in terror.

"This will teach you what you should have known," went on the hard voice, "that you cannot play the Scarecrow false. Look behind you."

The two small windows bristled with barrels held by the Night-riders and the servants of

Duloge. That colossal dandy had been quick and silent in attack.

"And now for the cause of this mutiny," said the Scarecrow. "I must have the reason and the ringleader. You have raised no complaint before. Fred Hart was the last to be condemned and sent here. Was it you, Fred Hart?"

Before he could answer another spoke for him. "No, Scarecrow. Fred Hart owned he deserved his punishment, and only asked us whether we thought the Scarecrow would keep his word and send over his wife and child. From the first he was against the mutiny, and only joined because we all did."

There was a long silence, during which the hideous head of the Scarecrow slowly faced each mutineer in turn.

Then he spoke again. "The ringleader in Handgrove. He has been betrayed two of his fellow Night-riders to the authorities, after extorting monies from them under threat of exposure. If you remember I rescued those tow men, his victims, from the Dymchurch cells, and sent Handgrove here for life. Handgrove is the ringleader, but Fred Hart is to blame. Now listen, Hart. Because of your wife and child, I am once more inclined to be merciful to you, and to you all. Not so to Handgrove. Where is he?"

No one answered.

"I see," went on the Scarecrow. "You do not know where he is, eh?"

A sullen chorus of 'No' from the mutineers.

"But you know where he has gone, eh?"

The mutineers looked at one another uneasily, but no one spoke.

The Scarecrow continued, "Monsieur Duloge, will you ask your servants who took your missing fishing boat?"

Duloge turned from the open window and jabbered in French to the servants behind him. Then, with no attempt to conceal his panic, he cried out through the window: "None of my people had the boat. My God! Then it means…"

The Scarecrow completed his sentence: "It means that these men shut themselves up in this store-house to conceal Handgrove's absence. It means that Fred Hart told his fellow-prisoners of the huge reward offered to anyone who could break up our gang. It also means the Handgrove has sailed in that boat to lay the information about this place. Am I right, Fred Hart?"

"Aye, Scarecrow," replied Hart. "He sailed last night. He is going to the Admiralty to appeal for a rescue ship to bring these missing families back to England. He will stipulate for a free pardon for all here."

"You will now lay down your arms," said the Scarecrow. "All of you will load the lugger. We will not sail with an empty cargo-hold. The women and children will return to the cottages, which, by the way, are all undermined, and Monsieur Duloge intends to blow them up if he perceives the least sign of mutiny again. Remember that you are in our hands, not we in yours. I sail tonight, but shall return in person for the next cargo which will be run in a few days' time, when I shall require all prisoners to attend the execution of Handgrove. Unbar the door and get to your work."

Leaving Mipps and the Night-riders to see to the loading of the contraband, the scarecrow and Duloge walked to the chateau for dinner.

"That was a good idea of yours," said Duloge, "about the undermining of the cottages. Shall I get my servants to put that work in hand?"

"Why worry?" asked the Scarecrow. "They believe it. But you look very troubled, my friend. Why?"

"Why?" repeated the Frenchman. "Is not this Handgrove on his way to your Admiralty?"

"But it is a long way to London by open boat," replied the Scarecrow. "He had provisions, of course, but no money for the road it he lands at a nearer point. Unless he sells the boat to buy a horse."

"He will do that if he is wise," said Duloge.

"But the price of a boat will not buy such an animal as I shall ride," laughed Doctor Syn. "The lugger, too, is fast. I think that I shall catch him."

"And if you do not?" asked Duloge ruefully.

"Then I shall wait for him inside the Admiralty," was Doctor Syn's reply. "Take heart, my friend," he added cheerily. "We have done well. Today we quell a mutiny. Tomorrow we must catch a traitor."

Lashed with spray, the tall gaunt figure of the scarecrow stood at the lugger's helm, as she spanked her way through the choppy waves of the Channel, with a ninety-mile gale behind her straining every stitch of her crowded canvas.

Behind the hideous mask of the scarecrow's fearsome disguise, his voice kept croaking out orders. "Strike nothing. She's lying low but she rides it bravely. I'll not lose a whistle of this gale. This change of weather is an omen for our good. Speed will save our necks. Brace up, my merry lads. Brace up."

On the other side of the tiller stood Sexton Mipps, masked like his master and answering to the name of Hellspite. He looked up at his tall companion and shouted above the wind: "Ain't you better turn in, Scarecrow? It's getting dark, and we'll make Dungeness this night, thanks to them mutineers loading us quicker than they've ever done, through fear of you. You've a hard night and day ahead of you. I can manage her now."

"I know it, Mipps," replied the Scarecrow. The men were forward, and it was safe to talk without being overheard. "Tell Curlew to keep the course. I must talk to you in the cabin, for I think we have never been in greater danger than we are at present, and the next two days will decide our fate."

As soon as the door of the aft cabin was locked behind them, master and man unmasked, and then Mipps realized by Doctor Syn's grave face that he took the situation very seriously.

"Aye, Mipps, the danger is as black as the night ahead of us. The occasion calls for brandy." Doctor Syn produced a bottle and two pewter measures, which he filled.

They drank in silence, and then Syn refilled the measures.

"Let us view circumstances calmly," he said, "and then, having settled our course of action, follow it as swiftly as this gale, which is so fiercely fighting on our side, against our present enemy, Time. First let us state what we know, then let us guess what we don't."

"Certainly, Vicar," replied Mipps, holding out his measure for replenishment. "Brandy puts heart into one, and helps us to remember what we know. What do we know?"

"This," said Syn decisively, pressing his long forefinger upon a chart of the Channel spread out on the cabin table. "Somewhere ahead of us is Handgrove speeding for London, in order to betray our organization to the Admiralty. If he succeeds, our contraband-running vessels will be blockaded in the mouth of the Somme, and it will be death to our vast brandy trade. This we know, and therefore know that Handgrove must be intercepted. Let us weigh his chances and ours. He had the start of us last night in an open boat. He has but one sail, and he is singlehanded. He sailed in calm weather, and not being too skilled a navigator we may take it that he wasted time in tacking which we would not have done. Remember, he was a farmer, not a fisherman."

"Perhaps this gale has caught him and him to Davey Jones," put in Mipps.

"We must not bank on that," went Doctor Syn. "We must suppose that he is still afloat, and by now the gale that is driving us is also helping him. But we can make more speed than any vessel in the Channel. Now let us put ourselves in his place. From what we know of him, let us translate his psychology to ourselves. Here is a desperate man, who for many weary years has been our prisoner back there in the mouth of the Somme. Under our faithful French lieutenant, Duloge, he has been worked hard, helping to load our cargoes with no thought of gain to himself.

"A little while back a fresh prisoner arrives. He is but one more of many who have betrayed the Scarecrow. This prisoner, Hart, tells his new companions of the great reward offered for information laid against the Scarecrow's organization. Covetous for the freedom and money, he determines to escape, and thinks of the chances he has of stealing one of Duloge's fishing boats and crossing the Channel. But he realizes that even could he get away in a boat, his absence would be discovered at the next roll-call. So he enlists the help of his fellow prisoners: organizes a mutiny, seizes the store-house on the quay, and with the arms and ammunition contained in it, declare a state of siege, knowing that there can be no rollcall, and that he can escape without being followed by a larger and faster boat.

"Of course he had to wait for a favourable night to escape, but he must have congratulated himself that he effected it before Duloge could get our help. Before leaving he exhorts his fellow mutineers to hold out at all costs till he brings them rescue from the British Navy. He will hurry, of course, because he is eager for his reward money, but he cannot know that Duloge and ourselves have acted so quickly, raised the siege, recaptured the mutineers, and are now on his heels. Still, he will hurry for all that, and having no money will sell the stolen boat and with the money take to the road."

"Or keep to the water and sail for the London river," interrupted Mipps.

"He might, but I think not," went on Doctor Syn. "He is a landlubber and will feel safer

ashore. Therefore, he will try to land this side of Dungeness, for he would not dare to show his face upon the Marsh, since he has too many enemies there in the men he tried to betray. I suggest he will make for the Sussex coast, and if successful take to the Hastings-London road. Hart will have told him that our bitter enemy, Admiral Troubridge, who has offered the reward against us, is at the Admiralty."

"It was to Troubridge he betrayed his two friends at Dover, and had we not rescued them from their cells, their necks would have been stretched. He knows that the irate old Admiral will have his face saved if he can discover our secret harbour in France, for we have fooled the old seadog too much in the past. So, Mipps, we will land and run our cargo as usual, and them make for the hidden stable. I shall be on my way to London before dawn, and at least far enough from the locality where Gehenna's magnificence might be recognized. You will follow by coach, catching the mail from Ashford. I will carry you as far, and drop you before dawn. Meanwhile our men must search for news of Handgrove. They must make enquiries as far as Hastings. If his boat has not arrive, then we have time to prevent Handgrove's interview with the Admiral."

"Aye, sir," replied Mipps, "and that will take him time. Didn't Captain Blain tell us the other day at the Vicarage, when he was dining with you, how difficult it was to get things settled quick-like at the Admiralty? We'll get time, with luck."

Before Mipps left his master to take over the watch, they discussed their plans in full detail. Mipps raised two objections.

"Even to save time, Vicar," he said, "it's madness for Doctor Syn to ride Gehenna. The

Scarecrow's horse should never be associated with you. Gehenna must attract attention. An animal in a thousand. Even by riding on the secluded road, as you must, someone is sure to notice you."

Doctor Syn shook his head. "I cannot borrow from the Squire's stable because I am believed to be in Rye.

Besides, he has nothing so fast or so strong as Gehenna. And certainly if I were to take side lanes and bridle paths, I should be noticed, as you say. No, I shall drop you at Ashford before dawn and then ride up on the Dover road. It will be faster going, and the turnpike keepers are well used to fast-mounted messengers riding on the King's business between Dover and London. And there is one man I can trust to hide Gehenna in the city. The landlord of the Mitre Inn will see to him. Is he not one of our biggest receivers? He would only put a rope round the his neck if he betrayed us. Besides, old Bubukles makes too much profit from us to do any such piece of stupidity. Any by the way, Mipps, I have always found that the truth is safer than a lie. In case the Squire takes it into his head to ride over to the Mermaid Inn at Rye to visit me, as he sometimes does, you will leave a letter for him at the Ashford coaching office for the down mail. I will write it now, telling him that I have to visit the Archbishop at Lambeth.

Fortunately His grace is there, and I shall make the confirmation candidates at Rye my excuse for being in London.

Now help me to finish this bottle and then on deck with you. I know that you can snatch some sleep upon the coach."

The bottle finished, Mipps left his master chuckling over his letter to the Squire of Dymchurch.

Now Captain Blain, billeted at the Vicarage as the guest of Doctor Syn, was most anxious to see his host come back from Rye, since during the night of his departure he had been awakened by the noise of horsemen. Cautiously peering through the shutters, he had seen the Scarecrow himself, with some half-dozen Night-riders. He had seen one of them dismount and write with a piece of chalk upon the stable door. Determining if possible to wing the Scarecrow, he had crossed to his bed to snatch his loaded pistol from under the pillow, but as he returned to open the shutters and the casement a shot had struck one of the diamond-shaped panes, and by the time he had recovered from his rage and his surprise, he saw the Phantom Horseman riding away into the Marsh. Groping his way downstairs, he had found a lantern and had gone out to examine the writing upon the stable door. Signed with the Crude sketch of a Scarecrow, the chalk message read, *"Friday, low, tide."*

He was glad he had crept from the house, because the next morning the chalk message had disappeared. So upon that Tuesday he told the Bos'n that the men would have no night duty till Friday. Clever as he had proved himself, Captain Blain never suspected that the message had been written for his benefit, and his alone. Anyway there were no revenue men out upon the Tuesday night when the lugger ran ashore at Littlestone, was met by the Highwayman, impersonating the Scarecrow, and all the valuable cargo of good brandy was landed safely and carried across the Marsh on pack-ponies to the 'hides' upon Lympne Hill.

Half an hour after the last keg had been safely stowed, and the pack-ponies had been dispersed to their various stables, Gehenna the Scarecrow's famous horse, was being saddled by Jimmie Bone, the Highwayman, in the secret underground stable, adjacent to Old Mother Handaway's hovel and farmyard, in the lonely centre of the Marshland.

The Scarecrow changed from his fantastic rage into the elegant black clericals of Doctor Syn. Hellspite similarly became once more the respectably dressed servant, Mipps, who had helped the Highwayman to attack loaded holsters and saddle-bags to Gehenna's harness. Into the deep pockets of guineas, and having given Mipps the letter which he was to post by the down mail from Ashford for the Squire, declared himself ready for the road. The great horse was led out of the stable. The door was secured behind them, and the Doctor leapt into the saddle, Mipps scrambling up behind him.

Bending down from the saddle, Doctor Syn gripped the Highwayman's hand and whispered: "See that further hints of a great run reach Captain Blain and the Kings's men for Friday. But there will be no run of course. It may take some days to run Handgrove to earth."

"I hope you may get him, sir, replied Jimmie Bone, "alive or dead."

"If he lives we shall get him alive," said Doctor Syn, "and after see him dead. Our luck will hold good. Within the last twenty-four hours we have crossed the Channel, put down a dangerous mutiny, unearthed the plot of a rascal, and run a good cargo of contraband. And now we ride on the track of the rascal, and I doubt not that we shall pull him down. Good-bye."

Despite his double load, Gehenna broke immediately into a gallop and thundered away across the Marsh.

It was still night when Mipps slid from Gehenna's back and bade his master farewell outside the town of Ashford.

The Doctor Syn rode hard. With his hat pulled well down over his eyes, and a black scarf hiding his chin, no one would have thought that this magnificently mounted gentleman in the black, well-cut riding coat, was a country parson. His rapid progress was misunderstood, for at every turnpike he would bend low in the saddle and whisper to the keeper: "There are French spies abroad. I ride on the King's business. Should any question you, as to whether I have passed on this black horse, you will shake your head. You are, I take it, loyal enough to welcome and bury King George's secrets with one of his guinea spades? You have not seen me pass, eh?"

The turnpike keepers only wished that such messengers could ride upon the King's business every day.

Gehenna reached Ely Place before dinner-time, and was safely lodged with mine host of the 'Mitre.' Half an hour later the Vicar of Dymchurch sat in the waiting-room of the Admiralty in Whitehall, having requested an interview with Admiral Troubridge.

Having the profoundest respect for the brave parson who had from every pulpit of the Romney Marsh, publicly attacked the crime of smuggling, the old sea-dog did not keep him waiting. In fact, he was delighted to see him.

"We are desolated, my dear Admiral," said the parson, "that you have left Dover for the Admiralty. I fear that your successor will not be interested enough to back me up against these smugglers that give our Marsh villages so bad a name. Had you remained in our vicinity, I think that between us we might have got the better of them. But I fear I tire you. You have now greater responsibilities, and cannot be interested, even in our notorious Scarecrow."

"On the contrary, Reverend Sir," beamed the Admiral, "I always asked you for information when I was at Dover, and I take it you have called upon me now to give me some. I shall welcome it and you, for I am still resolved to catch this Scarecrow of the Marsh."

"I fear, sir," replied Doctor Syn, "that my purpose in London is to call upon His Grace of Canterbury at Lambeth.

I shall have to repot to His Grace that since your leaving us the Scarecrow has been more daring than ever. I fear now that he will never be taken."

"You think so, eh?" chuckled the admiral. "You think also that I have abandoned you? No. Doctor Syn. I am expecting a visitor this very day who can give me information which will enable me to smash the Scarecrow's organization at the very source. I am to learn full details of his secret harbour in France. I shall be able to bottle up his ships before they enter British waters. Then what can he do?"

"That would indeed be a master-stroke, sir," was the Doctor's enthusiastic reply. "By the way, sir, I am expecting one of the Archbishop's servants to wait upon me here within the next quarter-hour. May I have you permission to wait for him in your enquiry-room?"

"Certainly, Doctor," said the Admiral. "You may come and go as you please. I will give orders for you. In the meantime read that." He threw a note across the table. Doctor Syn picked it up and read: *You may remember my name. I betrayed two of the Scarecrow's men to you, Admiral Troubridge, eleven years ago. You think I am dead. No sir, I have lived a living death as a prisoner of the Scarecrow. He was too clever for me and for you, sir, and the Navy. But now I can get my revenge and give you yours. I have escaped from his base in France. I can show you, just as soon as you have paid me the reward for such, the very spot in France he loads his ships with French contraband. When you pay me in golden guineas I will take you to the spot. A condition is a free pardon to certain Romney Marsh smugglers who fell foul of the scarecrow. They are not dead, as supposed.*

They are prisoners with their wives and children. It has been their lot and mine to load
the contraband fleet. For my information, I demand the reward and a rescue for my
unfortunate colleagues. Your honor may remember my name.
Your Servant, One Handgrove.

"This should prove most valuable," exclaimed Doctor Syn. "Through it I have no doubt but that you will take the Scarecrow himself. May I wait upon you later in the day?"

"We will sup together," said the Admiral. "By that time I may have something to tell you. Shall we say the Ship Tavern in Whitehall? At nine o'clock this night?"

"I shall be delighted," agreed Doctor Syn. "But if you will excuse me now, I will go and await the servant from Lambeth Palace. You expect this Handgrove today?"

"Aye, and he'll be here, too," explained the Admiral, "because a verbal message was given to me by his messenger who brought this note. He asked for an early appointment, and by the clock he should be in the enquiry-room within the next ten minutes. Do you remember Handgrove? Eleven years ago he was one of your flock."

"One of its blackest sheep, I fear, Admiral," replied the Vicar. "I recollect him well, though I doubt whether he would know me. He was not given to attending church."

"Why not stay and hear what he has got to tell me," suggested the Admiral.

Doctor Syn shook his head. "My presence would embarrass him. Besides I am awaiting the messenger from Lambeth, who is to tell me where I am to meet the Archbishop."

"Then I will not detain you," said the Admiral, ringing a bell, which was promptly answered by a petty officer.

"Conduct Doctor Syn to the enquiry room," he ordered. "He is expecting a messenger." The Admiral shook hands with his guest and added, "Nine o'clock, then, Parson, at the 'Ship' in Whitehall."

Doctor Syn found the enquiry-room a lively place. Groups of officers awaiting appointments with their Sea Lords, were renewing old acquaintances, and exchanging gossip of His Majesty's ships. Taking the elegant parson for a chaplain of the fleet they bowed politely as he made his way to the window overlooking the front courtyard.

He knew that Handgrove must come in that way and be directed by the sailor on guard to the enquiry-room.

Although Handgrove had not set eyes on the Vicar of Dymchurch for eleven years Doctor Syn had seen him many times, and recently from behind the Scarecrow's mask when the smuggling business had taken him to France.

He would have no difficulty in recognizing him. Neither did he, for after three minutes' vigil at the window, he saw his man creeping through the archway. Turing abruptly from the window Doctor Syn walked briskly to the door, and asked the petty officer acting as usher to order him a hackney coach. As he crossed the courtyard the approaching Handgrove saw the petty officer salute the parson and dash away. As he mounted the steps of the main entrance that led to the enquiry-room, the parson came down the steps to meet him.

"Your name is Handgrove, I believe," said he in a quiet, pleasant voice. "You are here by appointment to lay information before Admiral Troubridge concerning a certain party whom it is safer not to name. You may wonder how I knew you, but before I was made Chapla in to the Admiralty here I was Vicar of Dymchurch. You disappeared from my parish some eleven years ago, and were given out as dead. I am delighted to find you alive."

"I am here to see the Admiral," growled Handgrove sullenly.

"Who has appointed me to take you to him," replied the parson. 'It will be my duty to take your Bible oath upon the truth of what you tell us. I shall then hand you this bag of guineas in advance of your reward, to show you our good faith. The rest will be paid when we have proved your statement true." Doctor Syn drew a money-bag from his pocket, and Handgrove heard the chink of gold. "A hundred guineas, Handgrove, which you shall count after taking your oath. You will then be detained under the protection of the Admiralty till your story is proved."

"It's true enough as a certain party will find to his cost," snarled Handgrove. "I shall be glad when it's over, and hope the authorities won't delay. Where's this Admiral?"

"I am waiting for a coach to take us to him," replied Doctor Syn. "It may interest you to know that a certain party has sent him a threatening letter stating that if you enter the Admiralty you will be killed before you can utter a word. The Admiral, knowing as I do from bitter experience, that this unnamed one never utters idle threats, has commissioned me to take you to his private lodgings, and I think here is our conveyance."

Handgrove saw a coach with a sailor on the box seat beside the driver enter the yard. The petty officer sprang down and opened the door. Doctor Syn stepped in and told Handgrove to sit opposite him. He then called out, "Lambeth Palace."

"Lambeth Palace," repeated the saluting petty officer, and the coach rolled out of the yard.

"Why there?" asked Handgrove.

Doctor Syn smiled. "Because it is not where we are going, and when we are clear of Whitehall I shall change direction. We do not want to give information to the scarecrow's spies, and no doubt there are many now about the Admiralty, waiting for you."

"But how could he know that I've escaped?" asked Handgrove.

"My good fellow, don't ask me," replied Doctor Syn. "I begin to think, as many do, that there is something supernatural about him. I have striven against him in the past, just as the Admiral has, and if now you have it in your power to overthrow this devil, the government will owe you much, and you will deserve the large reward."

According to his changed direction the coachman at length pulled up his horses opposite the alleyway that led to the secluded Mitre Inn. Paying the coachman, Doctor Syn ordered Handgrove to follow him, and led the way to an upstairs sitting-room, where Handgrove saw a spread dining-table laid for three.

"The Admiral though it best for us to dine together here in private," explained Syn.

"I have no wish to dine with gentlemen," growled Handgrove.

"You will change your song when mine host brings in our covers," laughed the Doctor. "Now while we wait for the Admiral we will count these guineas." He drew a Bible and the bag of guineas from his pocket. "Here is the good Book ready for your oath, and here the guineas." He laid the Bible on the table, and then poured out the money on to the white cloth. "I have counted them at the Admiralty, but had better satisfy yourself. I will go and see if the Admiral is in the common-room below."

Closing the door behind him Doctor Syn beckoned to the waiting host of the 'Mitre.' You are sure you can do it?" whispered the Doctor. "Remember I want him alive. You must strike carefully."

Mine host nodded. "I have a heavy, lead-loaded, brass candlestick upon the sideboard behind his chair. I'll not kill him."

"I took him from under their noses without suspicion," chuckled Syn. "And good for us all that I did. If he had reached the Admiral you and I and some hundred others would have had our necks stretched. The cellar is ready? And the cellarmen?"

"Trust me, sir," whispered the landlord.

"Then bring up the tree covers as soon as you will," said Syn, "for if I have to look at that

traitorous dog much longer it will spoil my appetite. Mipps will be here by coach tonight, when we can shift the rogue from your cellar aboard the lugger in London Pool. Drunk sailors are a common enough sight upon the quays. We shall have no trouble. But once again let me remind you not to kill. I wish him to take his last voyage alive."

Doctor Syn re-entered his private sitting-room briskly. "The Admiral will join us in a moment, Handgrove. He has ordered dinner and begs us to start. You will sit there. Myself opposite, and the Admiral here. Is the money correct?"

"Aye. Ten piles of ten as you see," replied Handgrove.

"And here is mine host with the covers. Master Bubukle, the Admiral has ordered us to start. I will ask a blessing. 'May we who eat this food be faithful unto Thee, loyal to the King, and steadfast to our fellows. Amen.' Now, Handgrove, fall to with good appetite."

Mine host lifted the cover in front of Doctor Syn, as he saw the steam mount up into

Handgrove's face. Then a sickening thud, and Handgroves's head was on the table.

"Took it beautiful," chuckled the landlord. "Now a boozer's hoist to the dellars, and my

cellarmen will look to him."

Five minutes later Doctor Syn and mine host were doing full justice to the sucking-pig.

During that afternoon the Vicar of Dymchurch visited Lambeth Palace and took a dish of tea with the Archbishop.

At five minutes to nine the same Vicar was awaiting the arrival of Admiral Troubridge at the Ship Inn of Whitehall.

During those five minutes, for the Admiral was punctual at nine, Doctor Syn found occasion to leave a sealed letter addressed to the Admiral on the hall table reserved for patron's messages. That the Admiral was in a rage was apparent, but it was not till the waiter had left them to their soup that he explained.

"The rascal never turned up, Doctor Syn. Do you know, I think the Scarecrow's got him."

The Parson looked incredulous. "Come, come, Admiral. That is surely impossible."

The waiter brought the fish, and laid a letter by the Admiral's plate. As he read the contents the old sea-dog nearly had apoplexy. "It's true," he gasped. "I'm right! Read, read."

Doctor Syn adjusted his spectacles and read quietly: *"Handgrove cannot attempt to betray me again. Let his fate be a warning to you and that meddlesome Parson of Dymchurch. I will not brook your interference."*

It was signed by a rough sketch of a scarecrow.

Later that night, at the Mitre Inn, the Vicar of Dymchurch whispered to Mipps: "We shall have no more mutinies amongst our prisoners in France. I have a means of making Handgrove see to that. You will enjoy our next adventure, little Mipps, I promise you."

7

THE SCARECROW'S EXECUTION

The news spread like wildfire, and lost nothing in the telling. The bare facts of the case were that Admiral Troubridge, jubilant at finding an opportunity to smash the Scarecrow's brandyrunning from France, had had his valuable informer snatched from under his nose. One Handgrove, a desperate rascal, who had suffered eleven years' slavery for treachery against the Scarecrow's men, had escaped from the secret French harbour where the contraband was loaded, and had made appointment at the Admiralty to tell all he knew. There was no doubt as to the reason why he had failed to present himself, for instead of his man, the Admiral received a threatening letter from the scarecrow, stating that Handgrove's fate should be a warning to him, and to that 'meddlesome Parson', Doctor Syn of Dymchurch, who had for years been daring enough to attack the crime of smuggling from every pulpit of Romney Marsh. It was obvious, therefore, that the Scarecrow had retaken his prisoner on the way to Admiralty
House.

By this time the Scarecrow and the doings of his Night-riders had captured the public's imagination. No longer a mere local celebrity, his adventures were the chief topic of conversation throughout the inns and taverns of the London roads, the jokes and jibes of the coffee-houses, as well as the romantic gossips of the fashionable drawing-room. Not a man who did not envy him, neither maid nor mother who did not feel drawn towards his masculine effrontery. And yet was he masculine? Was he human? Was he not rather the Devil himself? When Doctor Syn first created the Scarecrow as the leader of the Romney Marsh smugglers, he had striven hard to give him a spiritual significance, and he was not disappointed in his creation. The Scarecrow was accounted uncanny.

Captain Blain, lodging temporarily at the Vicarage, with his score of sea-dogs billeted in the Tythe barn adjacent, thought otherwise. Although he had seen the fearful apparition of the Scarecrow, he did not share the superstitions of his men. He respected the Scarecrow as a dangerous and ingenious enemy whose clever head was joined to an agile body by a human neck round which he determined to place a hempen collar.

The news of Handgrove's disappearance came to him in a letter from Admiral Troubridge. The Captain was given authority to search every house and cottage in the Marsh and ordered to watch the shore, the dykes and the sluicegates for the body of the missing Handgrove. He was to apply to Admiral Chesham at Dover if he needed more men, and could inform those immediately under his command that extra pay was scheduled from the Admiralty, for every encounter with which they might engage the Night-riders of the Marsh. The Admiral also urged him to work in close cooperation with the Reverend Doctor Syn, whom he described as 'the bravest gentleman on Romney Marsh, in that at the risk of his own life he had never ceased to attack the nefarious smugglers'. He added that in his opinion the only trouble with the vicar of Dymchurch was that he took his parochial duties too conscientiously. Why could not the fellow find it in his heart to betray what he learned as a priest under the seal of confession? Not being Roman Catholic the Admiral could not understand why Doctor Syn was so very scrupulous about keeping secrets heard by him through the confessional comfort of the Church.

To his Bos'n, Captain Blain exclaimed: "Wish the Parson would come back, for I have a suggestion to make to him. Doctor Pepper tells me that one of his patients is dying. A hard-drinking old rascal of eighty, who seems to be very afraid of death. A Dymchurch man of that age, and a bad character from all accounts, must know a good deal about the smugglers. Under the fear of the next world what more easy than for Doctor Syn to make him talk. I shall try to persuade him that it is for the good of the Marsh parishes. I wonder how long he is staying in London. His housekeeper says some few days. I only hope old Pepper can keep his patient alive till then. Bos'n, I feel it in my bones that we can only take the Scarecrow through the help of Doctor Syn. So let us pray for his speedy return."

Although he did not know it, the Captain's prayer was answered, for Doctor Syn's return was certainly speedy.

Once more gratified turnpike keepers opened the road for the generous King's Messenger, whose magnificent black horse made short work of the highway. "French spies are on the road," he whispered, as he paid his toll with a guinea-piece. "It is not in the interests of the King that any should know I have passed this way. So forget you have seen a gentleman on a black horse."

After four and a half hours of hard riding, Doctor Syn turned Gehenna from the road on

Lympne Hill, and descended by a bridle-path to the Marsh Level. He entered his parish by a cross country gallop, avoiding the village and making straight for his hidden stables at old Mother Handaway's hovel. Here he was welcomed by Jimmie Bone, the Highwayman, who groomed the Scarecrow's horse, while his master roasted a fat chicken and opened a bottle of brandy.

"I must not return to the Vicarage," he said, "till I have crossed the Channel. The lugger, *Four Sisters* from London Pool, will lie off Littlestone tomorrow night. Mipps with ten of our London men are bringing her round.

We are unlikely to have any trouble from Captain Blain, since he thinks there is a 'run' planned for the next night, and he will be sparing his men for that encounter, which will not take place. By the way, am I right in thinking that none of our prisoners in France have ever seen your face?"

"The only ones who have seen me unmasked from Dymchurch," he replied, "are yourself, the Squire, Mipps and the Beadle. Why do you ask?"

"Only that I have a strange part for you to play in a somewhat grim adventure," chuckled Doctor Syn. "I think that after playing it we shall have no more trouble with our prisoners across the Channel. If Mipps is successful in carrying out my orders amongst the junk-shops along the quays of London river, we shall teach our enemies a lesson."

"But you have not told me what you have done to prevent Handgrove betraying us to the Admiralty," said the Highwayman.

"My plan was so simple," replied Syn, smiling, "that is must have tempted Providence to send It awry. But it worked, my good James, it worked. I took the rascal from the Admiralty before he had announced himself. He is at the moment a prisoner in chains below the cargo hatch of the *Four Sisters*. I will tell you all about it as we eat, and then I shall get you to sling me a hammock in the empty stall there and let me sleep."

Across the Channel, in the private harbour from which the Scarecrow's luggers sailed with their brandy cargoes, Monsieur Duloge waited anxiously for news from Romney Marsh. From the tower of his chateau above the quay he could sweep the mouth of the Somme with his spy-glass.

He knew that the Scarecrow had returned to England on an enterprise dangerous to them all, and his one thought since bidding him good-bye was whether his ingenious and brave colleague had succeeded in recapturing their escaped prisoner, the treacherous Handgrove. If he had failed and Handgrove had succeeded in laying his information before the Admiralty, at any moment the British Navy might be seen blockading the mouth of t he Somme. Once it were known that the Scarecrow's luggers loaded and sailed from his harbour, the brandy trade was finished as far as he was concerned, and any of his men who escaped with their lives would be fortunate.

Duloge was a rich French gentleman who loved surrounding himself with the expensive luxuries of the time.

The clothes with which he adorned his colossal body, were in the latest mode and cost a fortune. His chateau, harbour with quay and store-houses, and a fleet of boats, were his own property that had always brought in a considerable income, but since casting in his lot with the Scarecrow's organization across the channel, he was amassing an ever-increasing fortune. There was a large profit for him in every tub that crossed the water, since one half-anker, weighing when full some fifty-six pounds, and holding four gallons of brandy, could be bought in France for four shilling a gallon, the same costing in England thirty-six shillings with duty paid. The duty stood at four shillings a gallon, so that the run of a hundred tubs or half-ankers, was a clear profit of a hundred and twenty pounds.

Although it had been considered well worth while could one cargo out of three be safely placed, Duloge had found that since the Scarecrow had managed for him, not one cargo had been lost, though occasionally a decoy boat carrying a few tubs of inferior spirit was sacrificed for the safety of the cargo proper. The liquor being sometimes as much as a hundred and eight above proof, was uncolored, and called by the traders white brandy, so that the smugglers, by mixing it with burnt sugar, could make three full tubs out of one. Enormous profit and well worth the risk of capture by the Scarecrow for his success, he also had grown to regard him as a friend, and he trembled for his safety. Ships were scouring the Channel for him. On land, in England, the same search went on relentlessly, for the reward for his capture mounted as the failure to capture him increased.

Though confident in his colleague's skill, he had never waited so anxiously for his return. He had his own anxieties, too. Though the prisoners had worked with a will since the Scarecrow had quelled their mutiny, and a fleet of luggers were loaded in harbour for the next 'run,' he could not fail to notice a growing tension amongst his prisoners and his armed servants were urged to the greatest vigilance. He knew the cause of the prisoners' anxiety.

They were sharing with him the same speculation, 'Had Handgrove reached the Admiralty?' If the scarecrow had failed it meant to them a free pardon at home, and a rescue from their slavery by the British Navy. The Scarecrow had swindled the Government too much. He had defied the King's ships, and beaten them. Therefore the Navy was ranged against him. So with hope in their hearts the prisoners had worked cheerfully in loading the cargoes, hoping that every tub would fall into the Navy's hands.

All through the day Duloge watched from his tower. His lackeys for the first time noticed that their master did not linger over his elaborate meals. He took a mouthful, asked for the next course, and drank his wine hurriedly.

Then back to the tower with his spy-glass. As the night wore on he sent for a cloak, ignoring the comfort of his four-post bed.

"I shall not need my valet. He may retire. I shall watch this night."

At three in the morning he heard distant gunfire from beyond the river mouth.

At the same time Mipps came to Doctor Syn in the aft cabin of the *Four Sisters*, and said: "Shot across our bows, Scarecrow. British Revenue cutter in French waters. She's no right to tell us to heave-ho."

"Can you make her out?"

"Aye, it's light enough to see her lines, though she's some way off. She's the *Ferret*. Should be patrolling Hastings waters. What's she doing here?"

"Asking for death. Well, give it her," replied Syn. "She's dirty by her name. Give her a dirty end. Sink her."

"But we can avoid her by out-sailing. And there's a mist to creep into at the river mouth," objected Mipps. "And we have Handgrove aboard," went on the Sexton. "We have had the luck to get him so far, and we need not risk failure now."

"Engage the enemy," ordered Syn. "We have had luck with us for two days and nights. We have quelled a mutiny, recaptured a venomous prisoner, and now we'll play our third card, which will appall our enemies. Sink the *Ferret*."

"But, sir..." faltered Mipps.

Doctor Syn interrupted sharply, "Engage the enemy."

Mipps went out on deck saying to himself: "Well, when he gets captured, I shall follow him. But if I gets captured he'll rescue me. So engage the enemy it is."

The *Four Sisters* was a Littlestone boat, and could carry a crew of twenty-five. She was a vessel of good size, with roomy holds, and had once borne a French name, for she had been a privateer and had been taken by the Romney Marsh smugglers in a sea fight. She looked smart, was easily handled for speed and could show a quick stern when chased by anything more powerful in guns, carrying herself only four six-pound carronades.

As the first gun discharge shook the little cabin, Doctor Syn, dressed as the Scarecrow, went on deck to hear Mipps cry out: "We've unstepped her mast at the first shot. Now to bring down her other, and the Ferret will have on sea-legs."

"But she still has her teeth," laughed the Scarecrow, as a broadside fell short of the *Four Sisters*. "Give her the rest of the guns below the water-line and then make for the river mouth. Look out." As he spoke the cutter had swung round and delivered another broadside. Once more it fell short, though decidedly nearer. The cutter went about again, but before she could release another broadside the guns of the *Four Sisters* had struck her below the waterline.

"If we give her another chance she'll hit us," laughed The Scarecrow. "Show her our stern and head for the mist bank with every stitch we've got. The Ferret's boats are undamaged. There will be no drowning if she sinks. Cram on the canvas."

Duloge heard the gunfire and trembled. He calculated that it must be the Scarecrow's lugger being intercepted either by British or French patrols.

He would have trembled more had he been able to see the game little *Ferret*, though holed badly, turn once more and give chase, to the cheering of her sailors.

The prisoners heard the firing, and gathered it was the British ship sent to rescue them, trying conclusions with some French man-of-war. But they dared not leave their cottages for fear of being shot down by Duloge's armed sentries.

As the dawn stole in they had a pleasant surprise, for they were aroused by a British naval officer attended by two bluejackets, who ordered all prisoners to dress quickly and to muster on the quay in front of the main store-house.

Within a few minutes of such news a crowd of excited men, women and children were hurrying to the harbour side.

A strange and glorious sight awaited these poor exiles.

The servants of Monsieur Duloge were roped together on one side of the quay, with their captured muskets stacked in front of them.

Standing apart, roped and gagged, they saw the elegantly dressed Duloge. His sword had been taken from his sheath, and lay before him on the cobble-stones. To them his mighty bulk seemed shrunken with dejection. It was obvious that the British Navy had dealt quickly with him and his sentinels.

Lying in harbour they could see the *Four Sisters* with the White Ensign flying from her peak, telling them that the scarecrow's favorite lugger had been taken at last.

One thing puzzled them. The officer in charge of the King's men was inspecting a hole in the centre of the cobbled quay. It was about six-foot long and three broad. Two of his sailors were standing shoulder deep in it with spades.

"She'll do now, sir," said one of them.

"Then tumble up, and fall in with the others," ordered the officer.

The two men obeyed smartly, and joined four of their mates who stood on guard with drawn cutlasses.

Turning to the prisoners the officer said: "You are no doubt glad to see His Majesty's uniforms for once in you lives, eh? Well, you may thank your colleague Handgrove for braving escape with information. In a few minutes you will be given an opportunity to prove your loyalty by obeying an officer of the crown. Six of you who can handle a musket, and no doubt you all can, step forward. Master-gunner serve them out with the Frenchmen's arms."

While this order was being carried out he called down the quay steps, "Bring up your prisoner, and let us put an end once and for all with this Scarecrow nonsense."

Up the steps marched four sailors with drawn cutlasses. They had a prisoner limping in their midst, and at the sight of him the prisoners who held the muskets cried out, "The Scarecrow!"

"The Scarecrow is taken," laughed a woman from the back. "We are free! We are free! It is true."

"Quiet there," ordered the officer, as he picked up a board that had been lying near the ominous hole in the ground. He held it up so that all who knew their letters could read.

Those who could repeated the chalk inscription to those who were too ignorant: HERE LIES A TRAITOR
THE SCARECROW

The guards pushed the prisoner to the edge of the hole which was indeed to be his grave. He was bound and gagged over his famous mask. Addressing the armed prisoners the officer said, "You will cover him carefully and when I give the word, fire."

"Don't look so fearful now, does he?" laughed one of the armed prisoners. "Ain't so tall and upright as he was when bullying us."

"Poor devil," muttered Hart, the youngest of them. "I've had a bit of the torture they serve out to make men speak and betray. They've no doubt given him a taste of it."

"Quiet there," thundered the officer. "Present arms. Stand clear from him. Fire."

To the cries of hysterical women and frightened children the six muskets cracked. The figure of the Scarecrow sagged forwards on his knees and toppled into the open grave.

"Pile up those muskets," ordered the officer. "Ready with your spades, my lads, but first rip off the scarecrow's mask."

The two sailors with the spades jumped into the grave and ripped off the corpse's gag and mask.

"He's dead all right, sir," said one of them.

"Now all of you except the children file past this grave and look at this dead traitor's face," said the officer.

"Think, too, whether you were wise or foolish to betray your one-time leader."

The prisoners in morbid curiosity hurried to the open grave. And then screams of terror broke the silence of the chill morning. *For as they looked down upon the rag-clothed corpse they saw the glazed eyes of their colleague, Handgrove, looking up at them.*

Laughing, the sailors drove them in a herd from the grave at the point of their cutlasses, and then from the quay steps appeared the figure of the real Scarecrow.

"Fill in the grave and make his epitaph correct," he ordered.

The officer wrote tow letters more to the writing on the board, and held it out to that they could read the added word 'to'.

HERE LIES A TRAITOR
TO
THE SCARECROW

"Let this be a warning to you all," cried the scarecrow. "These sailors are my men from

London. Their uniforms were purchased by Hellspite from the junk-shops there. Disobey Monsieur Duloge again and there will be other graves upon this quay." Then turning to Duloge he added, "Let your men drive them back to their quarters."

As the wretched prisoners were surrounded by the Frenchmen, who had thrown aside their ropes, they saw the ensign being struck from the lugger's peak, and the two spades shoveling in the earth upon the corpse.

No sooner had they gone, however, but the filling of the grave stopped at the Scarecrow's orders, and the corpse was lifted out and carried back aboard the lugger.

Then the grave was filled up and the board placed as a headstone. Turning to the play-acting officer the Scarecrow whispered: "Very well done, my good Jimmie Bone. Admiral Troubridge might have spotted you, but to the laymen you surely had the manner born."

In the meantime, back in Dymchurch, Captain Blain's men searched to no avail for the body of Handgrove. But two days later they had their reward, for as Doctor Syn was supping with the Captain and describing his coach journey down form London, Mrs. Fowey, the Vicarage housekeeper, burst into the dining-room with the dreadful tidings that there was a body hanging from the gibbet outside the Court House.

"It must have got there after dark," she said, "for as I passed the spot at twilight there was never a smell of a corpse upon it."

Rushing out to investigate, Parson and Captain cleared their way through a group of fascinated though fearful villagers who were reading an inscription nailed to the post.

"THE SCARECROW'S COMPLIMENTS TO CAPTAIN BLAIN. IN FUTURE THE ADMIRALTY SHOULD GUARD THEIR INFORMERS WITH MORE CARE, FOR DEAD MEN CARRY NO TALES."

"I'll get the Scarecrow for this," cried the Captain.

"Dreadful," muttered Doctor Syn, shaking his head and shuddering with horror. "Really, something should be done."

"Is shall be, Parson," said the Captain. "Don't lose heart. We'll catch the rascal yet."

"Oh dear, oh dear," sighed Doctor Syn, "I wonder if you *ever* can."

8

THE DANDY SLEUTHS

Since that affair at the Admiralty, when the Scarecrow had prevented the informer,

Handgrove, from collecting the Government reward for betraying the secret base in France where his contraband boats were loaded, the Night-riders of Romney Marsh became more than ever the topic of popular conversation amongst the London gossips. The mysterious disappearance of Handgrove had not ceased to be the chief source of wonder at the scarecrow's skill, when the corpse was found hanging from the common gibbet outside the Court House in Dymchurch.

Amongst people of all classes a great fear had arisen concerning the Scarecrow. The average man, whether regaling himself in a club of fashion, a coffee-house, or a tavern, declared that if ever he had the opportunity to betray the Scarecrow, or his men, he would be too scared to do it, since what had happened to Handgrove might and probably would be the lot of any other who was dangerous towards the Scarecrow's schemes. However, this was but the opinion of the average man. A thousand golden guineas, which was now the reward offered for the Scarecrow alive or dead, was yet a great temptation to any man of courage who happened to be desperate for hard cash.

And such a one was Sir Harry Sales.

A young bachelor, clever, well dressed and attractive in manner as in face and form, he loved the ladies so well that he could never bring himself down to a one and only. His friends said of him that he would never marry in case his lady wife made him give up his gambling habits. Not that he was skilled in cards or dice, but he loved the excitement that they brought. He preferred to cut the pack for money, rather than to play a game of skill with them.

He liked to know quickly his gain or loss.

Having gone through a considerable fortune at the gaming clubs, he had retired to his country Seat, meaning to cut his losses by quiet living. But after a few weeks the gloom of his rambling old house got on his nerves, and the urge to return to the fashionable clubs of London compelled him to sell family pictures, jewelry and plate. With the funds thus obtained he drove to London in order to try a last conflict with the Goddess of Fate.

At them Bucks' Club in St. James's he was received back with open arms. He had been

missed for himself by his real friends, and by others because he played for high stakes and lost gamely. What was more to the point of pleasing them, he lost pretty persistently. Also he was overgenerous and when the wine mounted to his brain, which never made him quarrelsome, but the more jovial, he did not notice that he was doing all the paying.

His last funds sank as rapidly as he played. When luck was with him one night, it deserted him more disastrously the next. But he stuck to his purpose, hoping that he would be the gainer at the last. The crisis came when he had circulated the wine too freely, and his muddled, jolly head made a miscalculation of a thousand guineas. He cut for his last thousand, as he thought, not realizing that he had lost it on the round of bets before. His opponent made him see that he was wrong, after some argument in which high words were spoken. This attracted the interest of Admiral Troubridge, who, with his brother the General, and two guests, was playing a simple round of backgammon if they felt so disposed, though the younger members of the club wondered how they got any amusement from such games.

The Admiral had know Sir Harry's father, and had long grieved to see the son thus ruining himself. Thinking now to save the young man from a squabble which he thought might turn into a stupid affair of honor, he excused himself to his guests by saying that he wished to get the youngster out of an awkward corner which his so-called friends had forced him into.

" I'll bring him over and introduce him to you, my good Doctor," he said to the learned Vicar of Dymchurch, who had been his dinner guest.

As the Admiral approached he heard young Sir Harry say: "Well, then you are right, Major, and I take your word for it. Had I but kept a clear head I would not have always played for stakes that I could pay out of hand. I regret that I must ask you not to accept my I O U. I will get round tomorrow and see what can be done."

With a smile that thinly disguised a sneer, the Major replied: "I think you said that your stables were empty and everything not entailed disposed of for cash. Perhaps you were only exaggerating. I hope so from my heart."

The vicar of Dymchurch overheard and sized up the situation as the Admiral beckoned him to join the other group.

"My good friend, Harry," said the Admiral, "as your father's dearest friend I want to have the pleasure of introducing you to Doctor Syn, Vicar of Dymchurch, who also knew your father and would like to know his son."

"I am honored to meet you, Reverend Sir," replied Sir Harry. "Let me in my turn present you to my friends, who are all acquainted with the Admiral. This is Mr. Briston, Captain Tandyshall, Lord Strathway, Sir Peter Hemminge, and this Major Culland."

Doctor Syn noted that the last name was given with a formality that carried no friendship with it. Also that the other gentlemen seemed by their manner to hold the same view. It was obvious that his remarks about Sir Harry's stables being empty had offended their sense of decency. Even the Captain who served in the same regiment had edged away from his superior officer after bowing to Doctor Syn.

Lord Strathway, by reason of rank and seniority, became the spokesman.

"It is indeed an honor to the Bucks' Club to welcome you, Doctor Syn. Your name is on every one's lips for the courage you have shown in your parish against this Scarecrow. I marvel that you can appear so calm, for I confess that were I in your shoes, I should be shaking in them. I vow had I defied this outlaw as you have, I should be expecting him to leap out at me from the panels of this card-room."

"Doctor Syn of Dymchurch, is it?" drawled the Major, surveying the Parson with amusement through his quizzing-glass.

Doctor Syn bowed his assent.

"Well, well," went on the officer, "is the Bucks' Club turned into a Revenue Office that we have the scarecrow's enemies congregated together? The Admiral here, his brother the General there, with Major Faunce, and now the Parson. All four have been made the public butt of the Scarecrow's humor, and no doubt you are meeting here as a place of safety in which to form further plans against him. The old proverb, eh? Try, try again. 'Pon my soul the Scarecrow's head must be swollen with pride, when he has beaten the Navy, Army, Revenue officers, Bow Street Runners and the Church. Now, Sir Harry, here's a chance for you. A good idea. These gentlemen gathered here like ill-omented birds of prey against the Scarecrow gives me a hint. You owe a thousand guineas for that last cut.

A thousand guineas will be paid to whoever catches the Scarecrow. Significant that the sums coincide. Surely Fate challenges your courage and ingenuity, my good Sir Harry Sales? You have courage, eh? And certainly an ingenuity in dealing with the Jews. I am quite sure, too, that you have a desire to pay your debts, especially your debts of honor. Why don't you attempt the task that has beaten so many? Why not go down to this Romney Marsh place, play a lone hand, and bring back the guineas?"

Doctor Syn saw the challenge accepted in sir Harry's eye, and was secretly amused, but aloud he said very seriously, "You would be rendering a great service to the country, sir, if you were to succeed, and my poor parish could once more lift up its eyes unto the hills."

"Come now, sir," put in the Major, "I think we should not put pressure upon Sir Harry. He must follow his own discretion, for we must own that disaster has overtaken all who play a hand against this Scarecrow."

"There is no disaster greater in my mind," said Sir Harry quietly, "than to postpone the payment of a debt of honor. Give me a week. By that time I will do my best to confront the Scarecrow, and what will happen then is in the hands of Fate."

"You'll be more than ever the hero of the ladies if you succeed," laughed the Major, "and I need not add the envy of the men."

"I think that by accepting your challenge, Major Culland," said Doctor Syn, "Sir Harry Sales will earn great respect from all. It is undoubtedly a brave thing to play a one had against our local scoundrel."

"But he shall not play a lone hand as far as I'm concerned," replied Sir Peter Hemminge. "My sword and such brains as I can muster to the problem are at your service, Sir Harry."

"You mean that you'll join me?" asked Sales joyfully.

"There's my hand on it," declared Sir Peter.

"And mine too," put in Mr. Briston. "Hunting a Scarecrow will be a new sport, by gad."

"I think so, too," cried Lord Strathway. "What about you, Tandy? You're on furlough I think you said."

"I am, my lord," replied the Captain, "and not loving the cards as well as my Major here, I'll welcome anything more exciting than playing here night and day. You've no objection, Major?"

"Why should I?" asked his superior. "Your time is your own. Had I not business in Town to attend to I should have been delighted to join you in the enterprise."

"As to that," replied His Lordship, "there is a proverb about 'too many cooks'. Four is a concise number for such an undertaking. We will pledge ourselves to work under the leadership of Sir Harry, and he will at least be confident that his lieutenants are all loyal and sympathetic friends."

"And you may count on the old Parson for any help he may be able to give," said Doctor Syn. "At least I know the district, which may prove useful, and understand the temper of the parish, who are all members of my flock, black sheep and white. I think also I have shown sufficient spirit in declaring myself a public enemy to this troubler of our local peace."

"And since both my brother and myself are also his declared antagonists," added the Admiral, "and have guaranteed an equal reward to that offered officially against the Scarecrow, I'll write to Captain Blain, who is residing at Doctor Syn's vicarage, and my brother will write to the Dragoons encamped in the ship Field, to place themselves entirely at Sir Harry's disposal."

Doctor Syn smiled and shook his head. "I have the greatest respect for my guest, Captain Blain, but in his work he is, perhaps rightly, as close as an oyster. He is so determined to catch the scarecrow himself that I fancy we cannot look for much co-ordination in that quarter. It is another case of Lord Strathway's proverb, "Too many cooks."

"Well, join us at our table, gentlemen," said the Admiral. "You may as well know as much about the scarecrow as we can tell you, for remember, Doctor Syn, my brother, myself and Major Faunce have all had the experience of seeing him at work, and out testimony may be a service to you, Sir Harry."

"I shall welcome such a conversation," replied Sales warmly. Then changing his tone he bowed to Major Culland, saying, "I shall hope to settle our wager here in one week."

As the other gentlemen bowed stiffly and began to move, Major Culland stopped them. "Just a moment, gentlemen, before leaving me in this cold fashion. You convey plainly enough by your manners that you are displeased with mine. Yet I protest that I am willing to show that I have as much sporting instinct as Sir Harry Sales, who is about to risk his life as leader of this expedition to the Romney Marsh. Let us not deceive ourselves as to his danger. However secret we may be on the matter, and believe me I shall not breathe a word of it, the Scarecrow is likely to strike first. It is a way he has. Out of regard for this, I will raise the stakes against myself.

Suppose now Sir Harry's luck is better in adventure than in cutting cards, and that he wins the reward for the Scarecrow, alive or dead, I will tear up his I O U if today week at this hour of nine in the evening he shall bring the Scarecrow into this clubroom so that such members and guests who are then present shall have the fun of seeing the rascal unmasked for the first and last time. I am willing to forfeit my thousand guineas for such an honor to our Club."

"We can hardly bring such a dirty scoundrel into a respectable," club objected Lord Strathway, by way of excusing Sales from taking up such a difficult wager.

"But he may be a member, for all we know to the contrary," laughed the Major. "No one knows who the devil he is, though many think he is the devil himself. At least judging by his cleverness and grim humor, I incline to the opinion that he is a man of breeding and education."

"His handwriting hardly warrants such an assumption," said the Admiral.

"As to that, sir," suggested Doctor Syn, "his handwriting would be surely disguised, and as to His Lordship's suggestion that his distinguished club is hardly the place for such niceness as members might feel. The Major has suggested a wager that would be regarded in the best society as a piece of skylarking in the heroic vein."

"And a great feather in the club's cap, sir," agreed Mr. Briston.

"What do you say, Sales?" asked His Lordship.

"That I never refused a challenge yet, my lord," the young man replied stoutly. "I'll do my best, and with so many good friends at my back I see no reason why we should not be unmasking the outlaw here at this time next week. And now, Admiral, let us by all means talk it over with the General and Major Faunce. Good evening, Major Culland, and thank you for you stakes."

The group followed his example of another formal bow to the Major before leaving him alone. The Major surveyed them through his quizzing glass and with a smile of inward amusement strolled out of the club.

An hour later Doctor Syn also left the club, took a hackney coach to the Mitre Inn in the City, collected his baggage and his henchman, Sexton Mipps, and then took the night coach for the Kent coast.

The next evening the news spread round the village of Dymchurch that five gentlemen had booked the best rooms at the Ship Inn. Mrs. Waggetts, the landlady, informed Sexton Mipps that they were pleasant-spoken gentlemen and had bespoken the rooms for six nights. They had satisfied her curiosity as to their presence in such a remote village by stating that they sought sea air and quiet after a hectic season in Town, and that Dymchurch had attracted their attention owing to the much-talked of activities of the Scarecrow and his followers.

Mrs. Waggetts advised them for their own good not to venture on to the Marsh or sea-wall after dark.

"We thought we might see something of the fun, and have a good story to take back with us," laughed one of them.

Mrs. Waggetts shook her head and advised them to be cautious. Disregarding her motherly advice they put on their cloaks after supper and strolled out upon the sea-wall.

Here they were questioned by the naval patrol under command of Captain blain. To him they told much the same story, but the Captain rudely warned them to mind their own business and not to interfere with his plans for capturing the Scarecrow.

"Let us understand one another, sir," replied Sir Harry. "There is a public reward posted for the scoundrel. You can hardly prevent anyone from trying to earn it, and if you interfere with us you may find that you are interfering with the Law."

"And you may find yourselves with your throats cut in a dyke." Retorted Captain Blain, who on returning to the vicarage told the Vicar that things had come to a pretty pass when a party of dandy Sleuths were attempting to do his work.

The conversation had been carried on upon the sea-wall beneath the windows of the City of London Tavern, and the five dandies were unaware that a man who had followed their coach from London on horseback, and had taken a room at the 'Tavern' for six nights, had overheard all that had been said from behind the half-closed shutters.

News reaching Mipps of this man's arrival, the Sexton went round to the 'Tavern' for a drink, had a quick look at the stranger as he supped alone in the parlor, and then carried his description to the Vicar.

Applauding his factotum's eye for detail, Doctor Syn remarked: "So Major Cullund, so busy in Town, has taken a week off business to keep an eye upon his opponents in the wager. No doubt he will try to gain the reward himself. Well, the more the merrier, and we'll give them a run for their money. We will lie quiet for five nights, and then organize a spectacular 'run' of contraband upon the sixth. And we will see which of them can catch the wicked Scarecrow. I should prefer that Sir Harry's party had that honor, though for our own safety we must do what we can to prevent it. Tomorrow night we will ride out to the hidden stables and consult with our friend the Highwayman."

For five days and nights the party of Dandy Sleuths, as the Captain persisted in calling them, went out and about upon the Marsh. They visited all the ale houses and were lavish in their hospitalities. For free drinks the yokels were induced to talk, and made good use of their imaginations. The Dandies carried back with them more information than they had ever dreamed of getting, and as they discussed it over their wine in the Ship Inn they were of the opinion that the Scarecrow was not so popular amongst the men of Romney Marsh as they had been given to believe by reports in London.

Since Captain Blain refused to speak to any of them after his warning, Doctor Syn, out of regard for his guests, had to entertain the Dandy Sleuths for dinner at the inn, while the Captain was served in his house by the old Mrs. Fowey. It was during this meal on the second day of their stay that the Vicar showed them another threatening letter he had found upon the pulpit cushion of his church. It was written in the familiar scrawl of the scarecrow, and told him in plain terms to have no dealings with the town gentlemen staying at the 'Ship'. The old Vicar assured the gentlemen that he was not afraid.

Meantime Major Cullund kept to himself, and the Dandy sleuths were not aware that he was watching them. But the old Vicar went to the 'Tavern' and confronted him. Cullund told him that he hoped to take the Scarecrow himself, and so have the laugh against the men who had affronted the Bucks' Club. Doctor Syn, who owned that the Major had been in his opinion definitely affronted, gave his clerical word that he would not betray his presence in Dymchurch to the five gentlemen at the Ship Inn.

"As far as I can see," stated the Major, "there is small chance of anyone capturing the Scarecrow, since the inhabitants are so mortally afraid of him. So, Reverend Sir, I shall still get my thousand guineas, since Sir Harry has only to borrow the sum from his companions."

Doctor Syn told Mipps that his dislike for the Major increased.

Though the five from the 'Ship' worked according to their lights, indefatigably, they were bound to confess amongst themselves that after four days and nights of watching, listening and seeking, they were no nearer in finding out anything concrete to help them. And then, while supping late one night the door of the coffee-room opened and a tall man entered unannounced and closed the door quickly but quietly behind him. Placing his finger to his lips he tip-toed towards the table, motioning to Sir Harry Sales and Lord Strathway to give him room as he picked up a chair and placed it between theirs. In whispered tones he apologized for his intrusion, said there was no need to give his name, but instead could impart information which they would be glad to get, since it concerned the Scarecrow.

"His safety had always been that of fear amongst his men," he explained. "I know you gentlemen wish to get him from under the nose of Captain Blain. Well, I can help you to it. His men are tired of his tyranny and I know there is a plot to kill him after the next run on Friday night. Even for the sake of the reward his men dare not betray him, knowing he could inform against them all in the Law Courts. Therefore when the last keg is safely put to hiding they are binding him, and gagging him safe beneath his mask, and placing him in a disused oast house, which they intend to fire. At the first flame the conspirators will fly for their own safety, but if you dash into the oast house before the fire gets him you may carry him off alive. For myself I ask nothing, though a poor man, except that I hate the whole gang of them. I have reason, which only concerns me."

Closely questioned, and fortified with good wine and Lord Strathway's filled purse which was pressed upon him, the stranger gave them further details. The gentlemen, if hidden by the oast house, would see the landing on Littlestone Beach. The Captain had lapped up secret information that a landing was planned beyond Dungeness, and the Revenue cutter would be patrolling that water, where they would be delayed by a decoy of three harmlessly loaded luggers. Apparently the Night-riders had been cheated of many guineas for some time and were determined to appoint another leader. All of which information delighted the five gentlemen, who on the departure of the stranger became hilarious with joy, knowing that with a little dash and risk of burning they could win the almost impossible wager.

Hearing their laughter, Mrs. Waggetts remarked to Mipps in the tap-room that they were hardly the breed to score off the Scarecrow. The gentlemen, however, continued to drink and be merry, knowing that they were.

On the Friday afternoon Captain Blain, from information received, marched his men through the sea mists which were encircling the Marsh some two miles beyond Dungeness, closing in towards the promontory as darkness fell.

They heard the signal gun of the cutter ordering the luggers to heave-to. For two hours they waited for the revenue boat to report. At last it came grinding on to the shingle, and they learned that the luggers had nothing aboard but stinking fish shipped for manure. They had heaved the stuff overboard expecting to find brandy kegs beneath the cargo, and were now liable for heavy damages.

Meanwhile, Major Culland had seen the five gentlemen pass along the sea-wall, but when he tried to follow them found that he was locked in his room, and his casement was too small to squeeze through. His hammering and shouting were to no avail. For some reason he was being held from going after his club mates.

The five meantime saw much to astonish them. Their informer had been a man of his word. Hidden near the oast house they heard the distant gun of the cutter echoing across the water from miles away. They saw the signals from the landing party flashed in the darkness, and then the string of pack-ponies, guarded by the wild Night-riders.

Then they saw the Scarecrow himself ride up on his great black horse and give his orders, which were dutifully answered by many "Aye, aye, Scarecrow's."

In half an hour back came the loaded ponies from the beach, and then the Scarecrow himself. But this time, instead of leading his men he was led by them. Bound and gagged beneath his hideous mask he was dragged from his horse and hustled into the oast house. Out came the men again, and threw lighted torches into the building which began to blaze. Then away they galloped, laughing.

Into the flames dashed the five, saw the Scarecrow tied to a post, freed him, and carried him out. They took him up to the sea road, where a coach and riding horses were waiting, and putting him inside, under guard, with sir Harry on the box seat and two others riding by the windows, they dashed back through Dymchurch, making for the London road.

The next morning Doctor Syn was not at the Vicarage when the Squire called round to see him. The housekeeper could give no information of where the Vicar was.

"Been out all night amongst his sick parishioners, no doubt," thought Sir Antony Cobtree.

Now the news of Sir Harry's wager had not been kept secret. Major Culland had seen to that, for he wished Sir Harry and his friends to look foolish after so much boasting, and so at nine o'clock the card-room of the Bucks' Club was packed with members and their friends.

As the clock of St. James's chimed the hour a coach rolled up to the entrance. Two cloaked riders dismounted, the doors were opened, and from the interior of the vehicle a queer great figure was carried by Mr. Briston, Lord Strathway, Sir Peter Hemminge, Captain Tandyshall and Sir Harry Sales. Bearing their burden like a corpse they mounted the grand staircase and entered the card-room, where they called for a chair and dumped the burden into it.

A dead silence fell in the room as all saw the weird dress and mask of the Scarecrow.

"Well, gentlemen, we have succeeded, and have kept our word," cried Sir Harry. "You will now see the Scarecrow unmasked. We took him at his work when the King's men have been decoyed far away. Where they failed we have succeeded."

The mask was peeled from the head, and they saw a pale face gagged over mouth and nose. But the gag did not disguise the man. The Bucks' Club were gazing open-mouthed at their most unpopular member, Major Culland.

Two men pushed through the crowd. Admiral Troubridge followed by doctor Syn of Dymchurch.

The Admiral, not sorry to find that others could be fooled by the scarecrow as he had been, roared with laughter.

"I'm glad you are here, Parson," he laughed. "We are not the only ones the Scarecrow scores off."

"I am disappointed," said the Parson. "Do you know I came up to occupy the pulpit at St. Paul's, Covent Garden, tomorrow, and I dropped round here in the hopes of seeing our local celebrity. Do you know I nearly forgot my preaching date in London, and only just caught the coach in time. I did not even say good-bye to the Squire or to my servants. I sent them word though. I sent them word. I suppose this Major Culland is not really the Scarecrow?" At which remark the whole club except the gagged member roared with laughter.

9

DOCTOR SYN'S CHRISTMAS MUMMERS

In the days when Doctor Syn was Vicar of Dymchurch-under-the-Wall in the county of Kent, Yuletide was observed with the fullest ceremonial of ancient days.

Himself and Sir Antony Cobtree, the popular Squire and First Lord of the Level on Romney Marsh, had been students at Queen's College, Oxford, which has always maintained the Christmas ritual of the Boar's Head, so that it was not surprising to find in the hall of the Court House, the Squire's residence, that this delightful custom was carried out faithfully with the half-Latin, half-English carol, sung with due solemnity to the enjoyment of all the Squire's guests at Christmas dinner.

Both Squire and Vicar loved such curious whimsicalities, and perhaps the church choir who snag the carol, headed by "Doctor Syn himself in the part of the Cantor with a cook's cap upon his reverend head, and the great dish held by the Squire's servants above him at their arms'-length, was only eclipsed by the entertainment that followed on Christmas night. This was a play given by the local talent of the parish, and performed much as the old mummers had enacted if for generations upon other floors for stages than those on Romney Marsh. Doctor Syn, with a great love of drama, made a point of coaching the parishioners himself. They had enacted under his direction many old forms of Christmas Revels, but on the particular year when Captain Blain was guest at the Vicarage, and his men were quartered for the festival in the Tythe Barn, the good Doctor was determined to give his audience a more original entertainment that would in a spirit of Christmas fun hold out the finger of scorn at all the failings and failures of the year. The rehearsals had been carried out with the utmost secrecy, and all actors had been put under vow not to divulge anything of the matter to those not in the cast.

Now although the chief performance of the Dymchurch Mummers was the one presented at the Court House on Christmas evening, there were others held on other nights by the same players in other great houses. Indeed all the Lords of the Level extended Yuletide hospitality to their tenants, rich and poor, and the dates of such

festivities were fixed by the various hosts for the convenience of Doctor Syn's Mummers who came to form the chief item of entertainment.

At every manor where these players were asked to perform, there was more than enough food and drink for any who cared to attend, and those who could walk or ride followed the Mummers wherever they went in order to partake in yet another feast.

Next in importance to the Dymchurch performance (which was ever the most popular

because Sir Antony Cobtree was the host) was that given at Lympne Castle by Sir Henry Pembury upon the following night.

The castle hall was thronged not only by the tenants on the hills of Lympne and Aldington, but by everyone who could climb the inland cliff from the Lower Levels of the Marshes. Three districts these Marshes: Romney, Welland and Denge.

Sir Henry, Lord of Lympne, not only threw his castle doors open to all the common folk who cared to come, but took the occasion of this Boxing Night Revel to send invitations to all the immediate gentry, most of whom joined in the dancing that followed the play.

Long before the performance of the festivities about to be described, Sir Henry, hearing form Doctor Syn that since Dymchurch was honored by harboring so many King's men in the shape of hands from the Dover guard Ship and a squadron of Dragoons from Dover Castle, the play had been given extra attention, and was in his opinion well worth seeing, the fat and pompous Lord of Lympne sent out more invitations than ever before. He left nobody out, and begged all to come.

One and all gladly accepted with thanks except Captain Blain who curtly replied that he and his men would have witnessed the play the night previously at the Dymchurch Court House, and that he could not so far play into the Scarecrow's hands, as to leave the Marsh when no doubt all good citizens would have left it for Lympne Castle. "It is a great night for a 'run', and no doubt the scarecrow would have been delighted to think that I could leave my post and the road clear for him. But such a thing I do not intend to do, and should you have an inkling who the rascal is, you may tell him what I now write to you, declining your kind though misplaced invitation."

This reply naturally sent the Squire of Lympne into a great rage, and Doctor Syn, who knew something of the matter, mounted his fat white pony and jogged along to Lympne Castle as a mediator. He had told his guest, Captain Blain, that in his opinion he had failed to show tact or any tolerance towards an older man, which was reprehensible during the season of peace on earth and goodwill towards men, and finally he had ridden to the aggrieved Squire with something of an apology in the Captain's writing.

On entering the library of the castle, Doctor Syn at once perceived that the Squire was in one of his worst tempers. He was sitting before the great fire in a large chair with a table at its side, and upon the table lay a letter which the old lord seemed to be scowling at.

"Come in, and welcome, doctor," cried Sir Henry. "If you heard me muttering somewhat fretfully when you entered so quietly, it had nothing to do with you, whom I am always most happy to welcome to the castle. I dare say you did hear me muttering, eh?"

"To be perfectly frank," replied Doctor Syn with a smile, "I heard nothing of a fretful muttering, but a good deal of honest swearing. In fact, that is why I have mounted Lympne Hill. I guessed you would be swearing, and getting your good self into a high pother which Doctor Sennacharib Pepper declares is so bad for you, and so I came to help you by erasing the letters which have caused you so much ado."

The Squire picked up the letter from the table and shook it in the air. "This is the most impertinent letter I have ever received in my life, Doctor Syn. I should have thrown it into that fire on my first reading of it, but that the sheer effrontery of the words makes me read it over and over again."

"Then, sir, refrain from reading it any more," said Doctor Syn in a soothing tone. "This is a time of year when all good men like your honored self should be ready to hold out the hand of forgiveness to his worst enemy."

"That I will never do in this case," cried the Squire. 'Not even upon the advice of a saint like yourself, Reverend Sir. The writer is one that I hate, and shall always hate most fiercely. A traitor and an unmitigated scoundrel."

"Oh, come now, Sir Henry," went on the Vicar. "I think you wrong him there, upon my soul. No one who knows anything of him could question his bravery."

"Many a scoundrel has been brave," interrupted the Squire.

"And as to his being a traitor," went on the parson, "his whole life's career gives the lie to that."

"Oh, aye," nodded the Squire sarcastically. "He's loyal enough to his own men it is said, but then that is only to his own advantage. This letter to my mind is the saucy culmination of a million impertinences in a scandalous career."

"Now listen, sir," urged Doctor Syn. "I bring you a written apology from Captain Blain, and—"

"Damn the Captain and his apologies too," shouted the Squire.

"I am sorry you take it so badly,' replied the Parson.

"The Captain is small fry and don't matter a damn, Parson," retorted Sir Henry.

"He is at least big enough, sir to own his fault against you and ask pardon," argued the Vicar. "And to prove my words I have here a letter which I must ask you to read."

"I'll read no more letters," cried the Squire with rising irritation. "This one is quite enough to last me a lifetime."

"But I say that you should forget about it, sir, in view of the other letter I now bring you."

"Now see here, Doctor Syn. And I will endeavor to be calm while I convince you that you have no idea what you are talking about. The Captain's letter was merely silly."

"And he owns so much in this second one," said the Vicar.

"But this letter here," continued the Squire, "is not silly. It is terrifying. Yes, Parson, it is exasperating but terrifying too. And it is not from that disgruntled Captain who is trying to catch the Scarecrow while eating your good fare at Dymchurch Vicarage. No, it is not from that failure to catch the scoundrel and his smuggling gang, but it is from HIM. Him himself. I mean HE himself, or what is it?"

"But who is HIM or he himself?" asked the bewildered Parson.

"The Scarecrow, Doctor Syn," explained the Squire. "I keep telling you that his letter in not from Captain Blain or whatever his name is, but from the Scarecrow, and its impertinence is, as I have said, terrifying."

"Another letter from the Scarecrow?" asked Doctor Syn.

"Aye, Parson, and worse than the last one I received from him, as you will agree when you hear it, which you shall."

"Let me see; the last one you had from him," said the Vicar, "was a reproof that you had not invited him to the hunt with the Prince of Wales, and stating that he intended to come, which he did, and much to the Prince's amusement. That was bad enough, so please let me know what can be worse."

"He now invites himself into my house," replied the Squire. "Aye, he intends to visit Lympne Castle without an invitation. Before it was at least out of doors. This time it will be within doors. Think of my unmarried daughters.

The danger is frightful."

With an effort Doctor Syn repressed the smile which he felt inwardly at the thought of the Scarecrow having designs upon anything so unattractive as the Squire's unwieldy daughters. Aloud he said: "I think you may dismiss any fear of harm in that direction. Your young ladies have too many gallant followers, I should hope. So many who would protect them with their lives."

"Precious little good that would be," snorted the Squire. "None knows better than we that the Scarecrow does what he says he will and diddles everyone. Here, read the letter for yourself, and tell me what to do."

Doctor Syn adjusted his spectacles and smoothed out the paper which the Squire had crumpled in his rage. It was written in the usual scrawl that never had failed to disturb its receiver. A rough sketch of a scarecrow was the signature. The Doctor read it aloud.

"*We are informed that as Lord of Lympne Castle you have asked rich and poor alike to your Christmas junketing. Thanks to the poor attempts to put down the contraband traffic by all concerned, we count ourselves amongst the rich of this district. We therefore have been expecting to hear from you. Unless you wish us to attend in the wrong spirit, you had best nail and invitation to us upon the Lympne Hill signpost. When*

hunting with the Prince of Wales I did not have the honor of meeting your beautiful daughters, a pleasure I am looking forward to. It will also be a pleasure to drink a toast beneath the rafters of your historic home."

"And what do you think of that?" gasped the Squire, as though he had only just learned the contents which he knew by heart.

"I think that Captain Blain will now certainly accept your invitation," replied the Doctor. "His men will give confidence to us all by their presence, and he'll sit through the play twice without boredom if he thinks he has a chance of getting his prey."

"You think the Scarecrow will come, as he says?" asked the Squire.

The Doctor laughed and shook his head. "No, sir, I think the whole thing is a decoy to get the King's men to the junketing, as he calls it, in order that he may have a free hand upon the Marsh. But I advise you not to let Captain Blain think that, for then he will not attend, and in case of accidents it will be as well to have your guests protected from the scoundrel. Though come to think of it, sir, the rascally Scarecrow is too wise to prepare such a trap for himself and then, walk boldly into it."

"Yes, yes, but that's all very well," said the Squire testily. "Just the thing he'd enjoy. Prepare a trap, as you say, and walk into it, and then have the laugh of us all by walking out of it again."

"I think you will find that I am right this time," replied the Doctor. "Our play will go through without any disaster, because the Scarecrow will be busy shifting kegs of brandy on the beach. He will certainly have cause of a fresh quarrel with me, if he should see the play, for I am afraid that as author I have made many biting allusions against him, and the great Finale is framed especially to make him the laughing-stock of all that are good and true."

"But is that quite wise for your own safety, Doctor?" asked the Squire. "Even though he is not at the performance, as you think, he will be sure to hear of it, when it will be discussed by everybody. I think I should leave the Scarecrow out of it."

"I am too vain an author, sir," replied the smiling Vicar. "I could not think of cutting out the best scene in my play."

Before taking his leave, Doctor Syn penned a generous acceptance of Captain Blain's apology which the Squire of Lympne signed. It contained an urgent appeal for the Captain to bring his men to the festivity, in case the Scarecrow should be mad enough to make good his boast.

After many weeks of being baffled by the Scarecrow's wits, Captain Blain would not agree with Doctor Syn that the letter to Lympne was an idle piece of boasting. He pointed out that the rascal's threats had always been carried out, and he had every reason to think that this would be no exception, and he accepted the invitation to the castle on that ground.

During the days before Christmas, the Captain saw but little of his host, who was busy every evening training his Mummers in their parts behind the closed doors of the school house. Also the thick snow and severe wintry winds blowing across the bleak Marsh necessitated the Doctor walking on his parochial visits, which meant that his hours were fully occupied. But for all that

Doctor Syn was more than ever cheerful, and could be seen striding along chuckling to himself as he went, over the merry quips and satirical jokes that were going to be good-humoredly pronounced by his characters. Never before had the village play gone so well, or been more enthusiastically praised by the critical ones as on that first performance at the Court House.

Even the victims of the many jokes laughed uproariously at their own expense. But it was the final scene that caused the sensation. When Beelzebub entered shouting, "Here come I, old Beelzebub, and in my hand I carries my club," he was rigged out in rags similar to those worn by the Scarecrow. And when he claimed the hand of the fairest lady in the room, and led hew away to the gates of hell, St. George, throwing off his white battle-cloak, was seen to be dressed as an Excise officer. It was all voted grand foolery, though Mipps pointed out many an able-bodied parishioner who seemed to be fearful at laughing too much at the Vicar's attack upon the dread Scarecrow. He affirmed that this was even more noticeable amongst the audience during the performance on the next night at Lympne Castle.

He was right. Rumors of the Scarecrow's threat to attend had spread abroad, and even those who were most afraid were persuaded to attend out of curiosity and excitement.

The castle hall was packed. In the front sat Sir Henry Pembury, keeping an anxious eye upon his daughters, the eldest of whom was sitting next to Captain Blain, and obviously very piqued at his lack of interest in her. At the best of times the Captain was no man for the ladies, but the sight of Miss Fan, whom her detractors nicknamed the Dragoon, embarrassed him confoundedly, especially when she patted him playfully upon the sleeve whenever a flattering allusion was spoken about the King's good men. Blain was having no truck with such a she-dragon.

Unfortunately for the lady the other seat next to her was reserved for Doctor Syn, who, as the author, kept leaving it vacant in order to retire behind the great screens that backed the stage. But the last scene cheered her up. On the entrance of Beelzebub, attended by two Night-riders, she giggled hysterically, especially when the masked devils brought in a keg of brandy with No Duty chalked upon it, and made the Squire of Lympne take a glass with them.

"And who's the brave man acting the Scarecrow, miss?' asked Blain.

"I recognize his voice in spite of his disguise," she whispered loudly. "It is the eldest Upton boy from Dymchurch. Very well-looking, too. It is a pity he is masked so hideously. They are a very worthy family, as no doubt you know."

"The Scarecrow won't approve of him," growled the Captain. "He'll be needing my protection I fancy."

When this actor came to the front row and chose her as the fairest in the room, her delight and coyness knew no bounds. Everyone knew that this was but a compliment to their host, but Miss Fan took it as a compliment to her beauty. She accepted his hand and to the applause of the audience walked with him to the back of the stage so that the

Lord from darkness could salute her under the mistletoe. On their disappearance St. George came forward to make his heroic speech, and was applauded for some minutes, and the audience could hear the actors behind the screens whispering and asking for Doctor Syn.

After some minutes of an embarrassed wait the officious Mipps popped behind the screens to investigate. After another wait he reappeared, craving the audience's indulgence.

"The fact is, my lords, ladies and gentlemen," he said solemnly, "our principal actor appears to have disappeared.

What's more, he seems to have took off Miss Pembury with a-waiting to step forward at the conclusion of his play to accept your kind applause. He's gone, too. Perhaps he's achaperoning Miss Pembury, for the back door is open on to the terrace."

Suddenly Captain blain sprang to his feet. "Mr. Mipps," he cried out, "who was acting the part of the Devil?"

"We ain't supposed to tell," replied Mipps, "but if you must know it was one of them Uptons. Good, too."

"Was it?" replied the Captain. "Aye and he may be 'was' unless we're quick. Sir Henry

Pembury, I believe the Scarecrow has kept his word. I believe he has carried off your daughter under our noses. Quick, men. Fall in and follow me."

There followed a general stampede of those brave enough to venture out of the door to the terrace. The King's men with drawn cutlasses pushed their way out, and the first sight that met their eyes was a dishevelled Miss Fan lying in the snow on the terrace steps.

Captain Blain seized hold of her and gave her a rough shaking as he shouted, "Where did he go?"

Miss Fan pointed to a great tree at the foot of the terrace and then uttering a scream, fainted.

Leaving his heavy burden to be taken care of by others who were thronging out on to the terrace, the Captain, followed by his men, ran down the steps, and stumbled through the thick snow to the tree in question, where they found Doctor Syn and the eldest young Upton lashed to the trunk with coils of rope.

And away down the hill towards the Marsh they saw the hoof-marks of a horse.

Before the old Doctor could recover his speech, young Upton explained.

"We've been here for some minutes. We were seized, the Doctor and me, and dragged out here. It was Night-riders because we saw the great black horse, standing with three others which another Night-rider held. Presently out comes the Scarecrow with Miss Pembury in his arms. He seemed to be disentangling himself from her arms which were clutched round his neck. He finally got free of her and laid her in the snow, and then they all mounted and rode off single file down towards the Marsh."

When Doctor Syn recovered later in the castle, he smiled at Sir Henry and said: "You were right, sir. I was punished for making fun of the Scarecrow. What I cannot make out though is how did the rascal play his part so well according to you."

"Most likely he watched it last night in the Dymchurch Court House," suggested the Captain. "He was, in my opinion, a better actor than poor young Upton."

The next day Doctor Syn went out though the snow to visit a dying woman. On the way back, however, unknown to anyone, he visited Jimmie Bone, the Highwayman, in the Scarecrow's hidden stable.

"I hear, my good friend," laughed the Doctor, "that your performance was magnificent. I hope you enjoyed it as much as the audience."

"My very revered Scarecrow," replied the Highwayman, "had I known all, I fear I should not have obeyed you.

That Pembury woman, when I told her that I was the scarecrow in truth, clung to me tighter than ever. I can feel her heart beating against me now. I always had an eye for a pretty wench, but oh, that woman!"

"Avoid all such conceit," reproved the Parson. "No doubt she clung to you in order to get the thousand guineas on the Scarecrow's head. You must not misinterpret her motive."

"Wee, I'll never hold up old Pembury's coach again, in case she embraces me again," laughed the Highwayman.

Although the Scarecrow did not tolerate independent smuggling in his territory, and compelled any man or gang of men with such propensities to join his band of Night-riders or take the consequences, he had a soft spot for "old Katie," and made it possible for her to earn good money by the smuggling of Hollands.

"Old Katie" lived by herself in a little cottage at St. Mary's-on-the-Marsh. Although she had turned seventy, she was as strong as a horse and fearless. Many a Marsh farmhand or fisherman who displeased her, had received a blow on the nose that had staggered him and left 'Old Katie' victorious, since no retaliation was permitted by order of the Scarecrow who had proclaimed her as 'an old body that was to be left alone.' Maybe she took advantage of this privilege, for she herself left nobody alone, and would get what she wanted out of anybody, either by the sheer strength of her arm or through her engaging personality. She could outtalk the very devil himself, as she often boasted, 'and when I can't, I hits.' Despite this war-like tendency the old woman was popular, not only for her rough humor and quick retorts, but for what she could do for people in need.

Now amongst a large section of human beings there is no need so persistent as the craving for strong drink, and although most of the able-bodied men on Romney Marsh worked in secret for the Scarecrow, and were able to get for themselves and families plenty of spirits as part of their payment, there were many who were not so fortunate.

Sickly men whose strength could not cope with the laborious tub-carrying: women whose menfolk would have nothing to do with the Free Traders, either for fear of the scaffold, or though loyalty to the Government; and then those poor people who could not afford to buy spirits that were taxed.

To such folk 'Old Katie' was a ministering angel, and her jolly red face and vast bulk were eagerly looked for, since nobody ever suspected that she came in for anything else but a chat. To the sick and depressed she was always welcome, because she had the latest gossip of the neighborhood, and could embroider upon it in the drollest fashion.

But it was what Katie carried underneath the folds of her voluminous skirt and petticoats that made her most welcome. This was a pair of bladders each capable of holding a gallon of the best Hollands. They were ingeniously made with a three-inch tube in their necks made out of cuttings of elder boughs, the pith taken out and vent pegs inserted for corks. 'Old Katie' found this a handier contrivance than a bottle or keg could be, since it was lighter to carry, and whether full or empty, adapted itself to her figure.

Very often, when leaving her cottage for her Dymchurch clients, with her bladders full, she would encounter that sympathetic Vicar, Doctor Syn, who would ask her how she did, and whither bound.

"Oh, God bless you, Parson," the old rascal would answer, curtseying with the greatest difficulty by reason of the bladders, "and preserve you from ever being afflicted with the dropsy like 'Old Katie'. Aye, it's my dropsy you can walk it down after a bit. I calls in and sees someone for a sit down when I gets tired, and by the time I gets home I seems to have dispersed the liquid, and I feels thinner then."

When Doctor Syn used to suggest that the suffer should consult Doctor Pepper, who could no doubt relieve her, she would answer: "Not me. I'll come to you, Parson, for the good of my soul, but not to him for my dropsy. I knows it better than what he can."

"Well, Katie, I don't always agree with him myself," the Vicar would answer. "After all, by our own experience we should know what is best for our own bodies. Now some people maintain that any strong drink is bad for you complaint, and so it is if taken to excess, but in moderation, taken purely medicinally, I should recommend you try a little drop of good Hollands,. Believe me it is a very comforting drink, and if you would care to follow my prescription, why I will instruct my housekeeper to give you a drop or so to keep by you."

Katie was secretly amused at his suggestion, and recounting it to her clients would end up saying, "And there I was a-bulging with the stuff, and he looking that tired and overworked that I longed to give him a measureful there and then to keep the cold out and put the heart in him."

Doctor Syn was equally amused when recounting the same incident to Sexton Mipps.

"There she was, looking for all the world like Shakespeare's Fat Woman of Brentford, and complaining of her dropsy. Now had all that good Hollands been under her own skin instead of a sheep's, she would have been in the last stages of the disease. But since she gets the stuff for next to nothing by the scarecrow's orders, I thought it best to play the innocent by suggesting a few drops of the very stuff she was weighed down under. I don't grudge her the deceit, for she's a grand old sinner, though I shall not be surprised if one day we are put to it to save her from the gallows. She is the only one at the moment outside the Scarecrow's ruling."

"And the only one what rules the Scarecrow's men," retorted Mipps. "You say she gets the stuff for next to nothing every night there's a 'run'. I says she gets it for nothing now, and that there ain't no 'next' about it. Only the other night, when Curlew was filling up them bladders with the best, and expects her to fumble out payment farthing by farthing, she holds up them apple cheeks of hers, and says, 'A woman pays with her beauty, my lad, and you may kiss me.' Curlew refused, 'cos he was afraid she's tell his wife, whereupon Katie slaps him in the face for insulting her, and makes him give extra measure at his own expense. I told Curlew it was lucky he was a-wearing his mask, 'cos a woman's fingermarks across his face wouldn't have done him no good with his wife neither. But the crime of the whole transaction was that she paid nothing at all for the contraband, and Curlew, who we know ain't afraid of Preventive men, was too scared of Katie to ask her."

"Caution ain't cowardice, as you've often said yourself, sir," went on Mipps, "and I looks at Katie this way.

Suppose she gets caught by this Captain Blain, for instance, what is making himself such a nuisance, he might well force an old woman to talk the same as he made young Hart some time ago. No doubt you'd get us out of it somehow as usual, but is it wise to let Old Katie see too much? She can't wait for the stuff to be left at her cottage now, but just rolls up amongst the men when the pack-ponies are being loaded, and tell 'em she don't want to wait about all night. Now I considers that a cock on the steeple sort of attitude ain't one that would do us any good if the old girl got into a mess with that there Blain and his men.

"My good Mipps," soothed Doctor Syn, "although I admit that her drolleries many be irritating at times, I would stake my clerical wig that 'Old Katie' would never betray the Scarecrow. She's a good old soul with the stoutest heart, despite the sharpness of her ways."

Mipps went away shaking his head in doubt, but as things transpired, Doctor Syn was in the right.

Now Captain Blain was not having a happy time. Each day brought him letters of protest from his superiors.

Admiral Chesham, who had taken the place of Troubridge at Dover, was determined to spite his predecessor by smashing the Romney Marsh smuggling. Admiral Troubridge, at the Admiralty, was equally determined to get the Scarecrow and pay off many an old score, and being in London he planned to catch him by discovering, if possible, who was the Receiver in the city who paid such big money for the bulk of the Mash contraband. When his efforts brought in no result he worked off his spleen by writing taunting letters to his colleague at Dover and insulting ones to Captain Blain at Dymchurch.

In the ordinary way Blain would have retaliated, and possibly resigned; but the truth was

Blain's rage against his failure was leveled at the Scarecrow, who has so outwitted him, and he dreaded being recalled from his post till he had accomplished his purpose.

In this mood he did his best to conciliate Admiral Chesham's constant reprimands and applied for more men so that his net could be spread wider.

Burning for results which would stop him from being made a laughing-stock, the Admiral doubled the party of sailors billeted in the Tythe Barn.

These men were posted to watch every house and cottage in the village and the outlying farmsteads as well.

And it was from their observance that 'Old Katie" was first brought under the suspicion of the Law.

They watched her trudging along the St. Mary's road enormous with dropsy, and they watched her returning home after calling at the back-doors of houses and cottages, visibly thinner than when she set out.

The old woman, not being used to browbeating from sailors, went to the Captain and complained that his saucy devils were ever following her about, and that being a lone widow of attraction she objected.

Captain Blain retorted that his men were following every man, woman and child, in the hopes of getting some clue against the Scarecrow. He then gave orders to his men to watch 'Old Katie' more carefully, knowing that even the arrest of an old woman with proof against her would be better than no result at all.

The Bos'n, whose bulk had been the butt for Katie's sharp arrows of wit, which he knew

amused the men under him, made life the more miserable for himself by playing the spy on his enemy.

After a deal of creepings and wrigglings and waitings he went to his officer and told him that if he had authority to arrest the dangerous old hag, he would give the Captain full proof of her iniquities.

And so that very day a shouting and protesting old woman was hustled along the St. Mary's road before she had had time to make one call for a 'sitdown' and a gossip, and brought before the stern Captain in the Tythe Barn.

The poor old soul was more angry than frightened, and demanded that someone should inform Doctor Syn of the indignity which she was enduring.

The Captain replied that it had nothing to do with the Parson at the moment, though no doubt he would want to give her religious consolation before her end.

"Oh, so you've hanged me already, have you?" sneered Katie. "But only in your mind, that's all, and I wouldn't exchange anything so black as your mind for all the dropsy in my poor body."

"I dare say we'll be able to cure you of the dropsy before we hang you," laughed the Captain. "Now then hold her tight, you men. Two more of you grip her legs, and don't let her struggle while we examine her."

With a hefty sailor on each arm and leg the unfortunate woman was forced to stand still, while the Captain walked round to the Bos'n who was behind her.

"Ashamed to look an honest woman in the face, are you?" scoffed Katie.

The Captain did not reply to this taunt, because it was time to put to the proof his Bos'n suspicions.

With a spiker sharpened to a needle-point the Bos'n, who had been gingerly touching the back part of the heavy skirt about the right hip, suddenly pressed it home.

"It ain't her, sir," he whispered, " 'cos she don't cry out. Now let's tap the dropsy and see what it's made of."

He pulled out the spiker as Katie tried to spring forward. But the sailors were ready and pressed her against the Bos'n hand. The pressure released a stream of liquid which shot straight up into the Captain's face, which for the moment blinded him. Having lost one eye against the French, the other one gave him acute pain which made him curse loudly. At the same time one of the sailors standing by seized a tankard and half filling it with the precious stream took a gulp, and cried out, "Best Hollands, sweet and strong."

"Don't waste a drop, men," ordered the Bos'n, "for we'll need it for proof and tasting in the Court."

As soon as the Captain was sufficiently recovered to take up the command, he ordered his men to rig an old sail that they had been mending across a corner of the barn, and behind it the old woman was ordered to remove the other bladder of Hollands, and to push it intact under this temporary curtain.

The Bos'n whispered to the Captain that she would most likely attempt to empty it.

"Oh no, I won't," replied Katie proudly, who had overheard. I ain't one to squeal. I'm caught, and I may as well be hung for the death of a parcel of miserable sailors as for a couple of sheepskins."

"What do you mean by that?" demanded the Captain.

"Just this, you wretched fellow," answered Katie in triumph. "You have been here a good while, you and your sweepings from Chatham, and yet you ain't done nothing till now. And what have you done? As far as you know, arrested a poor old harmless woman for making an honest penny or two by retailing Hollands to poor folk what can't afford to buy it in duty tax in order to provide for the bloody-minded members of the dirty House of Commons. Mind you I says nothing against His Blessed Majesty, King George, God bless him. I only rails against them Commons, supposed to be elected by us, but who never stands by us. A lot of jumped-up puppets what orders your precious Navy and Army about I'll surprise you by handing over the undamaged sheepshskins full of good liquor you have stolen form the poor I gives it to, just to prove in Court that I gave 'em of the best. But I'll surprise you a good deal more in a minute or so, and that I will, but you first get paper and ink and pen so that you can write down what I says in evidence, and if it don't show you all up as a parcel of fools, well I've not been called 'Old Katie' all these years."

True to her word the full bladder was pushed under the screen of sail-cloth, and a few minutes later 'Old Katie' appeared in her tight figure. No semblance of dropsy about her. The only bulk she carried was hard muscle. The real Katie was hard, slim and virile, and her face, though still colored like a russet apple, was set in the grimmest expression. But her bright eyes still laughed as she walked proudly towards the Captain.

The Bos'n instinctively drew his cutlass and stood guard beside his chief. This seemed to amuse 'Old Katie.'

"You've caught me red-handed with the goods on me, Captain," she laughed, "and for that I am willing to take consequence. But I am about to give you the surprise of your life. However, Mister Captain Boils and Blains, as they say in the 'Oly Scriptures when talking of them plagues in Egypt, which, if I may say so, you so closely resembles, there's a little duty (and I knows how you values duty in the King's Navy), a very little piece of duty, what I owes to myself, and as it can't be you, since I has some sort of respect to an officer of King George, though only for his uniform, it just happens to be this dropsy-limbed Bos'n of yours whom I despises like this."

Quick as lighting her left shoulder swung round. Quick as thunder in a close-reefed storm came up her old gnarled fist right under the Bos'n's jaw, and down he went, cutlass and all, unconscious on the wooden floor of the vicarage barn. "and the blessed Lords of the Level will agree at my trial that I owed him that for his dirty sauce and followings of me about. And now for the surprise, Captain Boils. Ask me my name. Oh yes, I has a better name than 'Old Katie'."

"Yes, woman, I demand that," cried the astounded Captain. "If you were ever married I demand your married name so that I can charge you not only with the offense of smuggling, which can hang you, but with another grievous offence of striking a servant of the King when in execution of his duty."

"Well, Captain Boils or Blains or Blain, I'll tell you," replied the unruffled Katie. "My real name and the name I glories in is not Missus So and So, but the name you longs to get. *I am the Scarecrow.*"

"Nonsense," ejaculated the Captain.

"It ain't nonsense," replied 'Old Katie.' "And that you and you sweepings from the dirty dockyards will find to your cost. You will try me as the Scarecrow, but my followers will rescue me, by popping your corpses one by one upon the Dymchurch scaffold."

"And what do you suppose is the good of a lie like that?" he demanded.

"You're disappointed that I ain't a man, eh?" jeered the old woman. "But it was I that outrode the Prince of Wales when he hunted with the Romney foxhounds, and it was I who scored off you and a hundred better men than you who served the dirty Government. Being an old woman was my salvation. No one suspected me. But you must own that I'm powerful by the way I tapped out that fat old Bos'n of yours just now. I see the old bladder is recovering. So you'd best attend to him and then send a messenger to the admiralty that you have succeeded where so many have failed."

"I don't mind who the Scarecrow is so long as I hang him," cried the Captain. "I'll put you under guard and do as you wish. I'll call for Doctor Syn. You may confess to him, and on that evidence my work here is done. But what is your legal name?"

"Haven't one," replied Katie. "Only what you calls an illegal one. My name is THE SCARECROW."

And that was all that Captain Blain could get out of 'Old Katie.'

An hour later she was brought under escort to the Vicarage, and the Vicar of Dymchurch received her full confession that she was indeed the Scarecrow. She was then placed under Naval guard and locked in the cells of the Court House, while Sir Antony Cobtree, as First Magistrate of Romney Marsh, ordered her to be held till he could summon the Lords of the Level for her trial.

Doctor Syn seemed very upset that the Scarecrow should turn out to be one that he had

always had some regard for, and had viewed only as a dear, quaint, queer old character. He was more upset that he had been ordered to attend the Archbishop of Canterbury at Lambeth, who wished him to bring his wisdom of Ecclesiastical Law to the meetings of the House of Convocation. So after a long interview with Katie he departed by coach, but promised to be back to support her at her trial at the Court House, and to do what he could to save her neck.

"I cannot believe she is the Scarecrow," he declared to Captain Blain before taking his departure.

"She says she is, and as she is a remarkable old woman I take her word for it in thankfulness," he answered. "I want to catch the Scarecrow, and I have every reason to think I have. For my own credit I shall not be sorry to see her condemned."

Perhaps Doctor Syn's hurried exodus to London was not understood by all at Dymchurch. Perhaps the silence of the Scarecrow was misunderstood by his followers. 'Old Katie's' trial was due, and the Vicar, usually the most sympathetic of parsons, was not at hand to comfort the old soul in her trial. Also it seemed that since the Scarecrow, whom so many knew to be a virile man beneath his mask, had found another to suffer in his stead, he had taken no steps to effect her rescue.

And thus it was that for the first time in their history the Night-riders agreed to act without orders from their chief. In the early hours of the morning before the first day of trial, the Beadle was seized by a party of the Scarecrow's men, and he was forced to open the cell and release the old woman. They carried her away in triumph to the Oast House at Doubledyke, only to discover too late that Captain Blain had feared such a rescue and had fooled them, for the woman was discovered to be none other than the Bos'n tricked out in Katie's clothes. The unfortunate sea-dog was dumped into a filled dyke from whence he fortunately escaped by a miracle in time to be in Court as witness against Katie, whom the Captain has imprisoned at the Vicarage in Doctor Syn's absence. In the meantime the news of Captain Blain's success had spread to London, and broadsheets were being sold in the streets to tell of the Scarecrow being a woman of seventy.

Doctor Syn read them and laughed to himself, and then he busied himself, thinking with admiration of the Scarecrow's rival, 'Old Katie', the only retail smuggler on the Marshes. He reappeared in his parish upon the morning of her trial, and sat at the back listening to her condemnation. Despite her age and sex, she had done too many heinous crimes against the Realm to be pardoned, and much against his will and conscience Sir Antony had to bring in the verdict of hanging.

It was then the old Vicar's cue to stand up when asked by the clerk if there was anything anyone wished to say further.

"My Lords of the Level," he said quietly, "since this brave old lady has confessed her faults and told us something of her daring, there would no more to be said by me, or anyone who wishes the poop distracted old creature well. But I have had the honor to be received by the Prince of Wales, and have pointed out to His Royal Highness a promise he made on behalf of the scarecrow when he received the fox's brush after the Royal hunt Dinner at Lympne Castle. I reminded His Highness that he had praised the Scarecrow for his spirit of sport in giving praise where it should be, adding that he had stated publicly that if ever the Scarecrow were taken he would use his influence to set him free. His Highness is so astounded that the Scarecrow is neither man nor ghost but woman, that he has given me the signature of his Royal father the King, in pardon to 'Old Katie' known as the Scarecrow, so long as she in my opinion keeps the peace of the realm in future. I am sure my old friend Katie will give me that promise, and on this Royal authority I demand the release of one of my own misguided but brave flock.

I hope 'Old Katie's' promise to keep the peace will stamp out the evils of smuggling. That is if they really exist amongst my own parishioners."

There was no answer to the Royal command, and the authorities feared the joy and triumph of the whole parish.

And while Captain Blain swore revenge, though he hardly knew how to get it, Doctor Syn whispered to Mipps as they strolled with the released Katie to the Vicarage, "The 'run' goes forward next week as arranged, for 'Old Katie' here will be comfortably lodged in our place in France, and the Scarecrow will be free to show the world that she was lying out of loyalty, and that he, not she, still rides supreme on Romney Marsh."

Mipps grinned and nudged the old woman. "Told you he'd get you out of it, didn't I? And will you be comfortable in our place in France? My dear old girl, you'll love it there, and will they love you? "Old Katie', that they will."

11

THE CURSE OF ALDINGTON KNOLL

Above the wide extent of Romney Marsh, that pleasant territory reclaimed from the sea by wall and dykes, and but a few miles inland, stand two grim sentinels upon the old coastline cliffs. One is Lympne Castle, growing from the hill into a manmade high-perched cluster of fortifications, and the other Aldington Knoll, a naked hump of nature from whose grassy summit can be obtained a far-flung view of Marsh and Channel waters. An advantageous spy-glass look-out if ever there was one.

No wonder that there existed round it a local legendary curse proclaiming that should the Knoll at any time be leveled, it would bring a grave disaster upon shipping.

The reverence and awe attaching to this curse was well supported not only by navigators who used its sky-backed prominence when taking bearings, but by generation of smugglers who had ever availed themselves of the mound for signaling with flashers and beacon when giving orders to their incoming luggers.

The hill being privately owned for grazing purposes was often threatened by would-be levelers, and the Scarecrow, whose men used it to such good advantage, saw to it that any attempt at its removal by its owners should be met with the stoutest opposition.

Now in the days when Doctor Syn ruled the spiritual good of the Marsh, and the Scarecrow dominated the evil upon it, a certain Farmer Finn, inheriting the land from his father, became one of the most powerful holders in the district.

Full of energy and with a passion for farming he disregarded the local superstition by announcing his intention of leveling the Knoll in order to improve his cultivation.

A storm of protest arose when his word went out for labour. The local men of Aldington would not touch it.

Even those who worked on his land refused the task. Posting notices, distributing leaflets, sending out criers; all these methods brought no response. Not an able-bodied man from Lydd to Dymchurch would volunteer.

Doctor Syn who liked to keep in touch with all events connected with the Marsh, rode over to Aldington to visit Farmer Finn. He found him in an angry mood. Why, he demanded, should he be boycotted by local labour? He would show them that they could not dictate to him in a matter concerning his property. He was aware that the work was hard, but had he not raised the rate of pay to nearly double the amount which anyone else would offer? The right of way over the top would save pedestrians a stiff climb if the Knoll was level ground. Knowing that the height was used by the smugglers, he railed against the authorities for not having laid the Scarecrow by the heels. It was obvious that this same Scarecrow must have issued a manifesto that the work should not go forward.

"I think it goes deeper than that," suggested Doctor Syn. "You may scoff if you like, but people who live on or about the sea are superstitious as a class, and you know the ancient curse that some say was laid upon the Knoll by the Holy Maid of Kent."

"Aye, I know she was a local celebrity in the days of Henry the Eighth," sneered the farmer, "but she went to death at Tyburn, a confessed fraud. Besides, I doubt very much whether it was she who uttered this ridiculous curse.

More likely some scoundrelly smuggler-chief, like this Scarecrow, who finds it so useful. If bad luck comes of its removal, no doubt the ill-fortune will be mine to bear."

"The labourers you have approached evidently fear the curse will fall on them," said Doctor Syn.

"Well, I can tell you this, Reverend Sir," replied Finn. "The Knoll goes down with their help or without it. I can import men from another district, who will be glad enough to earn good money."

"But there is another point about this vexed question, which you may not have considered," went on Doctor Syn.

"Indeed I made this journey on purpose to discuss it with you. Captain Blain, who as you

know is in charge of the ferreting out of smugglers, and is staying at my Vicarage, informs me that the Knoll is given some importance upon all Admiralty charts of the Channel coast. Now I know something of the Law, and realizing the power of the Naval fellows in London, I should advise you to examine your ground very thoroughly before removing it. I mean it would be a vast expense and trouble if they made you put it back again, if you get me?"

"You can take it form me," retorted Finn, "that once the Knoll is down the expense will be theirs, since they will have to alter the existing charts. I know something of the Law too, and the most jealousy guarded rule of England is that an Englishman may do what he likes with his own. The Knoll is mine and I shall do what I like with it. Have you any objection, Reverend Sir?'

"I should be sorry to see it go, I confess," replied the Vicar of Dymchurch. "It is a pleasant spot to look at in fine weather, and in foul, why, it is pleasant to think of it as a safety guide to homing sailormen."

"Well, I am afraid both you and the Scarecrow will be disappointed by my action," snapped Finn.

"You may associate me with the scoundrel, if you please," said Doctor Syn. "But you must agree that our motives in this case of sane thinking are entirely different. His are selfish, while mine are altruistic."

"I have no wish to quarrel with you, Doctor Syn," replied Finn, more kindly. "You are an honest man, I know, and try to see things from other people's point of view. Therefore you are the only one I shall regret hurting when I pull down the Knoll. And, by the way, I wonder my ancestors have not been at it before me, for the antiquaries say that the mound on top is man-made: either Druid or Roman, and inside it there may be all manner of buried treasure."

"At least such discovery would go a little way to compensate us for its loss," said the Vicar. "But I do urge you, once more, to make sure how you stand with the Admiralty."

"Damn the Admiralty," exploded Finn. "Anyway, I am going to pull it down, and if needs be apologize for my act afterwards. I can at least give them the excuse that the Knoll is mine and not theirs."

Returning to Dymchurch the Vicar let Captain Blain know of Farmer Finn's attitude towards the Naval Rights, and when his guest had retired to bed saying that he would send a report the next day to Admiral Troubridge at the Admiralty concerning Finn's attitude, Doctor Syn admitted Mipps to the study, where, over a bottle of the best brandy, the two rascals put their heads together in order to find the best way in thwarting Finn's design.

Determined to carry out his project without further delay, Finn sent up into the weald of Kent for laborers. Here he was equally unsuccessful, for his agents found that the Scarecrow had been word-passing before him, instructing his agent in every village to let it be known that it would be highly dangerous for any man to accept Finn's offer of work.

Only one man disregarded the warning, and Finn welcomed him with open arms. A man of gigantic strength, Knarler had been a slaughterman at Cranbrook, but had been discharged from his post for cruelty. He was the type that Finn needed. A man not to be bullied by the local opinion against him, for he assured Finn in the strongest terms that he feared neither God nor man, and had no terror for old curses. He even expressed the hope that the scarecrow might oppose him in person so that he could knock him out and carry him before a Justice of the Peace.

"For I can do with that there reward upon his head," he laughed.

On inspecting the Knoll he assured the farmer that although he could do it singlehanded, if need be, it would take some time. Indeed he planned to make the job as long as possible, since it was double money an hour.

Needing money, Finn allowed him a little in advance, so that he could refresh himself at the 'Walnut Tree.'

The landlord of the inn, however, happened to be the Aldington agent for the Scarecrow, and told Knarler plainly that strangers were not very welcome by his patrons.

Knarler pointed out that so long as he kept sober and paid his way no landlord could refuse him service.

Shunned by the villagers, s though he had the plague, Knarler thought of a good way to retaliate. He went to his employer and asked for authority to make Finn's tenants help in the work.

"I tell you they are stubborn, and will neither be persuaded nor compelled," replied Finn.

"Besides, they are afraid of the Scarecrow. That's obvious. They will refuse."

"Not is you give them notice to give up their cottages," laughed Knarler. "If I begin throwing their furniture, women and children into the village street. You own the cottages and there would be no shelter for them. That would make their men work, and under me, as your foreman, they'll work hard."

To do him justice, Farmer Finn was horrified at the man's brutality. Angry and obstinate over the whole business, he would not tolerate such cruelty to gain his ends.

Knarler tried to persuade him to his way of thinking, because he had stupidly boasted of what was going to happen to the tenants at the inn, and when the farmer's refusal to this tyranny became known, they would laugh at him for his failure, and hate him for the instigation of such a plot.

When Knarler first mounted the Knoll, armed with pick, spade and shovel, he was conscious that every eye in the village was watching him, so to cheat them of a view of his proceedings, he climbed over the summit and started to work a few feet below upon the sea side. This was also more convenient as Finn's sheep were grazing on the land side. One of the Scarecrow's men was glad of this, since it saved him from a climb and having to bear a message to Knarler, for his orders had been explicit.

"It is necessary for the Scarecrow's plan that the cutting on the Knoll shall start on the sea side. Should this Knarler begin work upon the land side, you will take him orders from Farmer Finn to start on the sea side. As one of Finn's tenants and farm laborers, he will not suspect this order as coming from any other than your master."

For what reason the Scarecrow had given this order the fellow could not guess, but the loathing that everyone felt for Knarler since his plan of unhousing women and children, made him glad that he could avoid the contact of the message. Greatly relieved, he left his station at the foot of the Knoll, and went back to the 'Walnut Tree.'

He found the friendly old bar parlor filled with men discussing Knarler with animosity. They had begun to drink early because they knew he was away working and that the 'Walnut' would be sweet again without him.

"Why trouble yourselves with him?" advised the man who was to have been the Scarecrow's messenger. "He can only bring harm to himself by doing work for Finn's money that is accursed. And we mustn't blame Finn too much. He's obstinate over this, but he'd sooner be paying us his money that him from Cranbrook. At least Finn did not fall in with his devilry about turning us out under the sky. Finn has too much of his family in him to be a bad landlord to us."

"And that's true enough," echoed the landlord of the 'Walnut Tree.'

"And let us not trouble our peace about this Knarler," went on the other. "He'll work out his own damnation, you'll see."

Meanwhile Knarler worked on alone, and as he thought unwatched. He was determined to surprise his employer as to his capacity. At least on the first day of the job. He determined not to return to Cranbrook till he had money enough to make all envious, and with which to settle old scores. He would make himself a power with this Finn, and cause the lazy village of Aldington to dance vigorously to his tune. Every swinging stroke of his pick into the chalk he imagined to be the cleaving of one of their skulls.

Cleaning a filled-in pit of old rubbish, he picked out a large piece of broken pottery. It was the broken portion of an earthenware basin. He flung it vigorously over his head without looking round though he knew it would fall into the deep ravine behind him, and hoped that it might land on somebody's head and knock them senseless. He worked on with pick, spade and shovel. He would show these lazy ones what work he could do. He had climbed the Knoll with plenty of strong drink and hunks of bread and cheese. He vowed he would go on till dark.

He kept laughing to himself when he thought of the villagers' dread of the curse. That sort of nonsense would not worry him. But some little time after he had thrown away the pottery, he had a curiously uneasy feeling that he was being watched from behind. He told himself that he was not going to be upset by anyone. Neither was he the sort of man to get jumpy. So he filled another shovelful and turned to throw it into space. But he did not throw it, because what he saw so astonished him that he let the load slip from the tool. Close behind him stood a tall black-coated figure of a man, whose eyes seemed to be piercing his soul, or rather seeking for the soul which he had lost.

In his hands this arresting figure held the piece of broken basin. Knarler told himself that he had evidently hit this individual with the pottery, and that he had come up as an injured party to protest.

"What do you want?" growled Knarler.

"This piece of *terra-cotta,*" replied the other in a pleasant voice. "I am quite sure that Farmer Finn will let me have it, as I think such a relic will not interest him very much. Of course I want to reward you for having unearthed such a unique piece. See, my man, here is half a spade guinea. You shall have another if you can find the rest of this."

Knarler felt nothing but scorn for him now, though at first he had all but been frightened at his sudden appearance.

"You keep it if you've a fancy for broken crockery," he said. "But make good your promise. Where's the half guinea?"

The black-coated one casually tossed a gold coin across to him. It fell on the grass at Knarler's feet. The astounded ex-slaughterman picked it up, bit it, and found that it was good currency. Then this mad-brained generosity made him suspicious.

"Who are you, and where did you come from?" he demanded.

"I climbed the Knoll to see what kind of god was raining such treasures from above," he replied. "I climbed faster than my servant who is following me." He turned and addressed someone over the brink. "Let me lend you a hand, my good Mipps."

"I can manage nicely, sir," grunted another black-coated man who scrambled up into Knarler's sight. This second arrival was a wiry old fellow, who surveyed Knarler critically with sharp eyes.

"I am Doctor Syn, Vicar of Dymchurch, Mister Knarler, and this is my Sexton, Mipps. Look, my good Mipps, what I have achieved. A most illuminating example of the Roman period."

The little man looked at it with disgust. "It ain't much good, sir, surely? It looks to me broke."

"You keep your trap shut," warned Knarler. "If the gentleman likes it, what's that to you? I'll sell him some more at the same price. I can do with the other half of this guinea-piece."

"Half a spade?" echoed Mipps. "And I has to dig graves for a eightpence. Something wrong somewhere."

"Nothing is wrong," replied Syn. "In fact, everything is right if Mister Knarler of Cranbrook will only do me a favour."

"Mister Knarler of Cranbrook," repeated the digger. "You seem to have heard about me somehow."

"Do you know him, sir?" asked Mipps.

"I do, I do," went on the Vicar with enthusiasm. "He is the man who can remove mountains, and make rough places plain. Mister Knarler, you can help me, and then yourself to some more of my gold."

"Let's have it, and tell me what," said Knarler.

"This find from Roman days," whispered the Vicar, "is but the key to further treasures of equal value. If you will only dig as I ask you, how rich you can grow."

"I has to dig the lot away, so may as well clear the bit you want done first."

"I knew I should like you, Mister Knarler," laughed the Vicar. "They tell me you have no fear of this Scarecrow that has banned the moving of this hill. Well, I applaud your courage. I attack the Scarecrow, too, don't I Mipps?

Yes, Mister Knarler, I preach against him from my pulpit."

"And me always telling you not to, too," put in Mipps.

"Now see here," continued the Vicar. "This piece of pottery is part of a military wash pot. Finding it in the hollow there, tells me that in the face of the cliff behind it here we shall uncover the remains of a Roman captain. Clear all this grass, Knarler, and then cut the chalk into a level face. I have no doubt but that we shall find a tomb. All sorts of things buried with him. Sword, buckler, his personal properties, like wine flagon, milk-jug."

"And the rest of the wash-pot?" suggested Mipps.

"I think not, Mipps," corrected the Parson. "That should be where this piece came from, at his feet. He will be buried standing to attention. How splendid. If Mister Knarler works hard we shall see a dead man upon the face of the chalk. I will pace out where you must dig. From here to here. Show me a nice white face of cliff, and then I'll come along and help you. We'll have a corpse to show for our pains. Work well, Knarler. I fear I must leave you now for my duty. Clear the chalk, my good man."

"I will, and you of guineas, too, I hopes, sir. If his milk-jug's there, you'll have it and the rest of the wash-pot, too."

They left him hard at work.

Out of sight and at the bottom of the Knoll, Doctor Syn mounted his fat white pony that had been peacefully grazing. Mipps followed suit upon the churchyard donkey. As they rode off at a walk Mipps saw the piece of pottery that had cost his master half a guinea.

"Wait, sir," cried Mipps. "You've gone and dropt your wash-pot. I'll pick it up."

"Not worth the carrying," replied Syn. "Nothing Roman about it. Modern. Dumped there not more than a year or so."

"Then why pay gold for it?" whined Mipps.

"Because, as you know, the Scarecrow pays well for any work he wants done. And he happens to want a white facing of chalk upon the sea side of the Knoll. When that is done the work must be stopped, as we agreed it must be stopped. It is only that I have changed my plans slightly. Ride close beside me and you shall hear."

Meanwhile Knarler worked on feverishly, determined to find the Roman captain and his belongings that very day. The crazy Parson would pay him well. If not he would smash up such treasure as he found under his eyes unless the pay was double. The Parson would fall for such a threat. Although he did not waste time in eating, he constantly fortified his strength with copious gulps of spirit. By the time the sun set in Fairlight Bay he was drunk.

But he worked on, eyeing with pleasure the growing whiteness of the uncovered chalk. At twilight the Parson visited him, and after congratulations, encouraged him to go on.

"Plenty of time," growled the exhausted drunkard.

"But there is not," contradicted the Parson. "Farmer Finn had had a message from the Admiralty warning him to allay proceedings till Whitehall has looked into things. I had this from Finn himself. He is still obstinate, but their appeal to his loyalty has weakened him, It is not-pleasant to do a disservice to your country, and this landmark is of value when we are at war with the French yonder."

"Don't fret, sir," chuckled the digger. "I'll get that Roman before downing tools."

When Doctor Syn had gone, he drank more and worked harder. As the darkness deepened and the red in the west faded into black, he vowed that he'd work on in the gloom till the moon rose over the sea to give him light. As the Marsh turned black beneath him he quite welcomed the scattered little lights that began to twinkle up at him from distant farms and cottages. Ship's lanterns, too, moved slowly out on the distant fairway of the Channel.

He felt angry with himself for being capable of feeling lonely. He longed to see even the scowling faces eyeing him under the lights of the 'Walnut Tree' snug parlour. So he drank more till he glowed inwardly into a savage rage. Then his inflamed brain played tricks with him. It was not the sheep, for they were huddled together at the foot of the Knoll. Once he imagined that he saw horsemen below him on the level whose faces shone pale as they galloped. Cursing himself for a fool, he faced the whiteness of the chalk: drank deeper and worked on, his legs frequently giving under him as he swung his pick with greater effort. The moon would soon be up, he told himself.

Meanwhile, at the Vicarage of Dymchurch, Doctor Syn expressed mild surprise when his guest, Captain Blain, refused to linger over the port. His Bos'n was awaiting him, and he must go at once, he explained.

"Is it that you have heard rumours of a 'run', Captain?" asked the Parson anxiously.

"No, Doctor Syn," replied the Captain. "But I am taking no chance of losing a sight of the Scarecrow, and since he is so hot against this removal of the Knoll he may take steps in the matter. I think he may be attracted to the spot.

The moon will rise. I shall hide and through my spy-glass get a view of him perhaps."

The moment he had gone, Syn summoned Mipps from the kitchen.

"Just as I guessed," he whispered. "The Captain has gone with the Bos'n, and I can play my prank on him and punish this interfering Knarler at the same time. Is all ready?"

Mipps held out his left hand, began counting off items, "Strong rope attached to a sea-saving belt. Four lengths of thin cord. Two for arms. Two for legs. And we both knows the naval semaphore code. We've only to go.

Jimmie Bone is waiting for us with the horses and things, and the other lads at Aldington."

When the moon rose Captain Blain saw a strange sight upon the Knoll. Against the whiteness of the new-cut chalk stood out the black figure of the Scarecrow.

"Look," he whispered to the Bos'n. "He's doing it again. It says"—slowly he spelt out the sentence—"THE SCARECROW FORBIDS FURTHER DESTRUCTION TO THIS KNOLL. And look at him now. If he ain't adoing it with his legs. Look, he's dancing it out, sir. Same message. He'll be doing a hornpipe next."

"Come on, Bos'n," whispered the Captain. "We'll be taking a closer view."

Had the Captain been on the top of the Knoll, he might have heard whispered orders of: "Right, Right. Now again. Same order." But when he stood peering over a ledge and looking up at the Scarecrow he heard nothing.

The Scarecrow, hideously masked, was standing against the white cliff and seemingly looking out to sea. The Captain then acted on the instinct that he might never have such another chance again. He drew his pistol and fired.

There was a gurgling choke, and then four cords slid down across the face of the chalk and the ends trailed on the grass.

Come on, Bos'n. He's not standing on a ledge. He's hanging by a rope. Yes, from above. They'd let him down, and look, there's cords to his wrists and ankles. Up aloft we go."

When they reached the top they saw that the rope was fastened round the beacon post. There was no sign of anyone about, though the sound of galloping horses came up from the road beneath.

"We must have a look, Bos'n," said the Captain. "Lower him down, eh?"

They lowered the heavy weight to the ledge below, and then examined the features under the mask.

"I killed him. He's dead all right. Still warm. Is it the Scarecrow?"

The Bos'n shook his head at the Captain's query.

"No, sir. I've seen this cove. You ain't. It's Finn's man what was to level the Knoll."

Doctor Syn had just time to get into bed and blow out his candle before he heard the Captain return with the Bos'n. He heard him unlock the door below and tell Bos'n to wait. He then crept up the stairs and knocked on the Vicar's door.

As he told Doctor Syn the next day, it was the first time he had ever sought out a priest for confession. When he had told the whole story, he put his case before the Vicar in this way. "No one but the Bos'n knows of this. Even the Scarecrow's men who were obviously using this unfortunate scoundrel for their jest, and pulling his limbs this way and that in signals, will be wondering who fired the shot. Now if I confess, it will mean me being called for an Admiralty enquiry. I may be dismissed the service for rashness, though I think not, but I am sure to be taken from here, and, Doctor Syn, I want nothing to prevent me from catching this Scarecrow eventually. Can I in honour keep silent? I ask you as a wise man."

"My good Captain," replied Syn, "if we three keep silent the blame will fall on someone unknown who wished to prevent Farmer Finn from destroying our Knoll. The Scarecrow will no doubt be blamed. Well his crime-laden shoulders seem broad enough to bear another murder. Say nothing about it. Captain blain, if you leave us, we shall never catch the Scarecrow. Let us say no more, but make a compact that come what may we will work together to rid my beloved Marsh from this evil that rides by night."

"Thank you, Doctor," replied the Captain fervently. "You have given me a great relief. In return I will give you my full confidence. Perhaps I have kept you too much in the dark up to now, in spite of all your kindness. But this helpful act of yours makes me not only an obligated friend, but a sworn ally."

"Against the Scarecrow," completed the Vicar, nodding his tasseled nightcap. "Oh, Captain, do you think we shall ever unmask him? Do, *do* let us try."

Syn and Mipps chuckled next day when Finn rode over and said he repented he had ever gone against the Vicar's advice.

They chuckled more when they realized how well the plan had succeeded, for where Knarler had digged the chalk became in sunlight of moonlight a pilot light across the fairway of the Channel.

12

MYSTERIOUS COOPERAGE

After the death of Knarler, Doctor Syn expected his guest to keep his promise in giving him full confidence.

Captain Blain had purchased the Vicar's silence in regard to the matter of manslaughter, with an obligation to become his sworn ally against the Scarecrow, and yet as the days went by he kept his own consul and was more reserved with the Vicar than he had been before.

He seemed purposely to avoid speaking of the Scarecrow, and the closer he became, the more openly did the Vicar try to discuss. Indeed, Doctor Syn railed more than ever against the smuggling.

On the Sunday following Knarler's death, he preached twice against the ways of wicked men, who for the sake of gain, did not scruple to use the dreadful violence of sudden death. There had, he said, been too many tragedies upon their beloved Marsh, because certain men upon her had feared to disobey the orders of the arch fiend in their midst, and he urged all good Marshmen to support Captain Blain and his gallant followers, in their endeavour to stamp out the wickedness. At the conclusion of both sermons, he called his congregation to their knees, while he extemporized a prayer that the Captain's efforts would be blessed with success.

No one was louder with 'Amen' than Mr. Mipps, who was able to appreciate the humour of the situation, though his face showed nothing but righteous zeal for the destruction of the Scarecrow.

Since the Captain never referred to what he was himself planning, Doctor Syn, was certain that his guest was planning something very important.

Perhaps the Captain underestimated the Vicar's quick instinct for reading men's minds. He did not know that the Vicar was studying him all the time.

The Captain, pretending to be beaten by the Scarecrow, which he would not acknowledge in his mind, was under the impression that Doctor Syn was tricked into the belief that he could think of no plan of campaign, and was therefore content to mark time with carrying on the ordinary routine of a ship's company ashore. And yet as the days passed and they faced each other over the port, an occasion when conversation was demanded between host and guest, the Vicar could have staked his wig that Captain Blain was working secretly on lines that gave him inward satisfaction, but which he was not willing to divulge even to his supposed ally. The closer the Captain became, so did Doctor Syn become more communicative as to his own ideas on the subject.

Although many of these suggestions were sound and practical against the Scarecrow, the Vicar was well aware that the Captain, although politely pretending to consider them, merely discussed them in order to dismiss them in his own mind in favour of whatever scheme he was working upon, a scheme which he had decided not to impart to his host.

But if he was close about his own plans, he tried hard to draw Doctor Syn into conversing about his past travels in the Americas, which the Doctor at first thought was but politeness, until he began to wonder whether his guest was not trying to trip him up about his past. This amused the good Doctor, for he knew that the sea-dog would have to prove himself a lot cleverer to do that.

Doctor Syn knew how to deal with the past, but the Captain's campaign against the Scarecrow was a vital question of the immediate future, and it was very necessary that he should know beforehand which way the cat was going to jump when the Captain opened the bag.

As he confessed to Mipps: "I can of course take an opportunity of accusing the Captain that he is not keeping to his side of our bargain. If he persistently keeps me in the dark I have every excuse to do so. On the other hand, I would prefer not to show such a curiosity. I mean, I should like to discover his scheme, whatever it may be, without his knowledge."

An opportunity presented itself from an unexpected quarter. It was young George Lee, the cooper, who brought things to a head in the Vicarage, and enabled the vicar to discover and thwart the Captain's plan.

George Lee had been one of the Doctor's young parishioners, till he had left Dymchurch for Hythe in order to be apprenticed to the master cooper of the brewery.

He had been most solemnly initiated according to this ancient rights known as 'trussing the Cooper'. This consists of squaring up a cask with the help of his master, and then laying a cresset or iron bucket, wh ich when alight, warms the cask, and makes the staves pliable for shaping, which are then bound with the hoops and beaten with heavy hammers. The apprentice is then 'rung in'. This part of the ceremony is performed by hammering upon sheet iron. At the close of this pandemonium the willing, though nervous, apprentice, allows himself to become the victim to the masters of the craft, who bundle him, feet first, into the cask which he had helped to fashion. Gathered around him, as he crouches in the cask, the masters hammer upon the hoops, while the 'christening' ceremony is performed with sawdust, shavings and water.

The cask, still warm from the cresset, is then turned upon its side, and with the victim still inside it is rolled up and down the length of the shop.

The apprentice is then dragged out by his ankles and tossed into the air, when, to show that there is no personal animosity towards him, his particular master is tossed up by the same tormentors. His health is then drunk by all, and the apprentice has become a fully-fledged cooper.

Now George Lee had recently passed though this ordeal, and was justly proud in being a real member of his trade.

Meeting him outside the Brewery Cooperage in Hythe, Doctor Syn asked him whether he found his working hours too long, to which the lad had replied that he only wished he could be allowed to work longer, adding that he could forgo all recreation for the sake of his job. Therefore Doctor Syn was the more surprised to find him entering the Vicarage gate during the morning following his meeting with him in Hythe.

"Have you then an enforced holiday, my lad?" he asked. "From what you told me yesterday, I did not expect to see you so far from the cooper's shop upon a working day. You want to see me, eh?" And without waiting for an answer he added, with a smile: "I can guess at your purpose, I think. You are come to ask me to put up the banns for you and Polly Henley, eh? You find that you are prepared to face matrimony now that you are a cooper indeed."

The lad blushed and shook his head. "No, sir. Though in that respect I am only waiting Polly's permission to do so. But I did not come for that reason, though I wish I had. I am here, sir, under orders to see the naval gentleman, called Captain Blain, who I think is staying with you, sir."

"So you come to see my guest and not me, eh?" replied the Vicar, with another smile. "Well, I fancy you will find him inspecting his men in the old barn. This is his usual hour for that ceremony."

The lad thanked the Vicar, and was for passing on towards the large Tythe Barn, when the Vicar, wondering what business could be afoot between these two, stopped him with, "Has the Captain been commissioning you to make him a barrel, then?"

"No, sir," replied the cooper. For a moment he paused, as though uncertain what to say next. Then he added: "It is a business meeting, sir, which I am obliged to keep to myself, according to the Captain's express orders. Though to keep any secret from you, sir, seems all wrong, I admit."

"Nonsense," laughed the Vicar. "A promise is a promise, and a good man knows when to keep his mouth shut.

No doubt the good Captain has his reasons for secrecy, and you do quite right to respect them."

Just then the Captain came striding out from the darkness of the barn's great doors into the sunlight, and seeing the Vicar talking to the lad, whom he had been expecting, he came towards them with: "Ah, so you have intercepted my messenger from the cooperage, eh? A purely technical matter, Vicar. A contract for a sprung water-cask that they are to put right, that's all."

"And you have to worry about little things like that, Captain?" asked the Doctor innocently. "I thought such matters were arranged for you from the Supplies Office."

"And sink me, Parson, so they should be," responded the Captain with some warmth. "I fear they are not, however. At least not with any satisfaction. For any immediate service I find it better to put out a job direct, and send in the account to the Admiralty after."

Doctor Syn made a mental note of this, and later came to the conclusion that in reality Captain Blain would do no such thing. He knew enough of ships and shipping to be quite sure that such articles as casks, when faulty, would be supplied fresh from the dockyard coopers, and not from such a place as the brewery in Hythe.

"Do you mind if I take this lad into the house, so that I can refer to my order book?" asked the Captain.

"He does not wish me to overhear their conversation," thought the Vicar. "This 'order book' is but a blind drawn in front of my eyes." Which only made him the more determined to overhear what might pass between them.

Aloud he answered: "Certainly, Captain, with all my heart. You may have the use of my study undisturbed, if you will allow me but a minute to put on my gown to be in readiness for the reading of Morning Prayer. It is nearing my time, for the Sexton has already gone to the church and will be sounding the ten o'clock bell in a minute or so. And do you know, Captain, if I am not dead upon time, the old rascal will slip away quickly, glad of any excuse to escape going through the many responses and Amens."

Doctor Syn had already made up his mind. He led his companions to the Vicarage, entering by the front door and not by the study garden door, at the back. In the hall he went to a side-cupboard and produced the glasses, which he placed on the table, saying:

"I have not yet drunk our mutual friend, George Lee's, health, since he became a master of his craft. I am sure, Captain, you will join me in such a ceremony. I will open a bottle of sherry, for such an occasion demands the drawing of a fresh cork, and I can leave you to finish the contents, for if I stay too long my Sexton will abandon me.

Mipps is an excellent fellow, but he had his weaknesses. As he has not yet rung the bell I am safe for a minute or so before cutting off his retreat. You see, Captain, Mipps and I have frequent words about the necessity for carrying through the form of Morning and Evening Prayer, when there may be no one there but ourselves. You will understand that I am not in any way accusing my good flock of desertion, but they are busy fold upon week-days, and more often than not, we have not three gathered together, but only two, myself and Sexton. Not being in Holy Orders, Mipps is not obligated to say privately or publicly his Morning and Evening Form of Prayer, but I am. And although many clergy keep their churches closed during the week, I consider such to be a breach of discipline. Just a moment, Captain," he laughed.

Now Mrs. Fowey was in the habit of giving Mr. Mipps just one noggin of rum before service, 'just to give him strength to pull the heavy bell', she would say. So Doctor Syn knew that he could count upon finding the Sexton performing his part of this rite in the still-room. Mipps would no more have missed that ceremony than he would have missed accompanying the Vicar through the toils and trial of a Daily Service.

So now to the still-room Doctor Syn hurried, and found Mipps sitting by the rum barrel, with a pannikin in his hand, and being watched over by the housekeeper who wished to see that he did not help himself to a further allowance, which he would assuredly have done if left to his own devices.

"Ah, Mipps," exclaimed the vicar pleasantly. "I think it is nearing the time to ring the bell. I must go and robe.

I am glad to see that Mrs. Fowey is fortifying you to pull the bell rope. But before I go to the study there is just something I wish to point out to you in the kitchen garden. Oh, Mrs. Fowey, pray take your keys to the wine cellar and fetch me a bottle of sherry for the Captain and his guest. I find I could do with a glassful myself. I fear I an not so partial to rum as our good Sexton is."

As Mrs. Fowey strode away, Mipps favoured his master with a sly wink behind his back.

No sooner had the housekeeper taken herself from earshot than the Vicar whispered quickly: "Slip into the study by the garden door, Mipps. Conceal yourself in the usual spot behind the cloaks hanging in the alcove. I want you to listen to whatever the Captain is about to say to young George Lee, the cooper, who has come up to see him for some reason. That reason we have got to discover. It is very vital. Remember, he is making those special casks to the Scarecrow's orders, and before those casks are used for the purpose for which they have been planned, we must know exactly how much the Captain knows, and whether it has anything to do with the peculiarity of those casks.

Now, Mipps, remember, if by ill-chance he should discover you eavesdropping behind the cloaks, you must be asleep and very drunk. Then I shall reprimand you. The old dodge which has worked well before this."

Mipps nodded. "He may or mayn't look into the alcove, sir. In any case I shall be ready for him.

"I don't think he will," said Syn. "He will think you are at the church, and when he hears the bell, which I shall ring directly I get there, he will think you are safely out of the way. Make haste now."

Mipps went out to the garden, while the Vicar followed his housekeeper into the wine cellar with a "Make haste, my good woman."

Armed with the bottle of sherry he returned to the hall.

"Here you are, Captain," he said, putting the bottle on the table and laying a corkscrew beside it.

"Now while I put on my gown for church perhaps you, George, will draw that cork, and perhaps you, Captain will fill the glasses. At the risk of being abandoned by Mipps I will have a glass before I set off."

Having set them both a task which would keep them for the moment in the hall, the Vicar went towards the study door, taking off his long black jacket as he went. There was a hook upon the back of the door, so that he had every excuse to close the door in reaching for the peg.

Meanwhile George pulled the cork, and then the Captain signed to him to fill the glasses too.

In the study Doctor Syn saw that the garden door was fastened, and as he unhooked his Geneva gown, he was amused to see Mipps peeping out at him from the voluminous folds of cloaks and cassocks that hung in the alcove.

Mipps not only grinned, but winked, and then pulled a face of a drunkard feeling sleepy. Syn nodded approval and the folds fell back and covered Mipps.

This same hiding-place having served the rascals well in the past, caused the Vicar no anxiety, so that he did not bother to look down to see whether or no Mipps was fully concealed, for he knew that the riding cloaks were very ling and full, reaching the floor. Indeed he knew that his henchman was so well hidden that he purposely left the curtains drawn back, in order to appear the less suspicious.

Having pulled on his gown, he picked up a Bible from his table. Not that he would need this for reading from, since he would use the large one upon the pulpit cushion, but he thought it would lend a further tone of piety which would be good for the Captain to see. He realized that it would be policy to play the good man automatically on every occasion, since the Captain was not above suspecting even him.

Leaving the study door wide open he rejoined the others in the hall.

"Ah, I see that the glasses are charged. Splendid," he cried. "You are thirstily awaiting me to propose friend George's health, with a hope that he may have a long life in a settled trade." He picked up his glass. "I do wish you and honoured career, George, from my heart. Take after your grandfather and father in the business and you'll come to no harm. Also think sometimes of the teachings I was able to give you here, when you were a lad. Here's to you, George. You were a good boy, and I know you are now going to be a good man. Remember, too, the slogan of the Marsh: 'Serve God. Honour the King. But first, Maintain the Wall.' And the last sentence means this, my lad.

You must not only protect your home by maintaining the sea-wall with your strength and courage, but you must cheerfully pay such scotts as are imposed upon you by the Lords of the Level. And lastly, bear in mind that I christened you at the Dymchurch font with His Majesty's own name, and so you must obey his Government, as well as that of the Marsh."

"And have naught to do with the wicked smugglers, eh, Vicar," laughingly added the Captain, as he raised his glass to the cooper.

The Doctor shook his head. "I do not think that our young friend here will do aught to hinder the Revenue officers in their duty, eh, George? But I must be off, and at once. Recharge your glasses and carry them into the study where you can discuss your business undisturbed."

"Aye, it's good sherry," said the Captain. "So fill up, Master Cooper, and let us accept the Vicar's hospitality.

You will not take another glass yourself, Parson?"

"Good heavens, no," he replied, as though horrified at the idea. "I have a service to read, and who knows? There might be something of a congregation after all, and I assure you that some of our parochial ladies can be very quizzical."

As the laughing Vicar let himself out of the front door he had the satisfaction to seeing the Captain signing to George Lee to follow him into the study. Now he would soon know the Captain's business with the young cooper.

There happened to be no one about in the churchyard, and he know that the study windows had no view of it, so he ran across to the church, which he found empty, and pulled the bell rope three or four times, in order to give the Captain reminder that the Sexton was in the church. He then proceeded to the pulpit and began the service by himself, though shortly after he had started Lady Cobtree tiptoed in and supported him by reading the responses.

Meanwhile Mipps sat hunched up in the alcove. He heard the Captain come in with George Lee and close the door, and much to his relief heard also the noise of them both sitting in the Doctor's chairs.

"I am glad you took my warning seriously," began the Captain. "It shows you to be a young man of sense. You have now passed your apprenticeship, and have begun to take your place amongst your fellow-craftsmen. Well, I assure you that I have no wish to interrupt your career, though should you disobey my orders I shall not hesitate to have you pressed for naval service. You are a likely lad, and cooperage is a valuable asset on any ship. There would be no marrying with a Dymchurch lass then, for many a long year, and all the time you would be haunted with the thought that in your very prolonged absence the girl might have married another. So kindly answer my questions truthfully, and whatever I say keep strictly to yourself."

"I have every wish to be of service to the Government, sir," replied George Lee, is a voice which disgusted the listening Mipps because of its timidity. In truth the young cooper felt strangely nervous now that Doctor Syn had gone. He went on speaking slowly and humbly. "You heard our good Doctor Syn advise me so to do always, and I have tried to follow his advice. When I have succeeded in doing so only good has come of it, I assure you, sir."

The Captain grunted his approval to this sentiment, and continued: "Well, to begin with, perhaps you have been wondering why I watched you the other day at your work in the coopers' shop. It was chance that I happened to pick on you. I was determined to pick on whoever seemed most to wish to stick to his work in Hythe. A few questions about you, and I knew that you were happy and in love, and I recognized that you were the youngster who fitted in best with my plan. That has been, perhaps, an ill-chance for you. But my reason for going to the coopers' shop in the first place was not chance. I went there because I had had it brought to my notice that the Sexton of Dymchurch had visited the shop several times recently.

"Now, between ourselves, as all this conversation must be, please, I had kept a weather eye on him for some time, and he struck me as being a little man who could not keep that long, sharp nose of his out of any business. So, thought I, why should he not have poked it into this smuggling business? The moment I suspected him I set one of my men to watch him, and so checked up upon his goings and comings."

"Amongst other things I learnt that he had entered the coopers' shop several times, and I wondered whether he was carrying orders from the Scarecrow. No sooner had this idea occurred to me than I determined to pay a personal visit to the brewery, vowing that I would select an ally there to work for me: someone whom I could persuade to discover for me the purpose of the Sexton's visits. You were my selection. And now all you have to do is to tell me just what you know."

"Nothing, sir," replied George Lee timidly.

"That is very unfortunate," said the Captain slowly, adding the significant words, "for you."

"I wish to get no one into trouble, sir," faltered the cooper. "And least of all Mr. Mipps, who has always been good to me. It would be a dreadful thing to feel that one had sent an innocent man to the ordeal of a trial, and all that sort of torture, just because one may have thought things."

"Ah, and so you have 'thought things', eh? Rapped out the Captain with great emphasis upon the repetition. "I should like to know exactly what things you have thought, in order to save me from doing such a 'dreadful thing' as punishing you, an innocent lad, because I must take all possible steps to put down the enemies of the Crown. Now, come along. Be sensible, and speak up."

"Well, I think, sir," stammered the unfortunate cooper, "that it is permissible for my masters to make casks to an order without asking the purchaser for what purpose those casks are needed. That would surely be, sir, an inquisitive sort of trading?"

"You are prevaricating, my young friend," said the Captain gravely. "My business is to stamp out smuggling.

Others have failed to do so. I am going to succeed. And with that end in view, I shall not hesitate to be, and to make others, inquisitive to a degree. It is only by the inquisitiveness of every good citizen concerned that my object can be obtained. If I had my will not a barrel should be sold by firms like yours, unless that barrel had a clear port of call, as it were. I am confident that if the Scarecrow has placed an order with your firm, through the medium of Mipps, that your firm will know what Mipps wants them for.

"Now just to show you that once I have made up my mind to a thing, nobody will swerve me from attaining it, I'll tell you how I found the means to interview your head cooper. I ordered my Bos'n to spring a leak in one of our water-casks, and then told him to carry it to your shop for mending. This gave me the excuse for visiting your people. I called in to inquire if they could hurry with the job and what price my Bos'n had agreed on, saying I had to watch the leakages of money as sharply as leaky water-casks.

"I then expressed a lively interest in the mystery of cooperage, a craft that runs close along the art of ships-and-boat-building, which I have studied since I first took to the sea. Many a seafaring man sees no romance in the history of ships. To me a ship or boat is a romantic creation, and I have interested myself in each part of every craft I have sailed. And all the accessories of a vessel, too, such as ropes, casks, barrels and kegs. Sails, too.

There's little I cannot tell about canvas. The carrying of cooper upon every ship under my command made me wish to learn something of his trade, so that I could judge of his work and any difficulties that might arise. And that there were many difficulties upon a fighting ship I very soon did appreciate."

"I am not boasting that I could make a cask, for I could not, because, unlike you, I have not the advantage of five years' concentration upon it. But I know as much as you do about the job in theory. Perhaps a little more. Can you, for instance, tell me anything of the history of cooperage?"

Glad enough to talk of anything that did not necessitate telling tales, the cooper answered cheerfully: "Yes, sir, as little. It wan an honoured calling in the City of London as far back as the thirteenth century, and according to old Acts of Parliament, coopers were called 'good men of the mystery of coopers', and in the fifteenth century every cooper had to have his own mark, same as the stonemasons did."

The Captain nodded. "And that raises an important point. It is the custom still to put your mark upon a cask you make. Now suppose the tub, barrel, keg or cask is designed for some illegal work, such as smuggling, is the mark still put upon it by the good man cooper?"

"Well, sir," replied the cooper, becoming uneasy again, "if I make a cask I put my mark upon it in the ordinary way, and, at our shop, the head master-cooper puts his too, which shows that it has been passed with tests as the best our shop can turn out."

"I see," nodded the Captain. "And suppose I find tubs containing smuggled goods with your mark upon them, can I discover from any cooper that you were the maker? For I should wish to question you."

"Most likely, sir, since all our marks are registered in the trade," replied the cooper, wondering where the Captain was leading him. "No doubt, sir,' he added, "if you were to find smuggled goods in a cask I made, I could tell you to whom that cask had been sold, and would be justified in doing so, but that would surly, sir, be the end of my responsibility, except that it would have been guaranteed as a good cask, carrying with it an endurance test from the shop."

"Very well, then," cried the Captain. "Call your mind back to my visit. You remember that I sat in your part of the shop and watched you for some time at work, while my guide had gone to inquire about my cask? Well, now, what did I tell you?"

"You hinted, sit," replied the cooper with a fresh show of fear in his voice, "that if I wanted to escape the penalty of being pressed for service at sea, I was to call upon you here this morning, and not to let the other coopers know my destination. I made a good enough excuse for getting the morning off, sir, and her I am."

"And you are no doubt curious as to how you can serve His Majesty through me, eh?" asked the Captain.

The cooper nodded.

The Captain continued: "I saw you working upon what I knew was a finished barrel. You were adding to it.

You were fitting in straight staves from the top to the bottom. I thought this queer, and asked you why you were doing it. You said you were carrying out a special order: that the peculiar fashioning of that cask had been requisitioned, and you explained that it must be for packing something or other that did not need the bulge of a regular tub."

"That is so, sir, and that was all I knew of the matter," answered the cooper.

"Well, you must see to it that you know more about it in the next few days if you want to remain ashore," said the Captain. "Your liberty, which I take it you value, depends upon your finding out who is to receive that tub, and if there are to be more of them made in that odd fashion. You must also discover whether these casks or that cask are to be sent across Channel, what is going to be put into them, and whether they a re coming back again to this coast.

You will also find out why the contents have to be packed between staves unbent, and why they have to be put into an outwardly curved cask."

"Your last question is obvious, sir," replied the cooper. "The advantage of the curve outside a barrel makes it easier for rolling."

"True enough. A good answer," said the Captain with a note of approval. "But I suggest to you that the space occasioned between the outer barrel and the straight staves could carry a very considerable quantity of tightly pressed tobacco, for instance. The customs would open the top, and under the lid see nothing but the cargo which had been duly declared."

"Which in this case, sir, would be 'bones'," explained the cooper.

"Bones?" queried the Captain.

"I don't know why a large consignment of bones has to be shipped across the water, or that use they will put them. A mate I work with said something about bones being useful to farmers, who have some process of crushing them and using the powder obtained as a fertilizer for the soil. I never heard tell of that before."

"Very good," exclaimed the Captain. "We must then keep a weather eye open for the arrival of these bones, which will no doubt be the cause of stringing up some farmers' bones upon the Marsh. Farmers on the Marsh want bones, do they? I think the crows about here will be pecking at their own bones, too. And ordered by the Sexton. This is becoming interesting, George Lee."

"I think, sir, that you are wronging Mr. Mipps by suspecting him," put in the cooper. "I have known the Sexton all my life, and a kinder man you could not wish to find upon the Marsh. You accuse him of poking his nose into other people's advantage. He is one of those men who is always doing things for others. If Doctor Syn should send him on an errand to Hythe, why cannot he execute an order for a farmer friend at the same time? A farmer is a busy man, sir, in these parts, and would value the Sexton's help."

"The farmers here are very busy, I can well believe," retorted the Captain. "Especially those who work for the Scarecrow at night. But that is beside the mark at the moment, though there will come a time, and at no great distance, when these same farmers will be swinging as scarecrows above their own fields."

"I hope not, sir," replied the cooper. "I hope they are not so wicked as to serve under the Scarecrow."

"Let us keep to the point," ordered the Captain. "I presume that you have been preparing other casks in a similar way, eh? One barrel of bones would not fertilize the Marshlands. Many barrels of bones would, and many barrels could bring much tobacco in their innards. Now, exactly how many of these casks did the Sexton order?"

"My mate and I have orders to prepare fifty in that way," confessed the cooper.

"Fifty? You should have told me this at once," cried the Captain eagerly. "Now we are progressing. When must you complete this order for fifty barrels?"

"They are to be ready for a ship at Hythe to take them aboard by next Friday morning, sir. I don't think they will give me any more time off till then. Indeed I have to make up for this visit by working out the hours missed this evening."

"You mean you will not be able to visit me here again," said the Captain. "That will be as well, in any case. One of my men can meet you in Hythe for any further information. Far be it from me to hinder your work. The quicker the casks are shipped the quicker they will be back again. Can you give me any further information now? I want to know, for instance, the name of that ship that is to take the casks aboard at Hythe."

"To be exact, sir, there are two of them," went on the cooper. "Both smacks. One a Hythe boat named the *Plough,* and the other, so I heard, the *Strawberry* from Deal. They are to be shipped empty to some port in France."

" The *Plough* and the *Strawberry*, eh?" repeated the delighted Captain. "Do you know, my lad, I think you will be winning your security ashore all right. You seem to have done the Government good service already. Believe me, I have no wish for it to be otherwise. And the casks are to go out empty, eh? Well, I shall take no steps to prevent their shipment, I assure you. But I shall be awaiting their return most anxiously, I assure you. What a situation when I order them to be split open, and we take a look at those cavities! Now listen to me. You will hold no communication with your good friend, the Sexton, until such time as the *Plough* and the *Strawberry* return with their cargo of bones. Neither will you say a word of this matter to the Vicar here. It is a good thing that your work will keep you from Dymchurch. You must keep your ears and eyes wide open, Master Cooper, and your mouth as tight as a sealed keg."

"Yes, sir," assented the cooper. "I should not wish to come over to Dymchurch in any case."

"Not even to see the Dymchurch lass you are hoping to marry?" asked the Captain roguishly.

"She is also working at Hythe, sir," explained the cooper. "At the 'Red Lion', sir. She is in the kitchen there."

"Very convenient, too," replied the Captain, "and for your sake I am glad to hear it. Tell me, when will you be going to see her, on Thursday, which is the day before the casks are taken aboard?"

"I shall call there at six in the evening, sir. If she is busy and cannot get out, which is often the case, the landlady there lets me spend half an hour with her in the kitchen."

"Then go into the bar at a quarter to six," ordered the Captain, "and my Bos'n will be there. Anything further you may have learned, which you think I should know, tell him. Also he can give you any further orders that I may consider necessary."

This conversation was interrupted by the return of Doctor Syn from church. If he was surprised at finding them still there, he did not show it. But as both the Captain and the cooper stood up at his entrance, he apologized for his disturbance. "Forgive me, Captain," he said, "I have not come to turn you out of my study, which you are both heartily welcome to, but I know you will not mind my changing my gown for my jacket, before leaving you again."

"Indeed no, Parson," answered the Captain. "My business with this good fellow has been finished some time, concerning that cask of ours that had sprung a leak. But our friend here has been interesting me. He has let me into some of the mysteries of his craft. I thought I knew something of it, but when confronted by a master cooper, young though he is. Well, Master Lee, I must not detain you further. But I am your debtor for all that you have explained to me, and shall be able to be a lot more critical with my coopers when I get back to my ship."

"Poor fellows," laughed the Doctor.

"I suppose now, Parson," went on the Captain, "that you have never had the love for barrels and kegs, eh? Your profession hardly warrants it. But to one who loves ships as I do, well, a good cask is a fair thing."

"I agree with you, Captain," laughed the Doctor again, as he pulled his gown over his head and hung it up in the alcove, adding, as he took his jacket from the peg behind the door: "I love anything that is well fashioned. I can even admire a well-made coffin in my Sexton's shop. He's a good carpenter, is Mipps, but he cannot make a barrel like young George here. He told me only the other day that coopering is outside the scope of the carpenter, though I think it is the only thing made of wood that he could not make a good job of."

"Aye, Vicar," put in the cooper, "there's little else that Mipps cannot make, and I sometimes think that he could turn out a good cask too, if he had a mind to it."

"Well, a ship's carpenter no doubt has to lend a hand with the barrels should they go wrong, doesn't he, Captain?" asked the Vicar innocently.

"Aye, and they sometimes combine the two professions, though I have always carried a seacooper as well as a ship's carpenter and sailmaker. They pick up a good deal from one another, and can lend a hand, as you say. But I have no doubt that you wish to dismiss the subject of barrels in order to think of sermons, eh?"

"I fear I have to devote the rest of the morning to parochial accounts, Captain," said the Doctor, making a wry face. "A parson is expected to have a smattering of all professions. But I never could learn a love for figures myself. At Oxford I took classical languages and, my faith I begin to think that mathematics would have been more useful. Well not, I see that your glasses are empty, and that you left the bottle in the hall. Now that service is over I can take another glass myself, for a glass of good wine hurts nobody, I think."

Doctor Syn went out and brought back the bottle and his own glass, when once more the health of George Lee was drunk.

This time it was the Captain who proposed it with, "A word of advice, my young cooper. If you want to marry soon, and settle down to your craft, avoid walking out late in such a town as Hythe, for though I say it against a section of my own calling, the Press Gang have had orders to be active, and they are a rough lot of rascals, without a shred of sentiment. They possess no conscience at all, when they have to make up a complement of likely fellows."

"I have always felt the same, sir," replied the Vicar. "Take the Captain's advice, George, and if they should lay hands on you have no scruples at claiming protection from my guest here. I warrant he could free you quicker than most."

"And that's true enough," agreed the Captain.

"But unfortunately I might never get the word sent to me, so I still warn the youngster not to give the Press gang an opportunity. We know this about their ways, and that is that they know their own unpopularity. Consequently they work mostly at night when nobody is about, and a chance of rescue less likely."

"I will remember your warning, sir, thank you for it," replied the cooper, who then finished his wine and went towards the door. He knew full well that the Captain's warning was a threat which Doctor Syn could not appreciate.

To prevent any words passing between his victim and the Vicar, the Captain took up his hat and followed the cooper, but no sooner had they passed the Vicarage gate than Doctor Syn had begun to be made master of the whole situation by Mipps, and he then fully appreciated as much as the cooper did, that the Captain's warning was a threat indeed, and not only leveled at the cooper, but at his whole organization across the Channel and upon the Marsh.

13

CONCERNING A CARGO OF BONES

Mipps was glad enough to be released after so long a spell of being cooped up behind the Vicar's garments, and he took the excuse to point out that though his limbs were not so stiff, his throat was uncommonly dry with stifling a continuous desire to cough, which would have ruined all.

This was soon remedied by accepting the Vicar's offer to take a good pull at a half-finished bottle of brandy which the Vicar produced from behind a row of large tomes in the bookshelf.

The Sexton was then in trim to recount all that he had overheard.

"Well, it is a pity that the tobacco will not be able to be packed, s we had planned it for this voyage," whispered Doctor Syn. "Although the Scarecrow naturally depends upon the big landing, guarded by the Night-riders, these little runs upon this side keep our wits sharp and certainly increase the annual turnover of profit for the men. But I warrant I'll find a way to get the *Plough* and the *Strawberry* safely into port with the same weight of tobacco, for I have had another scheme in my head for that tobacco business, and when our ally across the Channel is informed of it, he will delight in carrying out my instructions. Although the casks must carry bones and nothing else upon this voyage, it will free them from any further suspicion. The Customs people always fear being made fools of twice in the same manner. Certainly the Captain will be blamed for the foolery this time, and they'll all feel shy of any future cargo of bones."

"We must be careful, however, not to implicate young Lee, for when no tobacco is found the Captain will be very angry, and suspect young George of having passed the word of warning to the Scarecrow's men. We must, of course, avoid Hythe till the empty casks have been shipped, and I don't think George will be so stupid as to come over Dymchurch way."

"He'll be far too busy fitting the casks for that, sir," said Mipps. "It's a pity we didn't have them casks made over in France, then none of this would have happened."

"Nonsense," laughed the Vicar. "They have to last for many a voyage, and the shop in Hythe turns out better work than they can manage over there. Besides, it is a lesson to us not to be too greedy. I was in two minds about the tobacco being packed with the first consignment of bones. And now fate has warned us to be cautious. I am right about the revenue men being reluctant at repeating an experiment that has failed them. They will not damage our casks a second time, believe me. The innocent bones will teach them a lesson."

Mipps chuckled. "They ain't forgot the lesson they learnt over the *Providence* of Folkestone."

Doctor Syn nodded. "Aye, that was a case in point. When we fitted her with a false bow we put no contraband inside it on the first trip. You remember that I feared information had leaked out, and we took no chances. In those days we employed one or two fellows who had not learnt to keep their mouths shut in the waterside taverns, and so our beautiful false bow was broken open upon her first arrival. But having to pay for wanton damage to the structure made them shy of unripping her again. And so it will be this time. The very sight of bones in casks will make the rascals sheer off, you'll see. They'll avoid bones as they avoided searching for kegs aboard the *Flower* of Rye. You recollect how we covered them with sprats, and delayed getting to port till they stank the harbour out?"

Mipps laughed. "Aye, that was a good trick of yours, Vicar. We've run some queer cargoes in the past."

"And have not lost our ingenuity, I hope," replied the Vicar. "So here's to us, and to the Captain's disappointment over the bones." Doctor Syn paused, and then added, "When does your onion-boy come here again?"

"Expected him today," replied Mipps, "but the Channel's choppy, and it may be tomorrow. Whatever the weather, he'll be here then."

"I'll have his parchment ready by tonight, then, said Syn. "I'll instruct Duloge to pack that tobacco in different fashion, this trip."

"Have you thought it out how, sir?" asked the Sexton.

Syn filled his churchwarden pipe and lighted it leisurely. He then sat down in his high-backed chair, and appeared to be merely enjoying the flavour of the smoke. Mipps, knowing this to be a sign that his master was thinking, kept silence. At last the Sexton saw his expression change to a frown, which lasted some thirty seconds, and then give place to a pleasant smile.

"He's thought of something," said the Sexton to himself.

The Doctor went on smiling and smoking, now and again giving vent to an audible chuckle.

"Aye, Master Carpenter," he said at last. "I have thought out 'how'. That tobacco shall come over on the decks of the *Plough* and *Strawberry*. What is more, should the Captain remain after he has examined the casks, he will see the tobacco slung ashore without any suspicion. He could even handle the stuff and not recognize it as contraband."

"And might one ask just how, sir?" asked the Sexton.

"You may," agreed the Vicar. "Duloge has not got a very satisfactory coopers' shop over yonder, but we cannot criticize his rope factory. That he can turn out good rope, you'll admit. Very well, then. The tobacco can be twisted tightly into rope lying aboard coming under suspicion. It can be slung on to the quay-side and removed under their very noses."

Mipps nodded, and then of a sudden looked doubtful as he remarked: "When connected with 'Free Trade' a rope ain't a pleasant thing to contemplate. It would be a bad thing to hang even with tobacco twist round one's throat.

Let's hope the Froggies threads it well."

"Duloge is proud of his rope, and justly so," replied Syn. "I don't anticipate that he will make it carelessly when there is good twist inside."

Mipps nodded once more. "Aye, he's clever enough for a Frenchman, and would be a man after my won heart if he could only speak the King's English. But he's got good English courage, as well as the cunning of a foreigner. I will say that for him."

"Courage and cunning are the two qualities that you and I must cultivate to the full," said Syn. "We must be very bold and very sly until such time as we can rid ourselves of this Captain Blain, for both these qualities he has very highly developed."

The eyes of the little Sexton twinkled, and his face became wreathed in smiles as he exclaimed: "Now you are talking sensible, Vicar. Rid ourselves of Captain Blain, eh? I've been waiting to hear them blessed words of comfort. And the sooner the better, I says. He seems to have got on to me with his nasty suspicions, and once on to me who knows as how it won't be you next, sir? And apart from us there's that poor young George. We wouldn't have him sent to sea by the Press Gang, I knows."

"We will not, Mipps," replied Syn. "We must watch the Captain closer than ever. He suspects you, and that means he'll watch you closer than ever. And what you say about me is right, too. I have become aware lately that he is trying hard to pump up from me the truth about my past. He is a great lover of the sea. He knows its history.

Only the other night he kept me up late telling me stories about Captain Clegg in the Caribbees. Tales of my old self, Mipps, and very creditably told too. They were painfully correct, and as I listened I lived some exciting times over again, I assure you. Here and there I longed to add details of which he had not heard. As it was I feigned a disbelief in such wild adventures. I had a longing to take him by the throat and to tell him that Clegg was never hanged at Rye, but had lived to choke the life out of an inquisitive sea captain. I found that feeling growing on me when he began to sing my old chanty, 'Here's to the feet what have walked the plank. Yo -ho for the dead man's throttle'. Little did he guess how near death he was at that moment. One pounce and the dead man's throttle would have been at his throat. Do you know what saved him, Mipps?"

"What did?" asked Mipps. "Whatever it was, was a pity."

"Aye, and a pity it was," nodded the vicar, with a smile. "He sang it so badly, Mipps, and all the while I thought of our roaring devils sending the same tune down the wind and waves, and my rage against him was blown away, because I felt he was not worth the killing."

"Well, I'm glad you thinks better of it now, sir," said Mipps. "I know that nothing would delight the Night-riders more than to get the word to take him off your hands. They resents him staying on at the vicarage, drinking you good liquor, though I has had it pointed out that it is the only way for me to keep an eye on him on behalf of the Scarecrow. There are lots of ways we can do it. We can come at night and take him from his bed, and then he can either be found a-hanging on the gallows, or not be found beneath the slime of the sluice-gates."

"My good Mipps," said the Vicar in reproving tone, "I happen to be very sane at the moment. My rage which was blown away, has not returned, and I shall not forget that the man is at least my guest."

"But you spoke just now of getting rid of him, sir," pleaded Mipps, at the same time producing his great clasp-knife and looking at it sorrowfully as it lay on the palm of his dirty hand. "There are some people whom I wouldn't pity at killing. Your guest happens to be one. If ever a man was ripe for the plucking, I thinks he is. And you've only to give me the hint, and he's as good as."

The Doctor shook his head. "He is at least a dangerous enemy, and I have ever had a regard for such a one. We have had many to deal with in our time. I think you'll agree with me there, Master Carpenter?"

Mipps grinned. "Aye, that we has, Cap'n. The other night, or rather the other early morning, 'cos it was after we'd got back from a secret meeting at the Oast house, I was a-swinging in my hammock, thinking as how a drop of sleep was overdue and badly needed, I starts in to count the individuals what we have had to remove from this terrestrial globe, because of their iniquities towards us, as the Bible says, and believe me, sir, I got into very high figures before I did get a wink of sleep, and there was a lot more victims waiting to be called for to show a leg."

"But none of them went unjustly, Mipps," said Syn sadly. "At least I like to think so."

"They all of 'em deserved a good deal more than what they got," declared Mipps with conviction. "And I'd so 'em all over again, only I'd do 'em a bit slower if possible."

"I sometimes suspect you of being a bloodthirsty little rascal, my good Mipps," said the Vicar reprovingly.

Mipps answered stoutly, "If I thought that my pet spider, Horace, was annoying you, sir, I'd tread on him, and not feel sorry neither."

Syn laughed. "I must confess that I do not share your affection for Horace, but every man to his tastes. Since you like spiders and I don't, no doubt I am the loser. Does he keep well, by the way? I have neglected to inquire after him lately, I think."

"As fat as ever, and could do with a shave on all eight legs," said Mipps with enthusiasm.

"I fear he would not last long were I to be accommodated in your hammock," laughed the Doctor. "I could sleep sounder in the condemned cell at Newgate than in proximity with that brute."

"Oh, I likes to see Horace run out and squint at me from the beam above me," went on Mipps.

"Never any tremors that he might fall upon you?" asked the Vicar.

"He wouldn't hurt hisself if he was to fall from the rigging," replied Mipps seriously. "But talking of Newgate, if my hands ain't as black as Newgate knocker. Must have been sitting down there in the corner."

"Mrs. Fowey would not take that as a compliment," laughed the Vicar. "But run along and wash 'em at the pump, and if she catches you at it tell her that it was dirt from the bell-rope when you pulled it for service. We must not fall out with our housekeeper."

Mipps chuckled and withdrew. Doctor Syn took from a drawer a sheaf of foolscap. On the top page of it were noted ideas for his next Sunday's sermon. But the Vicar did not look at them. He produced a tiny piece of parchment from another drawer, and laid it upon the sermon paper. He then selected the finest pointed quill from a silver tray, and began to write in minute letters instructions in French for his agent, Monsieur Duloge, who managed the Scarecrow's organization across the Channel. Before he had finished this, Mipps returned to the study, and was asked to wait.

The vicar chuckled as he wrote, and when the ink was dry he rolled the tiny missive tightly and said: "I think the fashioning of these ropes will be an artifice after our fat dandy's heart. I have also suggested the possibility of spare running-blocks with sheaves made of tobacco pressed very hard, instead of wood. Ever since I gave him the notion of shipping logs, hollowed out and packed with tobacco, he has been seeking in vain for fresh inspiration. Duloge is one of those lazy people who seems incapable of thinking out original things in his own head, but he is a rare one for perfecting the ideas of others. Let this go over with the onionboy, and g ood luck to our cargo of bones."

The onion-boy duly arrived upon the following morning, and carried back Doctor Syn's orders, signed by the figure of the Scarecrow. From the same bulb which concealed this list of instructions there had come over a note in French to the effect that a large consignment of bones was awaiting the empty casks for their shipment, and although the *Plough* and the *Strawberry* would only be delayed one day for the packing, the Scarecrow must not expect the next big run on their armed fleet for at least three weeks, for as the Scarecrow had himself pointed out, the vessels had been hard worked of late, and all keels needed careening. This job was now in hand and was a necessity in order to maintain the maximum of speed required for showing fast vanishing sterns to the revenue cutters. This meant a waiting time for the Scarecrow's men on the Marsh, so that things moved quietly enough in Dymchurch, and the Captain's men had a slack time of it too, with no rumours of a 'run' to stir them into action.

The Captain himself was well content to wait, knowing that

he would at least be able to show his zeal to the Admiralty just as soon as the casks of bones appeared from France. This proof of his ability he needed badly, for he had already been rapped over the knuckles by his chiefs at Whitehall for not showing any victory against the smugglers. He had also been reproved privately by the Admiral at Dover, who resented being worried by the bigwigs of London. And now, even the resident Revenue men at Dymchurch began to talk of his lack of initiative.

But Blain was a had man, and his shoulders were broad enough to bear the burden of abuse, for he was confident that in the long run he would show the bigwigs a thing or two.

The meeting between the Bos'n and George Lee, as arranged by the Captain, was duly kept upon the Thursday evening, when the cooper reported that the casks were not only finished, but were awaiting shipment that very night, and that the *Plough* and the *Strawberry* would be ready to leave the wharf on the early morning tide. George Lee was also able to inform the Bos'n of the approximate date for their return with the cargo. This he had learned from the longshoremen. This satisfactory news from the 'Red Lion' in Hythe caused the Captain to show his good faith towards his informant, by sending word to the Press Gang, who were being very busy along the coast, that although the young cooper might appear to them as a profitable victim, he was on no account to be touched, as he was secretly aiding the Admiralty by procuring certain information that was needed.

Unaware of this himself George Lee came into trouble from another source, but one from which Doctor Syn was eventually able to free him.

As it transpired later, someone in Dymchurch had seen the cooper enter the Vicarage with the Captain and Doctor Syn, and having watched the house saw him later come out and walk away with the officer, engaged in earnest conversation. Inquiries form the Henley family established the fact that George's visit had nothing to do with his wedding, since the girl had refused, so far, to set any date concerning that ceremony.

The man's story spread till certain members of the Scarecrow's gang put two and two together. Quickly suspicious they came to the conclusion that since the Captain and Doctor Syn were known to be the two arch-enemies of the Scarecrow and therefore of themselves, George Lee must be guilty of carrying secret information against them, and being in the know about the proposed tobacco run concealed in the cargo of bones, they guessed, perhaps naturally, that the news was out about the casks, and given away to their enemies by the young cooper.

Now as there had been no call from the Scarecrow to meet in full conclave at the deserted Oast House at Doubledyke Farm, a section of the gang resolved to take the matter into their own hands, arguing that it would delight the Scarecrow to find that an unknown enemy had not only been discovered, but very severely punished.

It happened to be customary for the lovesick young cooper to repair to the 'Red Lion', and to whistle under her window after she had been dispatched to bed, in the fond hope that she might be coyly encouraged to appear at the casement and signal, or better still whisper personally, a fond good-night.

When Polly Henley felt in a romantic mood herself, she would, if it seemed safe, actually open the casement of her bedchamber which looked not upon a side alleyway, in order to whisper sweet nothings to the upturned face of her swain.

Now this Friday night happened to be one of a pitch-dark sky, and there was no artificial light in the alleyway.

No lamp upon the wall. The only light which could cheer the sinister passage against the inn wall was from Polly's little candlelight, which shone through her small lead-rimmed casement.

Having heard the landlady about on the staircase, Polly contented herself, on this occasion, with appearing at the window, and waving to hew swain below, whose upturned white face was all that she could see. She thought it unwise to risk opening the casement, as the hinge squeaked. Having satisfied herself that her lover was loyally at his post, she drew one of the curtains, and undressed behind its protection. But the cooper, longing for a word with her, remained patiently beneath his shrine, hoping against hope that when she had extinguished her candle she would lean out and whisper a good-night.

His whole mind being riveted upon this expectation he was not alert to anything else, and utterly forgetful of the Captain's warning not to walk the town by night. He therefore neither heard nor saw the muffled-up figure of a man that stole along the alley. The cudgel that cracked him on the head brought him down unconscious and without so much as a groan.

The girl, hearing the noise of the blow, peeped out, but could see nothing, and since the upturned face had disappeared, she conjectured that the young cooper had been scared by the noise, whatever it might have been, and had wisely made himself scarce.

She waited a little, hoping that he would return. But his face was no longer to be seen in the candlelight, and when she blew it out she could see nothing at all, because of the thick darkness.

Although she would have been well content to slip into bed, leaving him to his vigil, she felt peeved that a little noise from someone around the inn could have frightened him away for good, though had he returned to his post she would not have been above reprimanding him the next day for risking a scandal to her good name. The assailant did not greatly care whether or no his victim was alive, since he had in his hand a paper, specially prepared, which he considered cleared him from any possible charge of murder. This paper he now pressed into the cooper's still hand.

By the time the landlord of the "Red Lion" opened the door to see what the noise might have been, the muffled figure had gone, and the landlord did not see the crumpled body.

When the cooper came to his senses with a throbbing head, it took him some little time to recollect where he was.

Indeed, his first thought was of the Captain, and that his warning had come tragically true. He imagined that he must be aboard some ship, a victim of the Press Gang.

Actually he had fallen against a wooden door, which suggested, as he touched it, the side of a ship. He began wondering whether his adored one had heard him fall, and whether he had cried out for help. It annoyed him to think that he had been given no chance to put up a fight. He would not have minded so much if he had gone down in the midst of a titanic struggle. She would have thought the better of him.

He had not told Polly of his journey to Dymchurch. Neither had he mentioned the warning which the Captain had given him in reference to the Press gang. He wished that he had at least told her that, so that she would guess what had happened and to the Captain on his behalf. If, on the other hand, she had heard nothing of the blow and his falling into their hands, she would be wondering why he had disappeared, always supposing that she had deigned to look out of the casement. Certainly when he failed to put in an appearance upon the next evening she would think him faithless and soon set her cap at some other man. This thought increased his mental anguish, while his physical pain increased as he began to move.

As soon as he discovered that he was not bound, he groped about with the intention of finding out in what sort of a place he was confined. Slowly and painfully he raised himself into a sitting position. He could detect no movement as of a ship at sea, so though that the vessel had not yet weighted anchor. Therefore, if escape was to be made, now was the time. In putting up his hand to feel if he could touch any ceiling or floor-deck above, he found that a crunched piece of paper was clutched in his hand. Although he could distinguish it as paper, it was too dark to examine it, to be one of the ribs of the ship, he raised himself slowly, fearful of striking his aching head against the deck above. Remembering tales of other men who had suffered at the hands of the Press Gang, but had escaped, he conjectured that he must be in the bilge, which was the common prison for victims previous to leaving harbour.

But he soon realized that the floor beneath him was not sloped like the bottom of a ship. Also it was not wood but earth at that. He eventually stood upright, and stretching up his arms could feel nothing above him. He began to edge his way along the side, and felt that the wood had given place to brick. And then, s his eyes became accustomed to the darkness, he made out that he was not confined at all, but was in the open air, and at last the building close to him resolved itself into the 'Red Lion'.

His thankfulness at this discovery knew no bounds, which compensated him for his throbbing head and aching limbs. He realized that he must have lain beneath Polly's window for a long time, for the inn was shut and quiet, and so with a gesture of good-night towards Polly's darkened casement, he made the best of his way back to his lodgings, taking every precaution to listen at every corner, so that he would not be surprised again. He could not imagine why he had been knocked out by the Press Gang, and then left for dead. Why had they not shipped him abroad after attacking him? Had he been rescued by some good Samaritans who bore a hatred for the Press Gang methods? There wee many such fellows in Hythe he well knew. But then, why had they left him after the rescue?

Had they in run been captured, and he forgotten in the darkness?

He made up his mind that he would tell Polly everything the next day, and he realized on reaching his lodgings that this course would be necessary, since not only the blow on his skull, but the bruises on his face, where he fell, would demand an explanation. It was not till after he had washed his wounds that he remembered the piece of paper which he had put into his pocket. He smoothed it out and read by the light of his candle, *Death to all spies by orders of...* And instead of a signature was the crude sketch of a scarecrow.

He had known others who had been warned in a similar fashion, and they had disappeared from the Marsh, and were never heard of again. The very next day he told Polly everything, under a pledge of silence. She took a very serious view of it, and made him promise to hold no further communication with Doctor Syn or the Captain, in case he was further suspected by the mysterious Night-riders, who had spies everywhere.

Strong as he was, the nasty crack on his head made him very ill. He became feverish, and Polly gave up her work at the 'Red Lion', so that she could nurse him at her parents' house in Dymchurch, promising to marry him as soon as he recovered. Her family liked him, and were more that satisfied that he would make Polly a good husband, now that he was a master cooper. They all agreed to keep his presence in Dymchurch a secret, and to that end one of Polly's brothers drove them from Hythe in their fish-cart after dark. So, in a few days George Lee began to think that his misfortune had been a blessing in disguise, and he made full use of his happiness in having his future bride for his name.

14

THE CAPTAIN SITS UP LATE

The news of the assault upon George Lee was brought to Mipps in the coffin Shop by the very man who had committed it. When he had finished describing the incident, which in his version spared no praise for himself, he told the Sexton that in his opinion the Scarecrow ought to be most grateful for his initiative.

"And what's more, Mister Sexton," he went on, "you must see to it that the scarecrow is told the full facts at once, so that he will not be caught out with that cargo of bones. He'll find some means of stopping it, I'll be bound, 'cos he's clever, just like what he'll say I be, when you tells him the true facts same as I've told you."

Mipps replied that the Scarecrow could always be trusted to thwart the Revenue men, and although he must himself decline to discuss this matter, which was the Scarecrow's business, he would promised that their mysterious leader would receive the information.

Directly the man had gone, Mipps sought out Doctor Syn and told him what he had heard, adding: "And no doubt, sir, this rascal is expecting a good reward for his zeal. What do we do?"

"Tell Percy to carry the two aces of clubs in his buckets this very evening, so that the Night-riders may meet at the Oast House tonight. Pass the word for an hour after midnight, Mipps."

"Aye, aye, sir," replied Mipps.

"I have always objected to any member acting violently without my express orders," went on the Vicar. "For that type of man becomes a menace to us all. And what is more that man must be punished."

"Death?" inquired Mipps with relish. "Well, I ain't sorry. Never took to him myself, I didn't."

"I am not at all sure that I should not bring in the same ruling against those like you, Mipps, who think violently without orders," replied Doctor Syn.

"Very well, sir. Sorry," replied Mipps promptly. He looked like a saint receiving a halo, which amused the Vicar, who promptly poured him out a drink with a sorry shake of his head. Then he smiled genially and added, "What a comical old rascal you are,

Mipps," and his tone had a note of real affection, "I believe no one delights in violence so much as you."

"I drinks your very good health, Vicar," returned the Sexton, with a grin. "I think we have both had our moments of violence on certain occasions that must be nameless."

Percy wa s duly sent out with the summons to attend at the Oast House. Everyone concerned noted the sign of two aces of clubs that floated in his water-buckets.

That night the Captain sat long over his drinks, and was more chatty than usual. As the clock struck midnight he still showed no signs of wishing to turn in, though the Vicar made a gallant show of suppressing his yawns that he was far from feeling. He presented a brave show of the polite host. In reality the Vicar was very anxious for the Captain to bid him good-night, in order that he might safely fasten his door from the outside against any possible exodus upon the Marsh. He had no wish for the Captain to take it into his head that an investigation outside the house might put a stop to some activity on the part of the Scarecrow's men.

Whether the Captain suspected that some such thing was planned for the night, the Vicar could not rightly determine.

To ask him deliberately to turn in would be to arouse unnecessary suspicion in his guest's mind, and yet to turn in himself, asking the Captain to turn out the lamp, and extinguish the candles, in no way suited his plan.

As a matter of fact, no sooner did the grandfather clock in the hall strike midnight than the Captain proposed this himself. He said pleasantly: "I see that you are most politely stifling your yawns, my good Parson. Now I happen to be finding this book most diverting, and as I never make a rule of reading in bed, which I take to be a most damnably dangerous practice so near the bedclothes, I should like to stay up and read a little further, if you have no objection?"

Doctor Syn bent down and glanced at the back of the volume which the Captain was reading. He then looked up at the space in the bookshelf, as though to verify the name of the volume. "Lawrence Sterne's *Tristram Shandy*, eh Captain?" he queried. "Well now, as a tutor I have ever had a quick eye for the student. I could always tell when some young student at the University was really reading or out making a pretence at it, and I rather think that I have caught you out this night. I can tell you that Sterne would be very disappointed at the desultory attention you have bestowed upon his pages. I rather think that it is just that you have no desire to go to bed. Perhaps you wish for another drink, eh?"

The Captain laughed. "You mean that half the time I have been reading I have been chatting about matters that have nothing to do with the opinions of Shandy, eh? Well, in a sense you may be right. If so it is small compliment to the author, eh? On the other hand, I should like to point out that our author has gripped me in spite of my inclinations and I should certainly like to finish this passage of Corporal Trim's account of the sick lieutenant."

The Vicar nodded with appreciation. "Well, I confess to being a little sleepy myself, but I will further encourage Morpheus to give me a sound night by fetching another bottle of brandy from the cellar. Any excuse is better than none, eh? If you will excuse me but for a minute we will both be at an advantage."

The suggestion pleased the Captain, since it meant detaining the Doctor a little longer before retiring. At least so thought the vicar, as with candle in hand he crossed the hall and entered the servants' quarters. Here he found Mipps anxiously awaiting him, sitting in the dark close to the rum cask, and with a handy pannikin clasped tightly in his fingers.

Doctor Syn smiled, and laid a warning finger to his lips. He then whispere d: "The Captain is for sitting up, damn him. He is, in fact, pretending to read. His manner the whole evening has aroused my suspicions, and yet it is time that we started for Mother Handaway's. I am taking in another bottle of brandy to encourage his sleepiness that shows as yet no signs of appearing. Give me but ten minutes or so, and then come round to the front door quietly and knock violently. I will admit you, and you can say in a loud voice that poor old Fletcher is dying, which I think will be no lie since Pepper told me this evening that his patient cannot be expected to last much longer. In fact, I will call upon alibi in case the Captain makes some awkward inquiries. Indeed we will set out that way, and then make a detour across the Marsh to the stables. It is necessary that we are at the Oast House by one o'clock."

As he whispered Doctor Syn had been selecting the bottle of brandy from his bin. He then repeated his instructions. "Ten minutes' time, Mipps," and went back to the library with candle and bottle. On his return he found the Captain pretending very well to be engrossed with his book, though on his host's entrance he sprang up and insisted upon drawing the cork for his host.

"Now I am just going to have one glass, and one lass only," said the vicar, "and then go straight up to bed. If I took more I might have to ask your assistance and disturb your reading, which I should be loath to do. I would sooner leave you to finish both the bottle and the book."

"I am a slow reader, Parson," said the Captain, "and I could finish more of your excellent brandy than the excellent reading set out upon your shelves. But in my own defense I must boast that I do remember what I read, and that is a thing that all students cannot say."

"Sow, but very sure, eh?" nodded the Vicar. "Well, let us hope that such a method enables you to catch our Scarecrow."

"Ah yes, indeed," replied the Captain sincerely.

For a few minutes Doctor Syn made a show of tidying up his table of papers which he had been poring over.

Parochial papers, of course. He then replaced certain volumes from the table to their allotted shelves. He also took some appreciative sips from his glass of brandy.

He then bade the Captain a good-night, and was just opening the door when there came a violent knocking from the hall.

"Now who on earth can that be at such a time?" he asked, showing a deal of disappointment. "Are you expecting a midnight report from that excellent Bos'n of yours?"

The Captain shook his head. "No, sir. I should be very disgruntled if he came to fetch me out now upon the Scarecrow's business. It would have to be a very important circumstance that would persuade me out at such an hour. No, Parson, I hate to depress you, but I rather fancy that this is a summons for the cure of souls."

"I must confess that I fear so, too," said Syn sadly. "There are of course plenty of sick folk upon the Marsh, but only one that I know of who is in danger of passing, and that is poor old Fletcher, whom I think I told you about during supper."

"Ah yes, indeed," replied the Captain. "Eighty-nine, isn't he? Well, perhaps it is his happy release knocking upon your door."

"Good gracious," exclaimed the Vicar, as a further pounding sounded upon the front door, "here I stand conjecturing when by opening the door I can find out the worst. How very stupid once becomes upon occasions."

"I should never accuse you of stupidity," said the Captain.

"But if I let that knocking continue, I shall be very stupid, for my old housekeeper will be aroused, and then we shall both suffer for it tomorrow with bad cooking." Saying which the Vicar went out of the library, crossed the hall and opened the door.

"Oh, it's Mister Mipps, is it?" he said in a loud voice. "Well, I presume I am right in my guess. Is it Fletcher?"

"It be," replied the Mipps promptly.

"Gone?" inquired the Vicar with a tone of anxiety.

"No, but just a-goin'," replied the Sexton.

"Dear, dear," exclaimed the Vicar. "Have you been over there?"

"No, sir, but young Jim was coming round to fetch you, but seeing as how I had my light on in the shop, since I was getting his old grand-dad's coffin ready just in case, I sends him back so as to be in at the death, which he wouldn't want to miss, being such a very dutiful grandson, sir."

"Come along in then, Mipps," ordered the Vicar, "and while I get ready you can take a glass of something to keep out the Marsh agues." So saying he led the Sexton into the library.

As Doctor Syn poured out a glass of brandy for the Sexton he told the Captain that his guess was correct and that it was indeed old Fletcher who was passing away, adding that he must set out immediately.

"I can't offer to go for you," laughed the Captain, "though I should welcome the chance of such courtesy to my good host. But I know that my uniform would scare the poor old fellow into his grave the quicker. I presume, however that he is too old to be one of the Scarecrow's active followers?"

Doctor Syn allowed himself to look pained at the joke. "Fletcher has ever been a very good parishioner. He will be sadly missed from his seat in church. His family occupies a whole pew, and has done ever since I have been in charge here. Is Doctor Pepper with him, my good Mipps?"

"No, sir, he ain't, and more shame to the old curmudgeon, I says," replied the Sexton. "Young Jim called around there before coming to me, and old Pepper said as how there was nothing he could do, so it was useless to turn out.

Jim told him too as how it was the end, seeing that the old boy keeps on a-singing a funeral hymn at the top of his voice which he says sounds very rattley."

"Their place is something of a distance too," went on the Vicar, "and it is essential that I get there in time for the end. I think you had best saddle up the pony if you will, Mipps."

"Certainly, sir, and then we can start at once."

"No, there's no need for you to accompany me, Mipps," said the Vicar.

"As to that, sir, I beg leave to disagree," replied the Sexton. "This hour of the morning ain't very healthy upon the Marsh. What with mists and agues that rise with 'em, to say nothing of the bad characters that roams about at such hours. In fact, sir, I've come on old Lightning, and bought my loaded blunderbuss."

"To take a pot at the March agues or at the bad characters, eh?" laughed the Vicar.

"Whatever presents itself first, sir." Replied the Sexton seriously. "There's them sailors, too, of the Captain's. I hear tell that they gets very nervous when on night-guards, and that they flourishes cutlasses at you, however innocent. Well, there's nothing like a blunderbuss for stopping that sort of behaviour. So I'll come with you, if you please, sir. Besides, I can't very well disappoint the old Lightning after having saddled him up. He'll want a canter."

"You meant that old donkey?" laughed the Captain. "Does it ever canter?"

"Does it? Why should it be called Lightning then?" responded the disgusted Sexton.

"Well, then, we'll get along together," said the Vicar. "I'll be glad of your company and you can look after the animals while I am in the cottage. Hurry then, Mipps."

In a few minutes the pony and donkey were carrying their masters along the Marsh road. The Captain watched them from the front door, and listened to the noise of the hoofs when there was nothing to be seen but the wreaths of mist into which the riders had disappeared.

"As queer a pair as ever I clapped my eyes on." He said to himself. "A couple of characters whatever they may be. And what, are they? Well, they could be simpletons. On the other hand, they could be as deep as the Indian Ocean. Now how can we determine just what they are? It seems that here is an opportunity. They may be thinking that I don't know the whereabouts of the cottage where old Fletcher is dying. But I do. In fact, I have the Marsh very well charted in my mind. But I am not at all sure whether old Fletcher is dying. Neither am I sure whether that queer pair are really bound to visit him. The Vicar seemed more than anxious to get me to bed. Was he anxious to get me safely into my room so that he could go out upon the Marsh without my knowing it?

"The more I think of it, the more it seems possible. Was that why he went to the cellar for that bottle of brandy?

We had already had sufficient, both of us. There was no necessity to open another. Now was that but an excuse to join his Sexton at the back of the house, so that he could send him to the front with the message about Fletcher?

Suppose now that they have not gone to Fletcher's. Suppose Fletcher is but an excuse for them to get out for some meeting upon the Marsh. Suppose Doctor Syn's animosity against the Scarecrow is just a deceit? Could that queer brace of birds be in league with the Scarecrow? Could they be in his power? Could one of them be the Scarecrow?

Or are they hunting the Scarecrow themselves and want me out of it? Well, I can find out if Fletcher is an excuse by going there myself, and taking a look round. If they are there the animals will be outside. If they are not there it will tell me that they have gone elsewhere to some place which they don't want me to locate. We'll get this Fletcher business cleared up anyway."

Thus arguing with himself, the Captain fastened on his sword, put on his cloak and hat, and making sure that he had the key of the front door in his pocket, closed the door after him and stepped out briskly towards the churchyard.

At the corner of the wall he halted and whistled.

This signal was immediately answered by an: "Aye, aye, sir. All's well."

"That, my good man, has yet to be determined," replied the Captain to the sailor who had miraculously appeared from the mist. "Indeed I am about to find out. Tell me now, what time did the Sexton enter the Vicarage? You were watching the house, I trust?"

"Must have been about an hour ago, sir, that I first saw him come round from the Ship Inn," replied the sailor. "I followed him at a safe distance to the back of the house yonder. The old housekeeper was closing up for the night, and instead of going straight to the back door to be admitted, the Sexton waits outside till all was dark and still.

Then he walks to the door and opens it. This puzzled me, sir, because I had distinctly heard the bolts shot-to. Did the old girl shoot 'em and then quietly open them up again? Or did someone else do it? Yet come to think of it there ain't no one living in the house but you and the Vicar beside the old lady."

"And since I did not shoot the bolts," said the Captain, "it only leaves Doctor Syn who could have done it, unless, as you suggest, it was the housekeeper herself."

"And another thing what puzzled me, sir," went on the sailor, "I see a candle light appear at the back some half and hour ago, but then it went. But a little after the Sexton, and he must have been sitting in the dark, comes out of the back door and goes round to the front door where he knocks and knocks. Now why does he want to let himself out of the back, I asks myself, in order that he can knock to get let in at the front? Seems to me."

"What does it seem to you?" rapped out the Captain.

"Why, sir, such as stealing of his drinks from the wine cellar, as it was the window of the wine cellar where I saw the light."

"There is no window to the wine cellar," retorted the Captain. "But there is one in the stillroom which leads to it. There may be something in what you say. Step along to the barn now and tell the Bos'n to bring round my horse."

When the Captain drew rein near the cottage and handed over his horse to the Bos'n, who was in no good temper after being awakened for this expedition and told to walk, which developed into a trot beside the Captain, the notes of a man singing reached their ears. The Captain approached the cottage cautiously on foot, and without being seen discovered that the singer was none other than the Sexton, who was regaling the night with a funeral hymn. One window was lighted up, and by its reflection the Captain could see both the pony and donkey in charge of Mipps.

Any doubts he may have entertained as to whether Doctor Syn was in the cottage were dispelled when he heard the Vicar's rich voice reading from the Scriptures. Disappointed he had been mistaken in the Vicar the Captain rejoined the Bos'n and went home to bed.

But he did not know that Mipps had sent Jimmie Bone the Highwayman to the Oast House with news that important business had detained the Scarecrow, but that the Night-riders were to await his coming.

An hour later the Scarecrow gave judgement against the member who had assaulted George Lee. A heavy fine was levied against him from his profits on the next run.

But if the Captain was disappointed at this failure, it was nothing to his rage when he was made the laughingstock of the district when he ordered the casks of bones to be emptied upon the quayside. But the laugh against him was even greater that he thought, for the crew, enraged against his unwarranted suspicions, carried their coils of rope to store under his nose, so that the full run of tobacco was safely landed and later distributed.

Against his own convictions, however, the Captain could not free himself of suspicion against the Vicar and his Sexton, and he made a habit of sitting up every night reading till the Vicar himself had gone to bed.

15

THE REMOVAL OF CAPTAIN BLAIN

One morning, during the smoking of his first pipe, Mipps received a visit from the onion-boy from France, who promptly unhooked one of the strings and laid it down on the lid of the coffin, pinching one of the bulbs as though to exploit his fine wares. Mipps opened the top skin of this onion and drew out a small roll of parchment. This he read through, and then unlocking a Bible box that served as a desk he drew out one of his ledgers. He turned up a list of names and numbers attached to them, and compared it with the parchment. The names were those of luggers harboured in the Scarecrow's base in France.

Having checked over the numbers, against the names, he took a quill and wrote at the foot of the list *the twenty-third of this month*. He then drew a few simple lines which gave the crude shape of a scarecrow, after which he replaced the list inside the onion, give it back to the boy, and bought another of the strings which he slung up to a hook in the beam.

The onion-boy was paid, and at once set off to the sea-wall where he took the direction to Rye.

An hour later Doctor Syn sat opposite Captain Blain at breakfast in the Vicarage.

"Do you know, Doctor," remarked the Captain casually, "that I have been on your hands for an unconscionable time, but you will be no doubt relieved to hear that my duties here are rapidly drawing to a close."

"So you are going to give up the idea of catching this elusive Scarecrow at last," said the Doctor.

"Rather better than that, Doctor," replied the Captain, with a smile. "In ten days I shall be handing him over to the gallows."

"Are you serious?" asked the Doctor.

The Captain nodded. "In ten days there is to be a great 'run'. You can look surprised, but I regret I cannot tell you how I know. But know I do. Ten days' time makes it the twenty-third, and it is an important date to me. It marks my fiftieth birthday, and what is more, my fiftieth year at sea, for previous to becoming a Royal Navy boy I was afloat at home, having been born on H.M.S. *Crocodile*, the Guard Ship of the Tower of London, of which my father was in command. I suppose, Parson, that I have done a good deal of good duty since those days, but somehow have not been in great favour at the Admiralty, for they have not yet given me an admiral's hat. So I take it as something ironical that on the day of this celebration I shall be able to do a job ashore that will give me a very wide notoriety. The arrest of the most impertinent scoundrel of our days is bound to create a big stir."

"You certainly whet my curiosity, Captain," interrupted the Vicar, "I hope you will tell me more."

The Captain shook his head. "No one knows just how much I know about this Scarecrow. I have kept my own counsel through all these months, during which I have had nothing but sneering and criticism. I have purposely not reported the great progress I have made to the authorities. I have let them rave at me to their hearts' content, and all the time I have been planning and plotting, working in the dark, alone, until I saw the first tiny thread of light, which I turned rapidly into a beam, and now has broadened into the full daylight. I should like to tell you of all men the whole remarkable story of how my deductions grew, forging themselves one by one into a chain for the Scarecrow on Execution Dock.

"But it is not my way to talk. I never believed in it as a policy. Not even my Bos'n realizes that I am going to put my hands on the Scarecrow upon the night of the twenty-third, or how I am going to do it. I shall give orders when the time comes, and then he and the men will be surprised at our success. I knew I could get him sooner or later, and so I could afford to ignore the scoffers. But what a hanging it will be, Doctor."

The Vicar repeated the word 'Hanging', and then added, "Have you remembered that the Prince of Wales has declared himself the rascal's protector from that fate?"

"Parson, Parson," laughed the Captain. "You forget that you used up that way of escape for your rascally parishioner when you saved that Old Katie from the gallows. I don't suppose even you would have the temerity to go to the Prince again with that request."

"I have quite a natural abhorrence for the gallows," returned the Doctor, "and would do anything to save even this Scarecrow from such a barbarous end."

It was after this conversation that Doctor Syn made a discovery which annoyed him. As he went about his lawful calling as spiritual head of the Marsh he found that two of the Captain's best men had been detailed to dog his steps.

He demanded an explanation.

"I suppose I owe you that at least, Parson," said the Captain. "I have every reason to believe that the Scarecrow knows that his number is up on the night of the twenty-third. What would I do in his place? Give up the planned landing? Perhaps, but that is not *his* way. He is too arrogant to give up anything o f his own planning. But knowing that it was you, Doctor Syn, who used influence with the Prince to save Katie, he will try to get into communication with you. He knows he can trust you as a person. He has the right to come to you for advice. Not that he would take it, but he might possibly be able to persuade you, with you natural abhorrence to hanging, to go once more to the Prince. Therefore since he may come to you I intend to know everyone who gets into contact with you, for your own protection, as well as for my own satisfaction."

The days that followed were anxious ones for the Vicar and his Sexton.

"How much did the Captain know? Was his confidence in his success merely a bluff?"

Doctor Syn thought not.

That he had something to go upon was obvious, as one of his first steps was to set a guard not only outside the Vicarage, but also within sight of Mother Handaway's upon the Marsh.

However, a watch upon the secret stable had been anticipated by Doctor Syn. Jimmie Bone was there to look after the horses, and there had been stored enough provisions for man and animals to cope with such an emergency.

Jimmie Bone could withstand a siege, but Mipps had a further comfort.

"There's this to it, sir," he said to the Vicar, as he helped him on with his Geneva gown before taking Evensong, "when we has to get into the stables and can't wait no more it will only mean that them good little sailors will have to get a crack on their heads."

"And a clumsy way it would be," replied the Vicar. "I imagine I shall be able to show the Captain a better trick than that."

The days followed without incident. Doctor Syn went about his parochial business escorted at a respectful distance by the sailors, and the Captain went about his, silently but with a growing attitude of confidence.

To avoid Mother Handaway's would have been to create suspicion. Doctor Syn rode over there as usual and the sailors had to wait outside and listen to his deep voice reading the old woman many a passage from the Scriptures.

Several times Mipps urged the Vicar to abandon the landing on the twenty0third, but Syn replied that if they were to be hindered by every danger that presented itself, they might just as well quit the business altogether.

A few days before the dreaded date, when Mipps nerves were stretched to the breaking-point, the Vicar patted him kindly on the shoulder, and told him that there was no cause to worry since he had solved the difficulty in his own mind.

To the Captain he said later: "I shall be giving your sailors a rest for three days, as far as watching me concerns them, for I am due to attend an important ecclesiastical meeting in the Lower House of Convocation, which means I must be in Westminster. The good Squire has placed his coach at my disposal, and he prefers his own armed servants to guard his vehicle from the dangers of the road, to sailors. The coach will not be able to accommodate my watchers, excellent fellows as they are."

"I have no jurisdiction to place my men on the Squire's coach, and unless I choose to ride behind you to London independently you will not be watched."

Doctor Syn could see that his departure for London annoyed the Captain for all that.

"I can promise you one thing," remarked the Vicar when he was ready to set off, "and that is I shall be back in my parish for the twenty-third. As a matter of fact I shall be with you the day before." He then added: "If you are contemplating a pitched battle against the Scarecrow's gang that night, there will be heavy casualties no doubt, and my ministrations to the suffering will be needed. I shall be ready to attend the sick and dying, whether amongst your men or the Scarecrow's."

Doctor Syn did not enter the Lower House at Westminster. He went instead to Carlton House, on a personal visit to the Prince of Wales.

Although the anteroom was thronged with notabilities, amongst whom were two bishops, he had the extreme satisfaction of being summoned to the Prince's presence before all others. The last to arrive, he was the first to be admitted.

The bishops, to be sure, put their bewigged heads together wondering why an obscure rural dean should be preferred before lawn sleeves. Neither could they understand why the Prince should be so far interested in one of their own cloth, since it was usually his way to admit first of all those rich enough to pay up some of his debts.

However, when, after some half-hour the striking-looking parson was brought to the Presence Chamber door by the Prince himself, they felt it incumbent upon them to pay court to him before he left the anteroom, and they eyed with a good deal of curiosity the sealed letter which the parson held, addressed to Admiral Troubridge, Admiralty House, Whitehall, in the Prince's own handwriting.

But Doctor Syn, though exceedingly polite and respectful to his superiors, was as tight as an oyster for communication as Captain Blain.

To be quite candid neither of the bishops had ever known the Prince to be so condescending to a member of the cloth, and his last words had puzzled them. Why had the Prince of Wales said to a country parson: "I have told the old boy to do exactly as you ask. A promise is a promise, Doctor, though I think you have been guilty of cheating.

You've kept me very strictly to the letter of it rather than to the motive which made me make it. You ask a favour for this fellow, and I don't really like what I've seen of him. Never mind. Have it your own way, and if you want to repeat the request at any time for yourself, it still holds good. And at a word, if things don't fall out as you planned 'em, tell me and there'll be the devil to pay for the old boy. If you come up to London for a sermon let me know. If you come up for any reason, apart from preaching, still do so, and you can regale me with some more of those tales about the heathen you have met. God bless you, Parson, and think well what I've told you about lawn sleeves. There'll be money enough to pay for their laundry, I promise you."

The bishops had not missed a word. They went home and repeated it to their wives. Who was this parson who asked favours for another fellow from the Prince? Who was the fellow for whom he begged? Was it his curate?

And why the letter to the Admiralty? All very puzzling, especially as the Prince had not appeared to them that day in at all a communicative mood. He had certainly taken no interest in the laundering of their lawn sleeves.

From Carlton House Doctor Syn strolled along to Whitehall and entered the Admiralty. He had to wait a good deal longer for Admiral Troubridge than he had had to do for the Prince. But he had far more confidence in being able to get what he wanted from the Admiral than he had ever entertained with reference to the Prince, although as it had turned out, nothing could have been easier. He had cleverly handled the very difficult First Gentlemen of Europe and had really made him behave like a gentleman, which not everyone was able to do.

What was more to the point he had not come away as so many had to do with an empty promise. There was no reason for him to quote that passage of scripture which says, 'Put not your trust in princes, nor in any child of man, for there is no help in them. He had come out of the Presence Chamber at Carlton House with a letter, the contents of which he had himself directed the Prince to write. It was couched in terms that could not be ignored by the Admiral.

Moreover, the old sea-dog was well acquainted with the Prince, and was very proud of the fact, and the tone of the Prince's correspondence being friendly and confidential, pleased him so vastly that he would have been willing to undertake a harder commission for His Royal Highness than was requested.

Doctor Syn owned that he knew the contents of the letter, saying that the Prince had insisted upon reading it to him, while he kept so many notabilities waiting for audiences.

He then tactfully recounted all the good things which the Prince had said of the Admiral, such extravagant praise that had never entered the Prince's head, much less issued from his mouth. Doctor Syn was perfectly aware that these exaggerations could never be repeated by the Admiral.

But though delighted to hear how very high he was in favour with the Prince himself, he was mystified at the Royal attitude towards such an officer as Captain Blain.

"It is quite conceivable that His Royal Highness might have recommended the fellow for promotion," he remarked to Doctor Syn, "but all these minute orders as to how it must be carried out seem very extraordinary under the circumstances. Besides although you say you have taken quite a liking for Blain, I assure you he is by no means looked upon as a likeable fellow in the Service."

"But surely, my dear Admiral," suggested Doctor Syn, "His Royal Highness has ever had the reputation for taking the queerest fancies for people."

"Well, he's carrying it very far in this case," went on the admiral. "He is treating Blain much as we treat a favourite child at Christmas. You know, 'Must make it a happy day for the nipper' sort of thing. I wonder he had not ordered the Admiralty to send him a cake with fifty candles round it. Of course, I must conform to the Prince's wishes as far as I am able, but the Prince should know more about the Service than to write a ridiculous sentence like *make him an Admiral or something and oblige.* I can't go making people Admirals at a moment's notice. We've too many as it is."

"He does say, 'An Admiral or something'," said the Doctor. "Perhaps there's something that he could be made."

"I know the very thing," the Admiral suddenly exclaimed. "I could get him the *Crocodile.* She had only a temporary officer in command, and the Guard Ship to the Tower of London is a step higher than a Guard Ship at Dover. I think that solves it. We'll send Blain on his fiftieth birthday, back to his nursery. His father had it and became an Admiral. It's a stepping-stone, and if I pop him on board the Prince will at least see that I am exerting myself for his protégé."

"He is certainly wasting his time, and that of his men, on Romney Marsh," said the doctor. "If I may say it, with all deference, you yourself were unable to string up our atrocious Scarecrow. No doubt you would have got him had you stayed at Dover, but Blain is hardly the man to succeed where even you failed, though he has been about the business for a considerable time, and unlike you, has been billeted on the spot."

"Aye, and as I have pointed out to him," put in the Admiral, "the landings have gone on all the time, and on a vaster scale that in my time. No one will catch the Scarecrow, Doctor Syn. I am sorry to say so, since I know how vigorously you have worked to get your territory clear of his tyranny. But I would rather be ordered to go down to hell and arrest the Devil himself than he expected again to catch that rascal. He's uncanny, and that's about the size of it."

"I begin to think so myself, sir," replied Doctor Syn.

With a great deal of importance the Admiral once more read aloud the Prince's letter, and then began to write out a memorandum on the details to be carried out.

"If I remember right Blain rides every tolerable, doesn't he?" he asked, looking up from his writing.

"An excellent horseman," replied the doctor. "It is an accomplishment that I envy. My little pony is about all I can manage."

"Well, I am not much of a hand at it myself," returned the Admiral. "Though I tell my brother, the General, that I cut a finer figure than he does in the saddle, for all his dragooning, especially when the animal is come to anchor.

Every man to his calling. The horse to the soldier; the dock to the sailor, eh?"

"And the pulpit to the parson," laughed Doctor Syn.

The Admiral returned to his notes. "So Blain rides. That means another horse. One for the Admiralty courier, and the other for him. He has a horse at Dymchurch, I see, from his reports, borrowed from the garrison on Dover, but that one must be returned. Better not trust it to the Bos'n neither. They must detail some officer who can ride to fetch it, from Dover. He can escort the men back at the same time. I'll not have them wasting any more time helping the Revenue men not to catch the Scarecrow. If they want to do it, they should do it properly and commission the Channel Fleet to sink his luggers."

"So my Tythe Barn will be able to return to its agricultural uses undisturbed at last, eh?" laughed the Doctor.

"Aye, Doctor, and you'll get no more Admiralty rentage for you Sick and Needy Fund from that source. Now wait a minute," went on the Admiral. "I must not forget the common dangers of the road. Not that I think your Gentleman James would hold up and Admiralty courier without getting as good as he gave, but..."

"Oh, our Jimmie Bone has gone into hiding, they say, sir," explained the Parson. "I think you can rule him out of this."

"But accidents will happen even to couriers," went on the Admiral. "So to prevent them I'll dispatch my best courier the day before, that is on the twenty-second, to Dover. He can carry dispatches to my successor there and save a journey. He can accompany the officer who is to fetch the horse and men, so that all can be clear at Dymchurch when Blain leaves it on the twentythird. I think, doctor, that settles everything which will ensure Captain Blain having a pleasant birthday and a surprise present when he arrives hot and dusty for orders here. I shall then hand him his credentials for the command of the *Crocodile* . And I hope for his own sake that he'll make a better job of it than he has over this Scarecrow business, which the Navy had far better have left alone."

When the Squire's coach rolled up before the Court House door in the evening of the twenty second, Captain Blain was pacing the front garden of the Vicarage, as though he were on his quarterdeck. The Squire, who had just returned from a run with the hounds, was chatting with Major Faunce who had accompanied him. Both men were in the saddle as Doctor Syn, neat and trim despite his long journey, stepped out of the vehicle.

"Welcome back from London, my good Christopher," cried the Squire. "And I hope my cattle behaved well?"

"A most comfortable journey, Squire," returned the Doctor. "And your good fellows did not have to use pistols or blunderbuss upon the road. I had the happiest time meeting many of my good colleagues. I also had the extreme honour of being entertained most graciously by the Heir Apparent, who received me before a brace of bishops, who were told to wait. So you see our Romney Marsh is of some importance in the Capital."

He spoke loud enough for the Captain to overhear, who out of politeness was forced to come forward to greet his host, though it was obvious he would have liked to have avoided meeting the Major of Dragoons. Doctor Syn noted this out of the tail of his eye. Neither has he missed the look of extreme surprise, and something of relief, when he had seen him step out of the coach.

The Squire invited them into the Court House, and they accepted his hospitality to the extent of a glass of wine, but declined to stay to supper. Doctor Syn pleading fatigue from his journey and the Captain saying that he had planned a long day with his men on the morrow and wished to turn in as early as possible.

So host and guest returned after a while together to the Vicarage, where over an early supper the Captain remarked that he had not expected to see doctor Syn so soon.

"I told you that I should be back for the twentythird," replied the Vicar.

"I thought you might wish to avoid the arrest of the Scarecrow," said the Captain, "since you expressed such an aversion to the gallows."

"I did not allow myself to think of things unpleasant," replied the Doctor. "But I did not forget that tomorrow is your fiftieth birthday. And do you know, I thought I ought to be here to see that my housekeeper puts the usual candles round a cake."

The Captain laughed at that, and as soon as politeness would allow, excused himself for bed.

Doctor Syn said that he would not be long behind him in seeking his own four posts, though he had to hear the parochial news first from his henchman, Mipps.

In the locked study by the candlelight, Mipps had to cram a corner of his handkerchief into his mouth to prevent his laughter becoming audible to the sleeping Captain. He owned, after many a good drop of brandy that had never paid its dues, that his master had surpassed himself, and only hoped that all would work out to the clock-work pattern set by him.

The next morning his doubts were dispersed, because the clock-work worked.

The Doctor was awakened by a violent hammering upon the front door. At least the Captain thought it had awakened him as it had himself. In reality the Vicar had not been without anxiety, and was lying awake to hear it.

But he let the Captain rise first, and when he appeared in a flowered dressing gown and nightcap, he looked down from the head of the stairs and saw his guest talking to a mud-bespattered courier. The front door was open, and there he saw a mounted naval officer holding the courier's horse. The Captain was holding an official document, and reading it by the light of dawn which illumined the hall window by the door.

"So as far as I'm concerned," the Captain was saying, "it means boot and saddle for Whitehall, and at once, eh?

And the officer outside is to take my men back to Dover. Well, orders are orders. I hope it means that they are sending me to fight the enemy on the high seas."

"What is all the trouble?" asked the Doctor innocently. The matter was explained rapidly by the Captain. Doctor Syn roused his housekeeper and ordered breakfast to be prepared while the Captain got into uniform.

At breakfast he not only wished his departing guest a very many happy returns of the day, but hoped that this change of front from the Whitehall spelt good fortune for him.

"It speaks of promotion," said the Captain during breakfast, as an explanation to his host. A coincidence that such an unlooked-for event should have occurred on my birthday, when I might well have expected to be shelved. I could have wished perhaps for one more day, which the courier tells me is impossible as the matter is of the greatest urgency. But I would sooner gain my laurels from my naval work that gain notoriety through the capture of a criminal. But it's a lucky happening for the Scarecrow. Any by the way, Vicar, it is also something of a coincidence that this should follow upon the heels of your visit to the Prince. I more than half suspect that I have you to thank for it, eh?"

"As to any conversations I had with His Royal Highness," returned the Vicar, "I can assure you of one thing. I took your advice and did not ask the Prince a second time to save the Scarecrow's life. On the other hand, though what I said to him and he to me I must think of as confidential, concerning his high rank. I will tell you that he seemed especially interested in your career. I told him that you had been born on H.M.S. *Crocodile* , and that today made your fifty years upon the waters complete. He really seemed most interested. But it does seem a pity that your work here should be so quickly terminated when you had apparently nearly completed it with the success for which you had worked."

"Aye, Parson," replied the Captain grimly. "I swear to you that I should have had him tonight. But will I pass on my information to that insufferable Dragoon? A thousand times, no. I would prefer to drink the good health of the Scarecrow, like the Prince commanded up at Lymphe. And what is more, that I shall do tonight as soon as I have left the purlieus of Whitehall. Good luck to him now. And good luck to you, too, Parson. Both clever fellows, on my soul. Perhaps one day we shall dine together, and perhaps then I might feel inclined to tell you all I have found out about your rascally parishioner. On the other hand, promotion may increase that habit I have ever had of knowing when to keep my ugly mouth shut tight."

So the Captain galloped off with the Whitehall courier, and soon after the sailors marched off behind the mounted officer to the tune of the drum and fife.

And to the tune of another song the Vicar of Dymchurch lifted a glass of brandy and toasted his Sexton across the study table. "The most dangerous situation of our long careers, eh, Master Carpenter?" he whispered. "And got over in such a simple fashion. We can now relieve poor Jimmie Bone and tell him that the run goes forward this night. And so I drink to you, old faithful sea-dog, in the well-remembered words of Clegg:

' *Here's to the feet wot have walked the plank;*
Yo-ho for the dead man's throttle:'"

Which in a piping whisper, was responded to by Mipps with:

" ' *Here's to the corpses afloat in the tank:*
And the dead man's teeth in the bottle'."